Published quarterly by the Popular Fiction Publishing Company, 2457 E. Washington Street, Indianapolis, Ind. Application made for entry at the postoffice at Indianapolis, Ind., as second class matter. Single copies, 25 cents. Subscription, $1.00 a year in the United States, $1.20 a year in Canada, $1.40 in other countries. English office: Charles Lavell, 13, Serjeant's Inn, Fleet St., E. C. 4, London. The publishers are not responsible for the loss of unsolicited manuscripts, although every care will be taken of such material while in their possession. The contents of this magazine are fully protected by copyright and must not be reproduced either wholly or in part without permission from the publishers. All manuscripts and communications should be addressed to the publisher's Chicago office at 840 North Michigan Avenue, Chicago, Ill. FARNSWORTH WRIGHT, Editor.

Contents of Summer Issue, 1931

579

The Dragoman's Slave Girl

By OTIS ADELBERT KLINE

A fascinating stor· of Hamed the Attar, which has all the glamor of the "Arabian Nights"

IT IS written and it has been said, *effendi,* that there are roses of many kinds. They grow in many lands, and many are the gardeners. But there is only one beauty of the rose—of the white rose or the red, the pink rose or the yellow. That beauty comes from Allah Almighty, and when once we have seen and smelt one beautiful and exquisite rose, then indeed have we sampled that perfect bliss which awaits all true believers in Paradise.

Like a flower from the very Gardens of the Blessed was Selma, Rose of Mosul. When the great Weaver of Destinies

crossed the threads of her life and mine, we were plunged together into a strange and wondrous adventure which came near to severing both, yet for a time they were entwined, each with the other. Then, indeed, did I sample that bliss which is reserved for the faithful in the Gardens of Allah.

You would hear the story? Tale-telling, *effendi,* parches the throat. Yet if you would listen, here is the coffee shop of Silat, who brews the best *ahhwi helwh* to be found in the Holy City, and who learned his art from the great Hashim, father of coffee brewers in no less a place than Estambul.

Let us take this cushioned *diwan.* Here we have both comfort and privacy.

Ho, Silat! Two *narghiles,* scented with your best rose attar and packed with golden Suryani leaf. And brew for us coffee, bitter as love's first estrangement, black as the throne of Shaitan the Damned, and hot as the molten lava that boils in the innermost lake of Laza.

Give ear, *effendi,* and I will unfold for you this wondrous adventure which befell me in the days of my youth.

Looking upon this bent and aged form and this white beard, you can scarce picture Hamed the Dragoman of those days. For then I was straight and strong as a

581

young cedar of Lebanon, with hair of midnight blackness and features that were not accounted unhandsome. Nor feared I man nor *jinni*.

I have related to you, *effendi*, my adventure with Mariam, Oracle of Ishtar, which left me with an empty heart and the opulence of a merchant prince. Hoping to find solace and forgetfulness in the curious scenes which other lands might afford, I decided to travel and see the world. I accordingly converted my wealth into gold and set out.

FOR more than a year I wandered, visiting the great cities of far Cathay and distant Hind, and spending with prodigal abandon. But there came a bleak dawn when I awoke in Singapore after a night spent in drinking the fiery liquors of the *Ferringeh* and watching the contortions of brown-skinned nautch girls. I found myself with a head that seemed as big as the Taj Mahal, and a purse that had shrunk alarmingly. I accordingly abandoned my intention to travel home overland, and took ship for Basra. From there I journeyed up the Tigris to Bagdad, and thence to Mosul.

Having crossed the stone bridge and the bridge of boats, I spent the morning wandering among the ruins of the buried city of Nineveh. Then I visited the grave of Jonah, on whom be peace, who was once rescued from the belly of a fish by Almighty Allah.

After I had viewed these wonders, I went to pray in the Great Mosque at the call of the *ezam*. Then, being hot and thirsty, I sought an airy coffee booth overlooking the *souk*.

My former great fortune, I found, had been reduced to a mere hundred *dinars*. It would be difficult to find employment as a dragoman, nor would it be lucrative, as few travelers of wealth were visiting the city at that time because of the oppressions and indignities heaped upon them by the new Governor, Mohammed Pasha, known as Keritli Oglu, the Cretan's son, whose cruel misdeeds had made him notorious throughout all Islam. Indeed it seemed to me that there were at least two dragomans for every traveler.

I had once been an *attar*, however, and with a hundred *dinars* might open a small drug and perfume shop, and at least manage to exist. This I resolved to do.

As I sat there sipping my coffee, puffing at my *shisha*, and gazing abstractedly across the market square, I noticed that a great number of people were entering the stall of a rug merchant opposite me, but though more went in than the stall could possibly have held, none came out.

Puzzled, I paid my host, and crossing the square, was surprized to see the place evidently deserted. But a tall, night-black Nubian eunuch had gone in just as I came up, and in a moment I heard a voice say:

"You have the word?"

"*Ayewah.*"

"Give it me."

"*Zemzem.*"

"Enter."

There was the sound of a latch, footsteps, and a door opening and closing. Then the merchant stepped from behind one of the rugs hanging in the back of the booth.

"*Salam alek'*," he greeted.

"*W'as salam*," I replied, stepping into the stall.

He drew the rug aside, and I went on into a tiny back room.

"You have the word?" he asked me.

"*Ayewah*," I replied, remembering what I had heard.

"Give it me."

"*Zemzem.*"

He pulled a tasseled cord, whereupon a curtain drew back disclosing a concealed door. Then a latch clicked, and the door swung open.

As soon as I stepped through that door I saw that I was in a slave mart. It seems that the British, the French and the Russians, all of whom had consulates in Mosul, frowned on the slave traffic. But so long as it was conducted behind locked doors through which none might enter without the secret word, it was impossible for them to take official cognizance of it.

I found myself in a walled enclosure, nearly filled with prospective buyers. They faced a great, flat-nosed, red-bearded fellow standing on an auction block, behind which was a door that opened in a small building at the far end of the lot.

FOR some time I stood there idly looking on, while he auctioned off girls and women, tall and short, young and old, fat and thin, willing and unwilling. There were slant-eyed, golden-skinned girls from Cathay, supple, brown-skinned nautch-girls from Hind, Nubian maids and matrons whose bodies were like polished ebony, and Abyssinians of the color of coffee. Then came the Circassians, Armenians, Persians, Nestorians and Yezidees, some quite good to look upon, and others distinctly ugly. But none interested me.

I turned to go, when suddenly I heard a chorus of "Oh's!" and "Ah's!" from the entire assembly. Looking back toward the auction block, I was smitten with admiration for the witching vision of feminine loveliness that stood thereon. Then, scarcely knowing what impelled me to do so, I elbowed and jostled my way to a position just in front of the platform and stood there like the others, gaping up at the wondrous frail creature who, standing there beside her auctioneer, was as a gazelle beside an overgrown wart-hog. Nor had Almighty Allah ever before vouchsafed me the privilege of beholding such grace and beauty.

Her eyes were large and brown, and their sleepy lids and lashes were kohled with Babylonian witchery. Her mouth was like the red seal of Suleiman Baalshem, Lord of the Name, on whom be peace, and her smile revealed teeth that were matched pearls. The rondure of her firm young breasts, strutting from her white bosom beneath the glittering, beaded shields, was as that of twin pomegranates. And her slender waist swayed with the grace of a branchlet of basil, above her rounded hips.

The flat-nosed auctioneer stooped for a moment for a few words with a well-dressed dignified graybeard who was evidently the owner of the little beauty. Then he straightened, and after clumsily describing the charms of her whose beauty defied description, stated that her master had stipulated that she should not be sold to any one against her will, but that if sold at all she would be accorded the right to choose who would be her new master from among those who would bid for her. Then he called for bids.

With but a hundred *dinars* in my purse, I knew it was useless for me to bid, for this girl would undoubtedly bring thousands. Yet so smitten was I with her loveliness that had I, at that moment, the vast wealth of Haroun al Rashid, I would gladly have bidden it all.

Over at my left a voice bid fifty *dinars*. I saw it was the huge black eunuch who had preceded me into the mart. It was a ridiculously low offer for the little beauty, whose rich clothing and jewels alone were worth twenty times the amount. But to my surprize not another voice was raised to increase it.

The girl glanced out over the sea of faces expectantly. Then her eyes found mine—clung for a moment—and in them was a look of appeal.

"Sixty *dinars*," I said.

A beetle-browed camel-driver who stood next me, nudged me with his elbow.

"Bid no more if you value your life, O stranger," he said. "You are competing with the eunuch of Mohammed Pasha."

Glancing about, I saw that several others were staring at me as if astounded at my temerity.

"Seventy *dinars*," said the eunuch, scowling at me. Then I felt the point of a dagger against my ribs. "Raise the bid, O dog of a *Badawi*," a voice grated in my ear, "and you die."

Again those lustrous brown eyes looked at me with a world of appeal in their glance. Suddenly I seized the wrist that held the dagger, swung it around in front of me, and twisted. The weapon clattered to the pavement, and I was glaring into the eyes of a villainous-looking Turk with a red *tarbush* and bag trousers. He grabbed for the dagger with his free hand, but I stepped on his fingers, so that he howled with pain. Then I flung him from me, along the length of the platform. He fell at the feet of the Nubian eunuch as I bid:

"Eighty *dinars*."

Half turning, I saw several more red *tarbushes* moving toward me through the packed crowd, and once I caught the glint of naked steel. I elbowed my way around the side of the platform so that I stood near the old man who seemed to be the girl's owner, with my back against the wall. Then I loosed my simitar in the scabbard.

The eunuch, who had evidently been waiting for the Turks to reach me, bid:

"Ninety *dinars*."

I whipped out my simitar and the *tarbushes* paused. A *jambiyah* hissed past my ear, snapping its point on the wall behind me before it clanked to the flagstones.

The Nubian frowned fiercely, rolling his eyes in my direction so that the whites gleamed against the black of his ebony skin.

I turned to the old man who was the girl's master.

"I have but a hundred *dinars*," I whispered.

"Then bid, in the name of Allah, and save her from worse than death," he replied. "Remember, the girl will choose her master."

"One hundred *dinars*," I shouted, and the Turks moved closer, while blades gleamed menacingly, hemming me in.

"One hundred fifty *dinars*," roared the eunuch.

"I would bid more, but I have it not," I called up to the auctioneer.

There was a look of triumph in the eyes of the Nubian. The ring of *tarbushes* around me began to move away.

The auctioneer shouted to the crowd, enumerating the charms of the girl, which were plain to any but a blind man.

"Two hundred *dinars*," he cried. "Who will pay two hundred *dinars* for this *houri* from Paradise? Why, her clothes, alone, are worth a thousand. One hundred seventy-five. Who bids one hundred seventy-five? Well then, sold to Mansur, chief eunuch of His Excellency, the Pasha, for——"

"One moment." The girl interrupted him with a voice as sweet and clear as the tinkle of a silver bell. "It was stipulated that I might choose my own master. I choose the young *Badawi* who has bidden his all—one hundred *dinars*."

"But you can not choose this pauper when His Excellency's servant has bid——"

"I choose the *Badawi*," persisted the girl.

"I will pay you *baksheesh* on the hundred and fifty," said the old man, *sotto voce*. "Make the sale quickly!"

"Sold to the young *Badawi* for one

hundred *dinars*, shouted Flat-Nose hurriedly, mindful of his extra commission.

While the girl was stepping down from the platform I tossed my purse to the graybeard, who promptly handed fifteen *dinars* to the auctioneer. The *tarbushes* were closing in again, and there was no mistaking their purpose.

The girl came up beside me. She had resumed her black street garments and donned her *yashmak*, over which her frightened eyes looked up at me.

"Master, we must get to the street quickly," she said, "for if the eunuch gives the word you will be cut down without mercy. I know a way through the house behind us. Follow me."

But she had scarcely finished speaking ere the Nubian shouted, and a half-dozen of the Pasha's cutthroats, who had only been awaiting the word, sprang at me with bared blades.

2

As the first of the Pasha's ruffians assailed me, I whipped out my simitar and made as if I would lay his head open. But when he raised his blade to parry, I changed the direction of my stroke, and dealt him a leg-cut that laid him low.

To my surprize, the graybeard to whom I had handed my purse drew his simitar and came on guard beside me as the others rushed up. With the girl behind us, we slowly backed toward the doorway, the old fellow at my side cutting and parrying with a skill that amazed me.

The crowd was in an uproar that all but drowned the noise of our clashing blades. Taunts and insults were hurled by the bolder of the onlookers at the Pasha's eunuch and his soldiery. Then suddenly, a tall *Badawin* sheik leaped to the platform, and with a push sent the flat-nose plunging into the crowd that milled below.

"I bear witness," he roared in a voice that thundered above the tumult, "that this is foul injustice. How long, O men of Mosul, will we stand idly by to see true believers robbed and murdered by the Pasha and his wolves?"

For a moment all voices were stilled. Then there were cries of: "Down with the Pasha!" "Down with the Cretan's son and his wolves!" Blades were drawn and brandished, and the mob which had stood idly by for the sole reason that it lacked a leader, was now ready to fly at our attackers.

Seeing the way things were going, Mansur the eunuch quickly called off his scoundrels, who picked up the man I had wounded and laying him at the feet of the castrado formed a semicircle in front of him.

But now the leader who had come so suddenly to our rescue, again demonstrated his ability to sway the mob, which, numbering well over a hundred, was ready to make short work of our persecutors. Flinging his hands aloft, he cried:

"Hold! Enough! We seek justice, nothing more."

Then, as the mob paused, he turned to the eunuch:

"I have a question to propound, O Mansur," he said. "Tell me, was this damsel lawfully purchased by the young *Badawi*, or was she not?"

"She was not, O Tafas," growled the eunuch. "He bid but a hundred *dinars*, while I——"

The Arab interrupted him:

"It was stipulated that she might choose her master, and she has done so. All is fair and according to law. However, it seems that you are like a walnut—must be cracked in order to be of use. Ho, men of Islam——"

A menacing roar from the crowd drowned his voice for a moment.

Seeing the way things were going, and realizing the peril in which he stood, Mansur quickly changed his tone.

"It may be that the sale was lawful," he admitted.

"You will bear witness?" asked Tafas.

"I bear witness that the sale was lawful," said the thoroughly cowed eunuch.

The Arab turned to where we stood— the old man, the girl, and I.

"Depart in peace," he said.

"May Allah requite you," I replied, and we turned and walked through the doorway, down a long, dimly lighted hallway, and into the street beyond. Here we all paused, I in considerable bewilderment.

"Lead on to your house quickly, Master," said the girl. "I will follow."

"But I have no house," I replied. "I am a stranger, sojourning in Mosul."

"You have a tent, then? A camel or a horse? Take me away swiftly, I beg of you."

"No tent, nor horse, nor camel have I. Nothing but my weapons and the clothes on my back."

"In that case," said the old man, "I invite you to my poor habitation. We must get off the street as soon as possible, for I am convinced we have not heard the last of this affair from the Pasha. Let us make haste."

WE SET off down the street, the girl following behind as is customary for slaves.

"By what name may I be permitted to call you," said the old man courteously, as we hurried along.

"I am Hamed bin Ayyub, late of Jerusalem," I replied, "where men once knew me as Hamed the Attar. Having lost my fortune through a scheming woman, I became a dragoman. Then, having won another fortune through a woman of quite a different sort, I became a traveler. You have witnessed the spending of the last of my latest fortune."

"My own fortune is in like case with yours," said the old fellow. "I am Hasan Aga, once the most opulent and powerful of the *agas* of Mosul. The girl you have just purchased is my niece, Selma Hanoum."

"Then you, an *aga*, have sold your niece into slavery."

"Necessity compelled it," he said. "She is a great lady, and was wealthy in her own right until Mohammed Pasha came to Mosul. Her father, who married my sister, may Allah grant them both peace, was a pasha, and she his only child. He left to her the finest house in Mosul with its palatial furnishings, slaves, and the wealth to maintain it. But Mohammed the plunderer quickly found a way to dispossess her by unjust levies, and by lawsuits with perjured witnesses, brought before the dishonest *kazi*.

"Not satisfied with acquiring her property, her slaves and her wealth, the Pasha, having heard of her great beauty, attempted to force her into his *harim*. With her sole remaining slave, a faithful *Magrhebi* eunuch named Musa, she fled to my house for protection. Whereupon, the Pasha, who had already deprived four of our leading *agas* of everything they possessed, including their heads, began his persecutions of me. Today, I was left only in possession of my house, my head and my niece, and certain that it would not be long before I should lose all three. At first I had concealed much of my wealth and that of my niece, but this I was forced to bring forth to save my head and to protect her. Four days ago I spent my last *para* for food. Destitute and starving, we could turn to no one for help, as nobody could offer us succor for fear of incurring the Pasha's wrath. And so terrorized were the merchants by the Pasha's wolves that they would not purchase the jewels and ornaments of Selma Hanoum, though I offered them at a small fraction of their worth.

"This morning, my niece, as a last resort, besought me to take her to the slave mart and sell her, making the stipulation that she should choose her own master. But the Pasha's spies must have followed us, and informed their master, who sent his eunuch and his ruffians to frustrate her plan for escaping his clutches. Knowing that many of the desert *Badawin* would be there, she planned to choose one as her master, hoping thus to get away from Mosul. Some weeks ago I sent a messenger to her cousin and my nephew, Ismail Pasha, in Estambul, requesting aid. As soon as help arrived, it was my intention to repurchase the daughter of my sister from the *Badawi* who would buy her."

"It is unfortunate that she chose a *Badawi* without wealth or followers," I said. "I have nothing but my blade and blood to give in her service."

"Women were ever wont to employ the heart rather than the head in such matters," he replied. "But here is my house. *Bismillah.* In the name of Allah, enter."

A *Magrhebi castrado* of about my own size and build admitted us.

"This is Musa, the slave of Selma Hanoum," said Hasan. "Musa, this is your mistress' master."

I exchanged *taslims* with the slave of my slave-girl, and we went into the magnificent *majlis*, now all but denuded of furnishings. The eunuch brought us water for washing our hands, and prepared pipes for us. Selma Hanoum had retired to the women's quarters, but returned presently, clad in filmy *harim* garments that covered, yet revealed, every curve of her perfect figure, and wearing a light face veil.

While we three discussed the perilous situation in which we found ourselves, Musa went to the *souk* for food and cof-

fee. He returned presently, and Selma prepared a meal for us that would have broadened the breast of a sultan. We regaled ourselves with deliciously grilled mutton, dolmas, leban, and an excellent *pilav*, after which came fruits, nuts and sweetmeats. Then, with pipes going, we made merry over our coffee and *'raki* despite our dangerous predicament.

But our merriment was cut short by a thunderous knocking at the door. Musa answered, and returned carrying a basket which he set on the floor before his mistress.

"A gift for Selma Hanoum with the compliments of the Pasha," he said.

"Open it," she directed.

He raised the lid, took out a napkin, then gasped in horrified amazement.

One look into that basket, and Selma drew back with a choking cry.

Wondering what gift could have so fearful an effect, I peered into the basket. The sightless, glassy eyes of an Arab stared up at me from a severed and gory head. I recognized the drawn features of Tafas, the *Badawi* who had championed our cause in the slave mart!

3

NATURALLY the grisly gift of the Pasha threw us into a panic. But strangely enough, the girl was the coolest of us all.

"It is written on our foreheads," said Hasan to me, "that we are not long for this world. I doubt if we two will see the light of another day. Following this warning will come the soldiers. We will be dragged before the Pasha. There will be perjured witnesses to swear to such charges as may have been trumped up against us. Then—the swift stroke of the headsman, and the daughter of my sister will be at the tyrant's mercy."

"I, for one, do not intend to submit

tamely," I replied. "When the soldiers come, I will fight."

"And I," agreed Hasan. "In our passing, we can thus take at least a few of the wolves with us."

"Valiant words, Master and Uncle," said Selma, "but how futile to rush into the jaws of death when, with a little planning, you may both live."

"A little planning? How?" asked Hasan, with the air of a drowning man clutching at a straw.

"There is the souterrain—the passageway which connects my house and yours."

"One can not exist for long in the souterrain without food and water," said Hasan. "Besides, if Hamed and I were to enter it, what would there be to prevent your being carried off by the Pasha?"

"Nothing," she replied, "nor would there be, were you to foolishly, if bravely, die fighting his soldiers." She turned to me. "Master," she said, "the house in which the Pasha lives is rightly mine. In the days when my father was governor of this pashalik, he dug an underground passageway leading from a secret panel in his *harim* to another secret panel in the *harim* of this house, which he also owned. He believed in being prepared for troublesome times, which are not uncommon hereabouts. More than one pasha has been murdered in his own house, so he planned this secret means of escape. In this house he established my uncle, who was apprised of the secret of the passageway.

"All this was done before I was born, yet before he died, my father told me of it, and showed me how to open the panel in his *harim*, and to travel through to this one. It has never been used, and to this day none knows of it but my uncle and I."

"And you would have me hide in a souterrain while you are carried off to the *harim* of the tyrant?" I asked. "No. I would rather——"

"But, Master, remember the souterrain connects with the Pasha's *harim*. Once inside, I can find a way to get food and drink to you and my uncle. Then we can plan our escape. I have already thought of a disguise for you. Come into the *harim* and I will apply it now, as we may not have the opportunity later."

She took my hand and led me into the *harim*. Then she bade me remove my upper garments and my slippers. While I was doing this she brought a bottle of brown liquid and a cloth.

"You and Musa are of one size and build," she said, "and were it not for his dark skin you might almost be twins. This is some walnut juice which I prepared some time ago, intending to use it myself in an attempt to escape. Now it would be useless to apply it, for any woman leaving this house would be seized. But if I disguise you as Musa, and arrange another disguise for my uncle, we may yet all find the means to escape."

I did not like the idea of even pretending to be a castrado, but despite my protests she began applying the walnut juice to my face with the cloth. After that it was useless to protest.

When my face, neck and ears were thoroughly stained, she skilfully colored my trunk, arms and hands, spreading the stain so evenly that I looked to be in very truth the Moor I was to pretend to be. While she was staining my feet and legs, I said:

"In applying this color to me, O fairest Rose of Mosul, you only make me look like that which I really am."

"You mean," she said, with manifest consternation, "that you are really a eunuch?"

"Not that," I replied laughingly. "I mean that I am really your slave. From the moment I saw you on the auction block, I have been your love-slave."

A telltale and most becoming flush

mounted to her temples above the *yash-mak*, but she only said, with a last dab at my thigh:

"There. That is as far as I may go. Musa will finish, and will furnish you with a suit of his raiment."

She clapped her hands to summon the castrado. When he arrived she gave him his instructions and rejoined her uncle in the *majlis*. A short time thereafter, without a white spot left on my body, and attired in garments like those worn by Musa, I returned to the *majlis* with the eunuch.

"By my head and beard!" exclaimed Hasan. "This is a wondrous transformation. It seems that Musa has suddenly become twins."

But Selma was not satisfied. She called for the walnut juice and standing on tiptoes, applied deft touches here and there to my swarthy countenance. I thrilled with the nearness of her, and could scarce refrain from crushing her in my arms. But she finished in a moment, and returned bottle and cloth to the eunuch, who took them away to conceal them with my clothing and weapons. The latter he had replaced with a huge, *harim* guard's simitar and a jewel-hilted *jambiyah* thrust in my sash.

WE THREE sat down to our coffee and pipes once more, and a few libations of '*raki* soon set us to chattering merrily. Musa, meanwhile, carried food and water into the souterrain.

Our merriment was short-lived, for there came a second summons at the door, more loud and threatening than the first.

"They have come!" cried Selma. "Into the souterrain with you, quickly!" She hastily donned her street attire.

"Go, Hasan! Take Musa with you," I said. "I'll answer the door."

"But Musa is to remain with me," said the girl.

"*I* am Musa," I told her. "I remain with you, and where you go, I will go."

"But you can not. They will detect and kill you."

"I remain," I persisted, giving the frightened Hasan a push toward the *harim* door. Bewildered, and muttering pious ejaculations in his beard, he fled. A moment later I heard him exchange a few words with Musa. Then the panel clicked, and they were gone.

The pounding on the door was by now so fierce that it threatened to fly from its hinges. Selma watched me with terror-stricken eyes as I went to the door and called:

"Who is it?"

"Daoud Aga, with soldiers. Open in the name of His Excellency, the Pasha," was the reply.

I slid the bar, flung the door wide, and stood with folded arms in the manner of a slave.

Simitar in hand, a young and self-important *aga* brushed past me, followed by a dozen soldiers with muskets. Daoud Aga was the highest ranking military officer in the pashalik, the *Yuz-bashi*, or Captain of the Irregulars, and he took no small pride in the fact.

Striding up to where Selma Hanoum sat, he demanded:

"Where is the dog of a *Badawi* who had the temerity to cut down one of my men?"

"I know of no such *Badawi*," replied Selma, demurely.

"Where is your master— the man who bought you this morning?"

"Oh, my master! He has gone to the *souk* to buy tobacco."

"So! And where is your uncle, Hasan Aga?"

"Why, my uncle went with him."

"Lies! This place has been watched continually. None but your eunuch went forth and returned. Search the house, men."

"Search if you will, but you will find no one here save my eunuch and me."

They searched the place thoroughly, but of course found no one.

"Once more," said Daoud Aga, "I give you the opportunity to tell me the whereabouts of your master and your uncle. If you will not answer me, then must you answer the Pasha."

"I can tell you no more," replied Selma.

"Very well. Then come with me." He turned to his men. "*Bismillah!*" he cried, with a wave of his hands. "Eat, in the name of Allah!"

The men responded with alacrity, and "ate" to their hearts' content, though with some quarreling among themselves, for this simply meant "to plunder." From the Pasha down, the entire governmental organization was a band of legalized freebooters, and it was said that only by permitting his men to "eat" on such occasions as this did Daoud Aga hold them together.

The loot must have been quite disappointing to them. The Pasha, by means of levies and false claims, had long since annexed nearly everything of value, and Hasan had sold most of what remained, in order to buy food.

Selma rose, and obediently followed the *aga,* while I, whom she had followed as master only a short while before, now followed her down that same street as her slave. Despite the perilous situation in which I found myself, I derived some small amusement from the idea of being the slave of my slave.

IT WAS only a short walk to the Pasha's house. Not more than six doors separated the two places. Yet, I reflected, considerable labor was required for the digging of a souterrain for even this distance.

We were ushered into the *salamlik,* where the Pasha sat, cross-legged on a *diwan,* smoking and talking to a half-dozen of his satellites. He proved as ugly in appearance as in reputation. His Excellency had but one eye. One ear had been torn off. He was short and of immense girth, and his features were deeply marked with smallpox pits. His gestures and mannerisms were as uncouth as his features, and his voice was harsh and strident.

With a wave of his hand, he dismissed his hangers-on as we entered.

Squinting up at Daoud Aga with his single good eye, he rasped:

"Well, captain?"

"I have brought Selma Hanoum into thy presence, in accordance with Your Excellency's commands."

"So? And where are the others? The traitorous *aga,* her uncle, and the murderous young *Badawi* who wounded one of my men this morning?"

"I could not find them, Excellency, and she refused to reveal their whereabouts; so I informed her she must answer to you."

The Pasha leered up at the slight cloaked and veiled form standing beside the captain.

"Where are your uncle and your master?" he demanded.

"If I knew I would not tell you," she replied.

"What? You defy me, the Pasha?"

He clapped his hands, and Mansur, the huge Nubian eunuch, came through a doorway at his left.

"Take this lady into the *harim,* Mansur," he said, "and prepare a room for her. She must be detained, and it will be more comfortable there than in the jail."

"Harkening and obedience, Excellency," responded the eunuch, and led her through the doorway.

The Pasha squinted up at me, then turned to the captain.

"Who is this fellow?" he asked.

"Musa the eunuch, slave of Selma Hanoum," replied Daoud Aga.

His Excellency smirked.

"Well come and welcome," he said. "I have use for you."

"I kiss the dust at your feet, O dispenser of justice and fountain of wisdom," I replied, with as much slavish humility as I could muster.

Once more he clapped his hands, and Mansur reappeared:

"Let this castrado be *bowab* of the rear door," he said, "and guard of the women's sleeping-quarters."

"I hear and obey, Excellency," responded Mansur. Then he beckoned to me, and I followed him through the doorway.

4

MANSUR led me through the *majlis* and up a stairway to a narrow balcony which fronted the women's quarters. Here a short, fat Nubian castrado whose shiny black torso was padded with rolls of flabby fat, stood guard.

"This is Sa'id, *bowab* of the *bab al harim*," said Mansur, to me, and to the fat one, he said: "This one is Musa, slave of Selma Hanoum, who will guard the rear door and the sleeping-quarters."

I exchanged *taslims* with the greasy Sa'id, and was conducted into the *harim*. In the front was a roomy and magnificently furnished apartment. Here were more than a score of women and girls, some merely lolling, some smoking and chatting, some busy at needlework which no whit interfered with the clatter of their tongues, and the rest plying hair-tweezers and cosmetics in their efforts to improve on the handiwork of nature.

I was somewhat abashed at this sudden sight of so many unveiled and lightly clad females—no Moslemah deeming it necessary to hide her charms in the presence of a eunuch, who is not considered a man—and found it difficult to maintain an imperturbable countenance as Mansur led me through the room. Moreover, they were all staring at me and commenting on my appearance as if I were some new bit of furniture of doubtful value added to the *harim* by the Pasha.

The Lady Selma I saw, unveiled like the others, seated near a window with one slave-girl brushing her lustrous tresses and another staining her dainty toenails with henna, both working under the direction of a wrinkled hag. These attentions, I knew full well, meant that His Excellency was expected to call on the damsel that evening.

My blood boiled at the thought, and unconsciously my hand stole to the hilt of my simitar. Though there were many girls of considerable beauty in the room, Selma's loveliness outshone them all. She was a lone, budding rose in a weed-choked garden.

Mansur led me down a long hallway on which opened the doors of the women's sleeping-apartments, each wife and favorite concubine having a room to herself. At the end of the hallway a larger door led to a balcony which overhung that part of the garden reserved for the inmates of the *harim*. The balcony was screened with lattice work so that those standing thereon could see without being seen. An enclosed stairway led down into the walled garden.

A portly eunuch acted as *bowab* of the garden gate. Mansur called him and introduced us. He was Sa'ud, twin brother of Sa'id, *bowab* of the *bab al harim*, and as like him as is one rice grain to another.

Sa'ud went back to his post, and the chief eunuch gave me my instructions. I was to stand guard at the rear door of the *harim,* and to patrol the hall at regular intervals. At night I would sleep on a *diwan* beside the rear door, keeping my simitar always by me.

I remained at the door until some time after Mansur had left. Then I sauntered down the corridor and looked for a moment into the women's *majlis.* The two slaves were still busy with Selma Hanoum, under the directions of the old trot, trying to improve on the beauty of a rose which Allah Almighty had made perfect. As I turned and sauntered back along the hallway, I knew that I was drowned in a sea without bottom or shore —head over heels in love.

Returning to my post, I seated myself on the *diwan* beside the door, and was lost in a maze of lover's dreams when there came to my ears the soft tones of a lute, then the sweet voice of a female singer. As I mooned there by the door, the words of her love song suited my mood:

"Thou hast made me ill, O my beloved!
And my desire is for nothing but thy medicine.
Perhaps, O fairest flower, thou wilt have mercy
    upon me;
For verily my heart loveth thee.
O thou blushing rose! O thou perfect rose!
Heal my bleeding heart with the perfume of thy
    presence."

Although it was not time for me to patrol the corridor again, I rose, and walked to the door of the *majlis* to see who was the singer.

Seated on a cushion near the door holding the lute, was a *Magrhebi* dancing-girl with slender waist, full, round breasts and exquisitely formed limbs. She was darker than Selma Hanoum, with hair that was black and lustrous, and eyes whose smoldering glances could kindle the flame of desire like a firebrand tossed among dry reeds. She turned those orbs on me while the other inmates of the *harim* cried their approval.

"Well done, O Fitnah! Allah approve you! Allah preserve your voice!"

"And do you like my song, O chamberlain?" she asked me, when the clamor of the others had subsided.

For a moment I was too astonished for speech at being thus addressed. But I recovered my voice, and said:

"Does a starving man dislike food,. or a thirst-parched desert traveler turn away at the sight of water? If these things be true then I can not abide your music. But if they be not true, then do I hunger and thirst after it."

The girl laughed, a low musical laugh. Looking at Selma, she said:

"Your slave has a gifted tongue. From what country came he, and what is his name?"

"He is from El Mogrheb," replied Selma, "and his name is Musa."

"Ah, from my own country!" said the girl. "I surmised as much. From what city, Musa?"

I thought fast, and remembering the name of a Moroccan city, replied:

"From Marrakesh."

"Why, this is amazing!" said Fitnah. "It was in that city I was born and reared. You remember the street of so and so that passed by the mosque of such and such?"

"Assuredly," I replied, though I had never heard, nor can I even now remember the names she mentioned, "as I went dow that street every Friday to worship at that very mosque."

"Marvel of marvels!" she exclaimed. "And to think that was the very street on which I lived! It may even be that we are cousins. You must tell me of your family and tribe some time. But now I will sing for you in memory of Marrakesh, that pearl among cities, which was your home and mine."

She sang again, stroking the lute softly and flashing at me from time to time such

O. S.—1

seductive glances that despite my love for Selma I was stirred by her witchery. Nor did her eyes look solely into mine, but swept over me appraisingly from head to foot, making me uncomfortably conscious of my bare limbs, naked torso and scant loin-cloth.

When she finished I applauded and returned to my *diwan*. This dancer, it seemed to me, had been well named. For "Fitnah" has several meanings, among which are: "beautiful girl," "seduction," and "aphrodisiac perfume." She was certainly a combination of all three—a lodestone to draw men's desires, well knowing how to shape them to suit her own ends. Such women are dangerous.

A NARGHILE stood beside my *diwan*, with tobacco and charcoal. I lighted it, and was puffing reflectively, meditating on the singular circumstances in which I found myself, when I heard the tinkle of anklets in the corridor. Looking up, I saw Fitnah, carrying her lute. She did not so much as glance in my direction, but raised a curtain and entered a near-by doorway.

A moment later, however, she peered out at me, and softly called: "Musa."

"What is it?" I asked.

"I have need of your strength. My *diwan* is heavy, and I would have it nearer the window. Will you help me move it?"

"Assuredly," I responded, and went into her apartment. To my surprise, I saw that her *diwan* was directly beneath the window.

She noticed my puzzled look, and smiled.

"Certainly," she said, "you are not as dense as you pretend to be." Then she came up to me, swaying her shapely hips in the wanton manner of the *gazeeyeh* dancing-girls of the bazars, and before I knew what she was about, had flung her

O. S.—2

arms about my neck, pressing her shapely body close to mine. I tried to draw away, but she clung the tighter, charming me with her smoldering eyes—fanning the flames of my desire. She was intoxicating! Overpowering! Maddening! Slowly our lips met, and clung. Rivers of fire coursed through my veins as I tried to shake off the spell of her accursed witchery.

Again I tried to push her away, repeating the formula:

"I seek refuge with Allah from Shaitan, the Stoned!"

But she only smiled up at me, stroking my face and murmuring:

"Musa, I love you."

Suddenly the door-curtain was drawn back and a slender figure stepped into the room. It was Selma. Surprized, she looked at us for a moment, then said:

"I am sorry to intrude, Fitnah. I thought you were alone."

I was too astonished and mortified to speak. And Fitnah did not. In a moment, Selma was gone.

Resolutely, now, I tore the temptress' arms from around my neck—pushed her away.

She flung back her head, hands on hips, eyes blazing. It seemed that she could be, at will, a cooing dove or a tigress.

"So," she said, "you do not relish the caresses of your little Moroccan cousin when Selma Hanoum is near. It may be, after all, that I shall report you to the Pasha. What are you doing in this *harim* masquerading as a *Magrhebi* eunuch? I knew you were no *Magrhebi* as soon as you spoke, by your accent. Then to test you further, I mentioned a certain street and mosque. You said that you walked that street and prayed at that mosque in Marrakesh. But unfortunately for the plausibility of your statement, both are in Cairo. I also suspected that you were no *castrado*. Now—I know."

"If it is gold you want as the price of silence, I have it not," I said.

She laughed harshly.

"Gold! I have enough for us both—for a dozen more like us, were all to live a hundred years. Until today I was the Pasha's favorite. He showered me with gold, jewels and presents. But today, Selma Hanoum robs me of my place. Today I must sit back with the others over whom I have lorded it, to be neglected—humiliated."

She snatched a dagger from her bosom—brandished it in my face.

"You see this? I had intended to sheathe it in the heart of Selma Hanoum, who was brought here to usurp my place. Then I saw you. It seemed a fair exchange. In taking the Pasha from me, she brought me you. My eyes are sharp, and I was not deceived like the others. Moreover, I was pleased with what I saw. But now—it seems that you would scorn me."

To my surprize, she dropped the dagger, burst into tears, and flung herself face down on the *diwan*.

My first impulse was to flee, but before I had taken three steps I thought better of it. Here, indeed, was a dangerous, headstrong girl. Capable of committing murder because her plans were thwarted, she certainly would not be above carrying out her threat and reporting me to the Pasha. She must be calmed somehow—pacified.

I knelt beside the *diwan,* laid my arm across her shaking shoulders.

"Dry your tears, my pretty one," I said. "It was not scorn that made me act as I did, for I have a profound admiration for your exquisite charms."

"Then—what—was it?" she asked, between sobs.

"Piety," I replied, "and humility. It is both unlawful and unseemly that I, a mere——"

"Oh Father of Lies!" she interrupted. "Do you think thus to deceive me? I will give you one chance, and one only. Tonight when the Pasha goes in to Selma Hanoum, come to me. If you do not, tomorrow will be the day of your death. You have until midnight to make your choice—the arms of Fitnah or the sword of the headsman."

"Why, that's a choice easy to make," I replied. "It will be a pleasure for me to see that, while the Pasha is engaged this evening, you do not lack a lover."

5

I REELED out of Fitnah's apartment, my brain awhirl. A plan had occurred to me on the spur of the moment, which had led me to make the rash promise that she would not lack an amorado that night. Yet this scheme, I now reflected, required the co-operation of Selma Hanoum if it were to have even a slight chance of success. And judging from the look of scorn with which she had favored me when she saw Fitnah in my arms, she was not in a mood to be of assistance to me.

Returning to my *diwan* beside the door, I flung myself down to think—to plan. What could I say to Selma? If I were to try to explain the compromising situation in which she had found me, would she listen?

So wrapped was I in the dark mantle of my gloomy meditations that I did not, at first, see that the object of my thoughts stood in her doorway and was endeavoring to attract my attention. But the persistent clinking of a bracelet against the door jamb caused me to raise my eyes. To my astonishment, I saw that Selma was beckoning to me. When she saw that I understood her signal, she stepped back, letting the curtain fall in front of her.

Rising, I hurried to her doorway, drew back the curtain, and entered.

Selma was reclining on her *diwan* in a pose that revealed every seductive curve of her perfectly modeled body. As my eyes drank in the glory of her loveliness, I mentally compared her with Fitnah, who, though she would have been accounted a great beauty even in the seraglio of the Sultan, was coarse and uninteresting when compared to my little slave girl. So filled was my heart with the love of Selma that the very thought of Fitnah in my arms brought revulsion. It seemed to me that I must have been *jinn*-mad to have even been tempted by the charms of the *Magrhebi* after having once seen the Rose of Mosul.

The voice of Selma recalled me from my ecstasy of adoration.

"There are some things that must be done quickly," she said, "and I can not accomplish them without your aid."

"Your slave but awaits instructions, *hanoum*," I replied. She seemed to have completely forgotten the Fitnah episode, and the explanations which I had planned to make were thereby postponed.

"The panel," she said, "is in the room directly across from this one, occupied by Jabala, the Kashmiri. I must have that room."

"Are you suggesting that I strangle this Kashmiri?" I asked.

"Hardly that," she replied. "You seem to have persuasive ways with women. Suppose you induce her to take another room. There are several others vacant."

"I will try, *hanoum*," I replied, and bowing, withdrew.

Throughout the short interview she had shown no emotion whatever. I could not tell whether she had been angered at sight of the girl in my arms, or was merely indifferent. Neither boded good for me.

CROSSING the corridor, I raised the curtain. Reclining on a *diwan* was a brown-skinned girl of voluptuous form and not unpleasing features. She was loaded down with jewelry and bangles of all descriptions. Finger rings, toe rings, anklets, bracelets, armlets and necklaces were hung on her person in such numbers that the aggregate would have been enough to start a small jeweler's shop. And not only were her body and limbs bedecked, but her face and head as well. Heavy rings hung from her ears, stretching the lobes. There was a diamond pasted to the middle of her forehead. And a large ruby flashed from one pierced nostril. Her headdress was decked with coins and metal ornaments.

"Is this the apartment of Jabala, the Kashmiri?" I asked.

"Jabala would not otherwise be using it, O chamberlain," she drawled, in a rich contralto voice with a husky undertone.

"I have been instructed, *ya sitt*," I said, "to assist you to move to another apartment."

"But I do not care to move," she replied. "I like this apartment."

"Is it your desire that I so inform the Pasha?" I asked.

"No, I will move. Here, carry this chest."

She pointed to an immense chest, which I upended and took on my back. My ruse had worked, thus far. It would be unfortunate if I should happen to stumble upon Mansur or the Pasha in the corridor.

I looked out. As there was no one in sight, I stepped forth into the hallway, and made for a room near the rear door, which I knew was vacant. It was poorly furnished, and much smaller than the one occupied by Jabala, who was evidently well liked by the Pasha. I wondered what the consequences would be when she complained, which she would undoubtedly do next time he visited her. Well, that would be a bridge to cross when the time should come.

As I lowered the chest, Jabala came in behind me, her ornaments tinkling and clattering with every step.

"It is a small room," she said, "and I dislike it, except for one thing."

"What is that?" I inquired, more out of politeness than curiosity.

"It is conveniently near your *diwan*," she replied, looking at me in a manner that reminded me of the appraising glances of Fitnah.

Horns of Eblis! Had she, too guessed? Or had Fitnah told her?

I backed hastily out of the room, ignoring the coquettish glance she cast at me from beneath long black lashes, and hurried to the apartment of Selma. She was gone. I stepped across the hall and found her already installed in the room just vacated by the Kashmiri.

She closed the door and bolted it.

"I'll show you the secret of the panel," she said. "You may have sudden need for it at any time."

Stepping up on the low *diwan*, she drew back a corner of the handsome Kashgar rug which hung in the nook behind it. Back of it was a panel that looked no different from the others in the room, surrounded by a molding on which were carved rosettes, spaced about three inches apart.

"Observe," she whispered, "that it is the fifth rosette from the bottom."

She pressed the center of the rosette. There was a click, and the panel slid to the left, revealing a dark opening into which the top of a ladder, nailed to the outer wall, projected from below. Leaning over, she softly called:

"Uncle."

"Coming," was the reply from below, and I heard some one ascending the lad-

der. In a moment the bearded face of Hasan Aga appeared in the opening.

"What is it?" he asked. "Musa waits below."

"Nothing, except to give you this food," she said, handing him a bundle which she carried, "and to ask you and Musa to remain near the ladder tonight. I may have sudden need of you both."

"We will stay within call," replied Hasan. "Do you plan to run away tonight?"

"My plans are uncertain, as yet," she answered.

"The Pasha's wolves have stripped my house," he told her, "and sealed the door with his seal. It may be, however, that we can escape over the garden wall without attracting attention. I go now, but we will be near the foot of the ladder, Musa and I. Allah guide and keep you."

"And you, *ya amm*," she replied.

He descended, and she again pressed the center of the fifth rosette, whereupon the panel slid back into place. I resolved to broach my plan.

"Fitnah has discovered that I am no eunuch," I said.

"I surmised as much," replied Selma, dropping to the *diwan*.

"She knew I was no Moor by my accent," I went on.

"Yes?"

"And she trapped me into recognizing a street and mosque in Marrakesh, which are really in Cairo. She guessed the rest."

Selma looked at me searchingly.

"Did you say: 'Guessed'?"

I felt myself blushing furiously, and for the first time was thankful for my walnut juice complexion.

"Selma, believe me," I pleaded. "I did not mean to make love to her—did not want her in my arms. I swear to you by the Most High Name——"

"Stop!" she commanded imperiously. She regarded me with a look of regal hauteur, eyes flashing furiously. Though fortune had made her my slave-girl she was still the daughter of a pasha. "How dare you mention the Most High Name in the same breath with that brazen adulteress? Go! Leave me! Do you think I am interested in your vulgar amours?"

"Only insofar as they concern our mutual desire to frustrate the Pasha," I replied, nettled. "I had a plan which involves this Fitnah. If you do not care to hear it, I will go. I came into this affair, risking my life, for one reason alone. I love you, and desire to serve you. From you, I have asked, and now ask—nothing."

"That is true," she admitted, softening. "Allah forgive me, I spoke without right or reason." She rose, and gently laid a hand on my arm. "I'm sorry," she murmured, contritely. "Please tell me of your plan."

"Tonight the Pasha comes to you," I said. "This Fitnah has threatened to betray me, unless——"

"Hush," she admonished. "Speak in a whisper. Some one may hear you."

And so I whispered in her shell-pink ear the plan that had occurred to me when I had, under compulsion, made a certain promise to the *Magrhebi* dancing-girl.

6

LATE that night I lay, turning and tossing on my *diwan* beside the rear door. Needless to say, I had not slept. Twice, earlier in the evening, the Kashmiri had appeared in her doorway, signing to me with her eyes. But I had pretended not to see. Once, as I patrolled the corridor, Sa'id, the fat *bowab* of the *bab al harim*, had called to me across the *majlis*, volunteering the information that the Pasha was drinking in the *salamlik* with boon companions. Faintly there had come to me the sound of dance music, followed by drunken shouts and ribald laughter.

The inmates of the *harim* had all retired. Many of them snored, but loudest of all snored the plump Kashmiri, whose room was near my *diwan*. Under other circumstances I should have cursed her for it, but that night I was thankful to be thus loudly apprised of the fact that she slept.

It had been a long, nerve-racking vigil. In the early morning stillness every sound was intensified. From some near-by roost a cock crowed. Others answered him, each in a different pitch. A young cockerel essayed to imitate them, but his voice broke in the middle with a choking sound, and he ended with a feeble squawk.

Suddenly I heard footsteps at the *bab al harim*, and some one gabbling loudly—drunkenly. Leaping up, I hurried to the women's *majlis*.

Across the room came the Pasha, leaning heavily on the brawny arm of Mansur. I made profound obeisance as he came up. He was very drunk and very maudlin.

"Peace upon you, lord of the bedchamber," he said to me. "Where's my little rosebud?"

"I kiss ground between your hands, O protector of the poor," I said. "The lady eagerly awaits Your Excellency's coming, and pines because you have remained away from her for so long."

"I was busy," he said with drunken gravity. "Very important conference. Take me to her." He turned to the big Nubian. "Go to bed, Mansur."

The huge eunuch bowed solemnly, but grinned derisively behind his back as Mohammed lurched over to support himself by clinging to my arm.

As Mansur moved away, the Pasha looked up at me, squinting his single, bloodshot eye.

"*Wallah!*" he said, swaying from side to side. "I've drunk enough *'raki* this night to float the Russian fleet. Did you say the lady was pining for my company?"

"She is devastated by Your Excellency's neglect of her," I replied.

He fumbled at his waistband—found and produced a piece of gold which he handed me.

"Allah increase your prosperity," I said, pouching the gold.

"Lead on," he ordered. "Don't want my little rosebud to suffer any longer than necessary."

"The lady has asked, as a special favor, that her room be kept in darkness this night," I said, as we strolled down the corridor. "You know she has——"

"Say no more," he interrupted. "Her wish shall be granted. Light or dark, it's all the same to me."

We stopped before the door of the apartment, and I drew back the curtain. The Pasha stumbled in. I closed the door behind him and dropped the curtain. Then I turned and crossed the corridor, entering the opposite room in which a single candle sputtered, and softly closing the door behind me.

The girl on the *diwan* sat up.

"I must have fallen asleep," she said. "Has he come?"

"Yes, *hanoum*," I replied. "He is very drunk, and has gone in to Fitnah. Thus far my plan has worked. The girl has discovered the trick by now, of course, but she will not dare to say anything. As for the Pasha, he is so overcome with *'raki* that I doubt if he could tell a woman from a camel, let alone one woman from another. Besides, the room is in darkness. I suggested this to Fitnah for safety's sake, then told the Pasha it was your wish that it be kept dark."

"Which was quite true," she said. "We must tell my uncle and Musa of this."

Turning, she raised the rug and pressed the button. The panel slid back, and a low call brought Hasan Aga and Musa

scrambling up the ladder. Then we four went into council. The *aga* and eunuch were convulsed with laughter when I told them how we had thus far outwitted the tyrant and his scheming concubine.

But after, Hasan grew grave.

"We are safe enough for the present," he said, "but when the Pasha wakens it will be a different story. Both of you will be in deadly peril."

"Perhaps it would be best if we would all go into the souterrain now," said Selma. "It might be that we could hold out there until the arrival of Ismail Pasha."

"Your cousin may arrive tomorrow," said Hasan. "On the other hand, he may be delayed for weeks or months. Or he may never come. It is possible that he has not been granted a firman. In this case, we should starve in the souterrain without help from outside. For who, in this city, would dare to help us? The fate of Tafas and others before him is a sufficient warning to prevent others trying to befriend us.

"On the other hand, we might try to escape under cover of darkness. But where could we go? And how? Without horses or camels or the means to hire or purchase any, we could not get far. We would only be apprehended and executed, and Selma would be returned to the Pasha's *harim* without hope of succor."

"Why not slit the throats of this Cretan's son and his wench, and hide their bodies in the souterrain?" asked Musa.

"There is nothing I would like better," said Hasan, "and there are thousands of true believers in this pashalik who would applaud the act. But it could only bring death to all of us in the end. The arm of the Sultan is long, and the majesty of his government must be maintained."

"It seems to me," I said, "that the *hanoum* and I should be able to carry on here for at least another day. The Pasha mentioned no names last night, and it was only natural for me to lead him to the door of his favorite. As for this *Magrhebi*, she will not dare to expose me to the Pasha for fear I might reveal her defection."

"One never knows what a woman will do," said Hasan. "However, if it is the wish of Selma that this be done, I see no serious objection. There is, after all, little choice between one course and another. Musa and I will be here within call if trouble arises, and as a last resort we can bolt the door of this room, pry out the window bars to make it appear that we escaped that way, and then enter the souterrain."

And so it was agreed. Hasan and Musa returned to the souterrain, and I to my *diwan* beside the door. I arrived just in time to make ablution and pray the dawn prayer. Presently a slave-girl brought me my breakfast. Soon the *harim* inmates began coming out of their rooms. Some went into the *majlis*, Selma among these. Others strolled out into the garden.

Presently Fitnah came out of her apartment and strode toward me, hands on hips, her brow a thundercloud of wrath.

"So, O consort of a flea-bitten camel," she snarled, "you thought to play a trick on your little Moorish cousin. For this, O mangy dog, shall your head and shoulders part company this day."

"I but carried out your wishes, *ya sitt*," I said, feigning bewilderment and great humility. "You feared that His Excellency's favor might be transferred to another, so I brought him to you. Now you reward me with threats and abuse."

But her anger was no whit abated.

"You will soon learn, O great blundering baboon," she predicted, "that Fitnah does not threaten idly. You well knew my desire, yet you brought me this old he-goat, too drunk for aught but sleep. What cared I if he went in to Selma on one night or another? My rule of this *harim* is ended, in any case, and I am not jealous of his maudlin caresses."

"Could I then disregard the wishes of the Pasha?" I asked.

"What do you mean?"

"Why he commanded that I conduct him to his little rosebud. Who, other than you, his favorite, would he name in such endearing terms?"

Fitnah looked at me long and searchingly.

"If this be true," she said, "I will forgive you. If not, your head shall be forfeit. We will know when the master wakens."

She turned and walked off into the *majlis*, hands on swaying hips, to mingle with the others.

Some three hours later the Pasha poked his ugly, pock-marked phiz and shaven poll out the door and bawled loudly for coffee. A half-dozen girls came running at his call, bearing steaming pots and cups. Among them were Fitnah and Jabala.

He squinted down the corridor at me. "Where is Selma Hanoum?" he asked.

"In the *majlis*, Excellency," I replied.

"Fetch her," he commanded, and withdrew into the room, followed by the girls.

I went into the *majlis* and quickly told Selma of what had occurred.

"If Fitnah tells," she whispered, "you must contrive some way to have Musa take your place." Then, aloud, she said: "Conduct me to His Excellency."

The Pasha was in a vile humor. It was evident that in his long bout with the '*raki* he had come off second best. Jabala was bathing his pock-marked brow with cold water while Fitnah poured coffee. The others were standing around, trying to curry favor by looking sympathetic. He tossed off a cup of searing hot coffee, then looked up with his single, bleary eye as I led Selma before him.

"How was it, Selma Hanoum," he demanded, "that you were not in attendance on me when I wakened this morning? Should I, the Pasha, be left alone, to die like a dog, unattended?"

"I leave you, Excellency?" said Selma, with a look of surprize. "I do not understand."

"It was my *diwan* you shared last evening, my lord," cooed Fitnah, proffering more coffee.

"What!"

The Pasha struck the cup from her hand, spattering her with the hot liquid and shattering it on the floor. Then he glared up at me.

"How came you to do this, you filthy blackamoor?" he demanded.

"I but obeyed your Excellency's orders," I replied. "Your command was that I conduct you to your little rosebud. It was my understanding that you meant none other than Fitnah, your favorite."

"So! You misunderstood! *Wallah!* We have something strange here."

"I can explain, my lord," said Fitnah. Cold chills chased up and down my spine as I saw the venomous looks with which she regarded Selma and me.

"Then do so, and make an end of it," growled the Pasha. "I am in no mood for mysteries this morning."

"This man brought you to me," continued Fitnah, "because he is an impostor. He is neither Moor nor eunuch, but the lover of Selma Hanoum, whom she has brazenly smuggled into your *harim.*"

It was a bold speech, and I could readily see the craft that lay behind it. For at one stroke, Fitnah planned thus to get rid of both me and her hated rival.

The Pasha's face went livid. For a moment he said nothing, but only glared at me, making little choking noises in his throat.

"Mansur! Get Mansur!" he finally managed to articulate. "We'll soon test the truth of this statement."

One of the girls dashed out of the room to call the chief eunuch.

"Permit me to suggest, Excellency," I said, "that Mansur's ministrations might prove embarrassing here before your ladies. With your permission, I will await him in the room across the corridor. In the meantime, I might suggest that you make inquiry of Fitnah as to how she acquired the intimate knowledge that she seems so sure of, and also learn why, if she possessed this knowledge, she did not denounce me before."

With this parting shot, I bowed and withdrew. Once outside, I leaped across the corridor, entered the room opposite, and softly bolted the door behind me. Then I opened the panel and called Musa. He must have been at the very foot of the ladder, for he arrived at the opening in a few seconds.

"Unbolt the door," I told him, "and wait here. Mansur will come to examine you, for you have been accused of being an impostor — neither a Moor nor a eunuch. Talk no more than necessary, but if you are questioned, remember what I told you of last night's adventures, and stick to the story."

Musa chuckled.

"Who accuses me?" he asked.

"You are accused by Fitnah, the *Magrhebi* dancing-girl," I replied. "Remember the story. I'll be waiting behind the panel."

While Musa unbolted the door, I crawled through the opening and closed the panel behind me. To my surprise, I saw a small peephole, cut beneath the panel, which I had not noticed from the outside. To this I applied my eye. Scarcely had I done so ere the giant Mansur burst into the room.

Glaring at Musa, he roared: "So! You are neither *Magrhebi* nor eunuch!"

"On the contrary," said Musa, stripping off his loin-cloth and dropping it to the floor, "I am both."

Mansur stared at him for a moment, then laughed uproariously.

"*Waha!*" he exclaimed. "Behold! If I mistake not, the Moorish girl will get forty stripes for her pains."

Just then the Pasha lumbered through the door.

"What's this talk of stripes, Mansur?" he asked, "and why this boisterous laughter?"

"*Billah!*" replied the Nubian, "if this man be not a eunuch then am I a flaxen-haired *Ferringeh*. Your Excellency can see for yourself that the girl lied."

"Why, so she did," said the Pasha. "The stripes will be in order, Mansur. Lay them on without stint, but take her to a room at the end of the corridor and close the door so her cries will not disturb me."

"Harkening and obedience, Excellency," replied the Nubian, hurrying away with a broad grin on his face.

Mohammed turned to Musa.

"Resume your loin-cloth, O lord of the bedchamber," he said. "Then fetch Selma Hanoum to me here. I like this room better than the other."

"To hear is to obey, my lord," replied Musa, donning his loin-cloth. Then he went out.

Swiftly I descended the ladder. Hasan Aga was waiting in the darkness at the bottom.

"What mischief is afoot now?" he asked.

"The Pasha has ordered Musa to bring your sister's daughter to the room above," I said. "The time has come to strike."

"Agreed," he answered. "Lead on, and I will follow."

7

I MOUNTED the ladder swiftly, Hasan at my heels.

Scarcely had I reached the top and applied my eye to the peephole, ere I saw Musa enter the room with Selma Hanoum. The Pasha was seated on one end of the *diwan*.

As the two came before him, he said: "Stand guard outside, chamberlain, and close the door. See that I am not disturbed."

"I hear and obey, Excellency," replied Musa, but looked questioningly at Selma as he said it. She nodded slightly, and he went out. I could see that she was deathly pale. Evidently she had strong faith in those of us who waited behind the panel or she would not have permitted Musa to go.

The Pasha took a bottle of *'raki* from the taboret and poured himself a stiff drink. Raising the glass to the girl who stood before him, he said: "With health and gladness!" Then he gulped it down, and seized her wrist.

"Sit here beside me, little rosebud," he said. "Be not afraid."

She jerked her arm free, eyes blazing.

"What! You resist me?" he bellowed, leaping to his feet. "Why then, I'll tame you, little tigress."

Quickly I slid the panel back and sprang through the opening. The Pasha heard me, and half turned, whipping out his simitar.

"Treason!" he shouted. "Assassins! To me, Mansur! To me, Sa'id!"

With bared blade I leaped at him, intending to stop his mouth for good. I slashed at his bull neck, but his steel was there to meet mine, and he countered with a stroke so swift and sure that only my skill and extreme quickness of wrist averted my entrance into Paradise at that instant. Despite his age and girth, he proved to be a master of cut and parry.

"Fool," he grated. "Think you to best a seasoned swordsman like me? I have slain of youths like you, a thousand save one, and you shall make up the thousand."

Too eager to end the contest with dispatch, I received a slashed shoulder for my carelessness. Presently, however, I managed to bind his blade with mine—a trick I had once learned from a *Ferringeh* swordsman—and whirling it from his grasp sent it clattering into a corner.

Weaponless, and expecting instant death, he sank to his knees, groveling before me, crying:

"Mercy, lord chamberlain! Spare me, and I will make you rich and mighty."

"Bind, gag and hoodwink this whining dog," I told Hasan.

This the *aga* did with great good will, while I stood over him with the simitar. Meanwhile, I heard the clash of steel on steel outside, and knew that Musa was engaged. I was about to go to his assistance when the noise ceased, and he came in, grinning.

"The fat *bowab* of the *bab al harim* attacked me," he said, "but my point raked his cheek, and he turned and ran, screaming that he had been murdered."

"Bolt the door," I told him.

But I spoke too late, for at that moment, Mansur rushed through the doorway, brandishing his huge simitar.

Swinging his heavy weapon with both hands, the giant Nubian struck at me—a mighty blow that, had it landed, must have split me in twain. But I sidestepped, and brought my blade down on his head with all my might. It bit deep into his wooly skull, and he pitched to the floor without a sound, dead.

Musa sprang to the door and slid the bolt. Outside I could hear the frightened screams of the *harim* inmates, the heavy footfalls of running men, and the clank of weapons.

"The guards are coming," I said. "Into the souterrain, all of you. We'll take this fat pig with us. You first, Musa. Then the Pasha, followed by Hasan. I'll follow Selma Hanoum in case they break down the door before we close the panel."

We bundled the bound, gagged and blindfolded Pasha through the opening, and placed his feet on the rounds of the ladder. Then, Musa supporting him from beneath and Hasan steadying him from above, they took him down into the souterrain.

Selma, who had donned her street attire, quickly followed them. The door was splintering beneath the blows of the soldiers as I closed the panel and descended the ladder.

At the bottom, Musa took up a lantern he had left there, and led the way between gray stone walls down a dank and musty passageway. Presently we came to the foot of another ladder. Here Musa passed his lantern to Hasan, and together, he and I got the Pasha up to the top. When we were through the panel opening, the *aga* and his niece followed.

We took the Pasha into Hasan's *majlis*, and removing his hoodwink and gag, but leaving his hands bound, seated him on the floor.

"I regret, Excellency," said Hasan Aga, "that I can not seat you on a *diwan*, or even a rug. But, as you can see, your soldiers ate from my house with their usual thoroughness."

The Pasha looked up sullenly.

"I'm a man of few words," he said. "Name your price, and let us get down to business."

"As you may have surmised," said Hasan Aga, "we are desirous of leaving Mosul. We will require horses, camels, slaves and traveling equipment, and, let us say, five thousand pounds Turkish."

"Five thousand pounds!" groaned the

Pasha. "There is not so much wealth in all my pashalik."

"We will also require your company for at least three days on the road," continued Hasan, "after which you will be given a horse and our blessing."

"Release his hands, that he may write," he told Musa.

The eunuch removed his bonds, but before he could begin there came sounds of a tremendous commotion in the street outside. First we heard much cheering and the barking of dogs. Then came the thunder of hoofbeats, the shouts of riding men, and the clank of weapons.

Selma ran to the window—peered out through the lattice.

"No need to bargain with this Cretan dog, now," she said. "It's Cousin Ismail Pasha and his brave riders."

She hurried to the door and flung it wide, then rushed out into the street with Hasan and me hurrying after her in wild excitement. Behind us came the Pasha, with Musa, bared blade in hand, watching him as a cat watches a mouse.

"*Alhamdolillah!*" exclaimed Hasan. "Allah be praised! It is indeed Ismail Pasha!"

The young Pasha, a handsome, richly dressed youth mounted on a prancing jet-black stallion, pulled his steed to a halt before us.

Springing lightly from the saddle and tossing his reins to an attendant, he warmly greeted Hasan and Selma.

"I have the firman," he said, exhibiting an official-looking packet. "Mohammed Pasha is deposed and I am to govern in his stead until the arrival of the new appointee, Hafiz Pasha."

LATE the next day, Hasan Aga and I were seated in his refurnished *majlis*, smoking and sipping coffee. Outside, the rain poured down in torrents, as from the mouths of water-skins. Presently there came a knocking at the door. A moment later a servant ushered in Musa.

Leaving his dripping *aba* and muddy shoes at the door, he came up, and bowing low before me, said:

"*Saidi*, I bear a message for you from my lady. She bids me inform you that, having rid her house of the Cretan and put it once more in order, she would feel honored if you would visit her this afternoon."

"At what time?" I asked.

"At such time as suits your convenience, my lord," he replied.

"Tell her to expect me in half an hour," I told him.

He bowed, and withdrew.

A half-hour later, with my cloak drawn tightly about me to keep off the pelting rain, I was picking my way up the muddy street toward Selma's house, when I saw a short, rotund and quite familiar figure hurrying toward me in bedraggled garments, followed by a number of urchins who were shouting insults and pelting him with mud balls. It was Mohammed Pasha.

In order to escape his young tormentors, he dodged into the doorway of a deserted and nearly roofless house. Coming up, I checked the youngsters as they were about to follow him inside. Then, giving them a handful of coppers, I told them to be off.

The deposed Pasha squinted at me without recognition, for I had succeeded in removing most of the walnut juice from my skin and was now dressed with the splendor of an *aga*, from Hasan's own wardrobe.

"May Allah reward you, *saidi*," he said, "but not as I have been rewarded. Yesterday all those dogs were kissing my feet. Today, every one and every thing falls upon me, even the rain."

He was a picture of dejection, standing

(Please turn to page 719)

Mr. Munn Makes Money

By RAY CARR

The story of a lascar's attempt to make trouble for the serang of a Burmese sailing-vessel—the Orient divested of its glamor

MR. MUNN was chief officer of the *Hispaniola,* that diminutive and wholly unkempt steamer which plied uncertainly between the lesser ports upon the coasts of Burma and Malaya. She went where rumors of freights and the dictates of her Armenian owners sent her, and picked up unconsidered trifles of cargo and such deck passengers as had been unfortunate enough to miss the regular British India sailing.

Standing in the sun, his mean features shadowed by a battered solar topee, Mr. Munn presented an appearance entirely in keeping with that of the *Hispaniola.* He was small, like the ship, and similarly, too, he seemed unwashed. His white drill uniform was creased and unclean, and the unbuttoned collar of his jacket revealed the fact that his singlet was one that had been in use for many days.

He stood above an open hatch supervising the work of a gang of vociferous Tamil coolies who were filling the half-empty hold with a miscellaneous cargo of bags of rice, corrugated iron sheeting and cases of rubber. And from time to time he glanced toward the gangway leading to the jetty and noted with satisfaction the stream of deck passengers coming aboard. He was peculiarly interested in deck passengers, and more than once he made a rapid mental calculation of the number that had boarded the steamer.

Suddenly, at the sound of his name being called, he turned and looked up toward the bridge deck upon which stood Captain Padwick.

"Mr. Munn! Just a minute, please." And the captain, a fat man, beckoned to him with a pudgy hand.

"I found this on my cabin table. Anonymous letter." Captain Padwick held out between finger and thumb a grimy document. "It seems to be some complaint about the serang—says he smuggles deck passengers on board for a small bribe and does the owners out of the proper passage-money. Inquire into the matter, please."

The chief officer took the letter and placed it in his pocket.

"Nothing in it, I expect. Probably one of the lascars trying to get even with the serang. But when I've finished down there I'll make inquiries, sir." And he returned to his place beside the open hatch in the well deck.

But this matter of the letter annoyed him; for, in spite of his assertion that there was nothing in it, there was a great deal in it. And he knew it, too. In fact, to put the matter plainly, Mr. Munn was hand in glove with the serang, and for every deck passenger who avoided paying the proper fare he levied toll upon his subordinate. However, he must make some show of an inquiry.

The same evening the *Hispaniola* sailed from the little Burmese port at which she had spent several hours. Her decks were littered with groups of deck passengers and their many baskets and bundles; and the whole steamer was pervaded with the evil scents of salt fish and that strong-smelling fruit, the durian.

And as the golden pagoda on the hill above the town, and the godowns and palm trees vanished in the distance, Mr. Munn recollected the anonymous letter and ordered a passing lascar to tell the serang, Ashraff Ali, that he desired to see him in his cabin.

Ashraff Ali was a personage of some importance on the *Hispaniola,* and he ruled his lascars with a rod of iron. Like the European officers above him, he, too, profited improperly by the voyaging of the *Hispaniola,* but he permitted none of those who served under him to do so.

Saluting gravely he presented himself at the door of Mr. Munn's cabin, having previously straightened the red sash about the middle of his loose blue tunic and given a flick to the tassel of his scarlet fez.

"Come in, serang."

Ashraff Ali entered the small apartment and faced the chief officer, who was seated upon his bunk.

"Serang, somebody has complained to the captain that you are in the habit of cheating the company. You accept money from deck passengers and then help them to evade me when I go to collect their fares. Is this true?" Mr. Munn spoke in *lascaribat,* that pidgin Hindustani inevitably employed by ship's officers when addressing their native crews.

"Sahib, Allah knows that this thing is false. Who tells this lie?"

"It was contained in an unsigned letter which the captain found on his table." The chief officer unfolded the letter and turned it over in his hands. It was written in green ink upon cheap, ruled paper. "Here is the document. It would seem to be the work of a bazar petition writer."

Ashraff Ali took the letter and, although he could not read it, he affected to examine it closely.

"Without doubt this was written in the bazar. And it was written by the order of one who bears me a grudge. There is such a one on board this ship, sahib."

"Ah! And who is that?"

"The lascar, Gunu Meah. It is a family quarrel. If your honor will permit, I will punish him myself. This complaint he makes against me is entirely false."

Mr. Munn nodded.

"It is for you to maintain discipline amongst the men. I will report that you have explained the matter satisfactorily."

From his pocket he produced a black Burma cheroot, and lit it carefully. Then he reached up to the rack above his bunk and took out a small black-covered exercise book. Opening it he examined it, and then turned again to address the serang.

"What is due to me for today?"

"There are, perhaps, twenty people who are unable to pay the fare, sahib. For the sake of charity I have allowed them to board the ship."

Mr. Munn leant back and puffed contemplatively at his cheroot. With half-closed eyes he calculated his share of the profit.

"I will take thirty rupees."

"Sahib!" The serang made a gesture of despair with his hands.

"Thirty rupees. . . . Remember the complaint. . . . I will expect the money in the morning." And, with a wave of the hand, he dismissed the serang. Then he turned once more to a contemplation of the entries in the little book with the black cover.

The present voyage was proving profitable to Mr. Munn.

2

LASCAR Gunu Meah was elated. His letter, for the inscribing of which he had paid eight annas to a Madrassi petition writer, he had seen in the hands of the captain. And the captain had conferred over it with the chief officer. Assuredly would there be trouble for the serang, Ashraff Ali. And Gunu Meah, his heart beating high beneath his tattered and greasy suit of blue dungarees, went about his work with a cheerful grin.

His feud with the serang was a family affair. Both men hailed from the same small village near Chittagong, and in that village Ashraff Ali was a notable. True, he did not rank as high as a serang in the employ of the British India or the Clan Line. But a serang is a serang, and infinitely above a mere lascar.

Now Ashraff Ali had a brother named Mahomed, and Mahomed had cast eyes upon a girl who was the daughter of Gunu Meah's sister. The girl, a willing captive, had allowed herself to be abducted by Mahomed and there ensued the inevitable proceedings in the courts. Feeling ran high between the families concerned, but the real root of the trouble was that Mahomed stoutly refused to pay the usual dowry to the girl's parents. Ashraff Ali had been besought to bring his influence to bear upon his brother, but he had repulsed the approaches of the girl's family with contumely and vulgar abuse.

And it was to avenge these insults that Gunu Meah deliberately sought employment upon the *Hispaniola* and for this purpose abandoned another steamer in which he usually sailed. His family had been disgraced by the abduction of the girl Halima Bibi. It was his duty, therefore, to humble the swaggering brother of the abductor.

But Gunu Meah's elation was short-lived, for he was in entire ignorance of the alliance which existed between Mr. Munn and the serang. And it was within a few minutes of the interview between these two worthies that he began to doubt the wisdom of the revenge he had planned.

He was cleaning some brass work in a leisurely manner and dreaming happily of the early discomfiture of his enemy, when he was almost stunned by a sudden and severe blow on the side of his head. As he picked himself up from the deck he became aware of the fact that the serang was cursing him fluently.

"Son of a pig! Is that how you were taught to work on your last ship? Have I not sufficient to see to without checking your task, thou unclean animal?" And Ashraff Ali spat noisily and with much ostentation over the ship's side.

Later in the same evening, at sunset, Gunu Meah again met with defeat at the hands of the serang. Together with half a dozen other lascars he was squatted on the deck outside the small deck house in which lived the native crew. The men were busy with their evening meal and Gunu Meah was dipping eager fingers into a large bowl which contained his ration of curry and rice.

"Ho! Gunu Meah! There is a man required immediately upon the bridge. Go thou at once." Serang Ashraff Ali pushed his way through the seated men.

"But, serang, I am feeding——"

"Dog! Do as you are bidden."

And Gunu Meah fled obediently along the deck. When he returned, having found of course that he was not wanted upon the bridge, his bowl of curry and rice had vanished. His shipmates, when questioned about its disappearance, affected a supreme ignorance and even seemed to doubt that he had been forced away from his evening meal. More than ever did he feel that he had made a mistake in attempting to depose the serang. Nevertheless, with a certain swagger, he went into the dark and frowzy hutch which he shared with the other lascars and proceeded to unlock the little tin box which contained all his worldly belongings. From the box he withdrew a large clasp-knife, and taking it on deck he began to sharpen it. The blade flickered and gleamed in the light of a hurricane lantern which hung above him, and the lascar grinned and made much ado of the sharpening. But the serang who was passing removed the lantern and laughed insultingly.

3

It was an hour before dawn.

Gunu Meah was awakened by a pressure upon his chest and the sharp pricking of a knife at the base of his throat. He moved uneasily and a harsh voice whispered in his ear:

"Quiet, thou son of Hell."

Rough arms gripped him and he was jerked to his feet to find himself standing between Ashraff Ali and a lascar.

A dim light burnt in the deck house and revealed amid deep shadows the sleeping forms in the narrow bunks. Gunu Meah's companions slept; almost too obviously did they sleep.

But he was given no time for speculation. The knife-point was pressed against his side and his captors impelled him toward the gray blur of the open door.

On deck the gleam of a waning moon illumined all things with a pale and ghastly light. In particular it lit with an unnatural brightness the churned white wake of the steamer. And Gunu Meah, standing at the stern of the *Hispaniola* behind the deck house, was fascinated by the frothing, bubbling stream which seemed to emerge from the screw thudding immediately beneath him. He stared in silence at the ever-changing and yet unchanged wake. Perhaps he sensed what was about to happen to him.

Ashraff Ali spoke.

"There must be no tale-bearing liars aboard this ship. Silence, dog!" And he moved his knife threateningly as Gunu Meah gave vent to a half-hearted exclamation. "See, there is the shore." He pointed to a line of palms which made a dark smudge between sea and purple sky. "If you would live you must swim to it." He chuckled quietly, for he knew that the lascar could never reach the land.

"Oh, serang! Have pity. I——"

"Quiet. Climb up upon the rail and jump."

And Gunu Meah, the knife-point ever touching his back, mounted the rail. There followed a deft push, and he was struggling in the foaming wake.

Once, twice, his black head appeared above the white wrack of water. Then it vanished.

"It is well." Ashraff Ali closed his knife and returned to his bunk to complete his night's rest.

Next morning Mr. Munn collected his thirty rupees from the serang. Methodically he made a note in his small black book. And while he wrote, the serang hovered uncertainly about the door of the cabin.

"What is it?" inquired the officer.

"Gunu Meah, lascar, is missing. He it was who wrote that letter, sahib."

"What has happened to him?"

Ashraff Ali made a vague gesture.

"He was frightened. Perhaps he has deserted the ship. The shore is not far distant."

Mr. Munn nodded and dismissed him. Then he placed the thirty rupees in his locker. The fate of Gunu Meah, lascar, did not trouble him unduly.

An hour later he reported the absence of the lascar to the captain.

"Damn the fellow! Why in Hades should he jump overboard? He could easily have waited until we touched port. . . . Well, I suppose we must report when we reach Moulmein. Queer birds, the Chittagonians."

"Yes, sir."

"And, while I think of it, we have been warned that we are to be prepared for an unusually large number of deck passengers. Something wrong with the B. I. boat."

"Indeed, sir." Mr. Munn grinned happily. He thought with pleasure of the next entry he would make in his little exercise book with the black cover.

O Pioneers!

By WARREN HASTINGS MILLER

A stirring tale of adventure and death in the Borneo jungle, and the burning love of a Dyak woman for her man

THEIR trysting-place was out under the stars, where the dark jungle bordered the rice fields back of the Bornean kampong of Long Nayah. A huge and high thatch roof on piles rose blackly beyond the *ladang* embankments, Long Nayah, that communal Dyak village of twenty doors on the banks of the Makkaham. The flat mirror of a rice pond reflected dimly the faint star-glow overhead, the penciling of rice-stalks, and the lone figure of Mata-Manis awaiting impatiently her lover, Migi Siak. Her ears were intent upon the jungle, unmindful of the boom of great Bornean frogs in the lowlands, the occasional bark of an uneasy dog under the kampong, the soft drone of cicada and gecko lizard. She jumped and her hands crossed in front of her bare bosom as a stick cracked in the undergrowth. The bushes parted and Migi stood before her.

Mata-Manis greeted him with a silent and ominous gesture. Her sleek head lifted to his appealingly in its Malayan beauty of incurved and elfish nose, its black tresses drawn back in a tight knot that bared the soft curves of her cheek and chin. Her brown eyes flashed tragically as she announced her bad news:

"Oh, Migi! The gods frown on us, my own! We must fly from here. Bukit Bruang has visited my father this day, bearing gifts!"

Migi drew in his breath with a sudden gasp of anger. He was but a stripling, scarce older than Mata-Manis herself. A nude figure of a youth, his graceful body hidden only by the embroidered *chawat* or loin-cloth whose tails hung down before and behind quite to his knees, and was ornamented solely by the red rattan amulets on biceps and calves. The sudden glare of Dyak ferocity distorted his usually merry and carefree features: "What! He that has three wives already would now buy thee? He knows well that thou and I are betrothed!"

"Thou art but a youth, dear one!" said Mata-Manis tenderly. "What cares he about thee? He that is rich and powerful and the greatest warrior in the kampong! *Ya Allah* but I hate him! There is but one way, Migi; we must fly from here"

"Nay!" said Migi stoutly. "It is not for thee, Sweet-Eyes. A new room in the kampong thou shalt have. The presents, the feasts, the merry-making, the grand wedding, such as is due the beauty of all the girls of the kampong! I shall outbid Bukit Bruang for thee, dear one!"

Mata-Manis shook her head. Beautiful she was, under the faint light of the stars shining on her corselet of polished red rattan hoops, on the gold threads in her necklace of knotted white embroidery that set off her brown shoulders. Beautiful, and the belle of the kampong, and she knew it. But Migi was poor. It would cost more than he or his father owned if her wedding was to be done up in the style that the position of her family in the kampong demanded. All the men of the community would have to join forces in erecting new piles at the end of the long communal dwelling, in extending the great thatch roof, in splitting wide boards and hewing rafters for their new "door," room. All this in addition to the sum required to buy her from

"*She stared fixedly at the but on the knoll above her.*"

her father. Bukit Bruang could afford that, but not Migi.

"How wilt thou pay, beloved?" she asked him despondently.

"Debt-slave will I become to thy father for thee, Sweet-Eyes!" replied Migi. "Is not a man worth more than all Bukit Bruang's rattan and rubber and gongs and vases? Thy father can not refuse. In time we shall buy our freedom. It is the only way, dearest."

Mata-Manis eyed him tenderly. "O kingling!" she murmured, for her heart knew what a sacrifice this was that Migi was making for her. Years of toil . . . perhaps *never* free . . . for the toils of debt-slavery were endless. And they would be nobodies in the kampong, slaves in her father's house, they and their children. It would take years to repay such a sum as her father would demand, once Bukit Bruang began bidding for her against him.

"Nay! Not even for me, my heart!"

O. S.—**3**

she protested. "To see thee toil thy young life away! And the humiliation, for both of us!"

"What else?" asked Migi. "I might challenge Bukit Bruang and kill him," he spoke up more brightly.

Mata-Manis gave a stifled scream, suddenly hushed lest the kampong should hear them. But she gripped him frantically. "Never, my own!" she whispered tensely. "Thou, a mere youth, against his war-wise experience? *Phoo!* He would like nothing better!" she laughed harshly.

"Well?" said Migi. He was at his wits' end for ways and means.

"The jungle is free," said Mata-Manis meaningly.

Migi considered that a new and somewhat startlingly original idea, for a girl of

Mata-Manis' communal bringing up. He had his ax and his parang, and with them could build a home for her, out in the jungle. He had his weapons, the sumpitan and spear, for hunting. Clearing for a rice field was an easy matter. Nothing in all that that he could not do with his own two hands! But that she, the belle of the kampong, would consent to go and live in such a home with him, forsake the protection of the rooms in the high and strong kampong, risk the dangers of wild beasts and wandering head-hunters and Arab slave-catchers, seemed unbelievable.

"If I build thee a home, wilt thou come, Sweet-Eyes?" he asked her.

"I'd do anything for you, Migi!"

Migi gasped as her eyes glowed upon him. Here was love, strong as his own, love that would do and dare anything that they might be together. Her idea grew in attractiveness, too, as it sank in. Why *not* start a new kampong himself? Other young fellows would soon come and join them, and the place become strong against the myriad enemies of the jungle. And, a home of his own! The call of it was as strong in him as in her, he soon realized.

"So be it!" he said finally. "I go. Tell no one anything. For a week I labor. Then, at night, when thou hearest the call of the minah thrush from this spot, bring all that thou hast and come!"

She went to his arms; and then at a harsh feminine call from the kampong tripped away lightly and was gone in the night.

MIGI retraced his way through the jungle to where his canoe was hauled up among the others on the river bank. All night he paddled up the Makkaham. By dawn he had landed on a jungly point and was looking for a site. He chose a knoll in the forest, back somewhat from the river and looking down upon a ravine full of bamboo and sago palms. A brook trickled in it. Here grew a slender and straight young tapang tree a little over a foot in diameter, not one of those mighty tapangs of which his people hollowed out their long proas. This the ax bit and in an hour it had crashed to earth. Migi cut its trunk into sections and split those into wide boards with ironwood gluts. He was very happy in spite of all this unaccustomed and perspiring labor. Home! How good the jungle was! Here was his house, this tapang split into boards. Here was food, bread from the pith of these sago palms. Their leaves gave attap for his thatch, too. Here was fruit, wild banana, lansat, durian, and mangosteen. Here was meat, wild pig, rusa deer, fish from the river. Yonder cane simply needed clearing for a rice patch. He whistled as he worked.

With his sumpitan he shot a large crowned fruit-pigeon for lunch and cooked up some of the rice in his belt in a green bamboo joint set up in the fire. By evening he had a quantity of boards split and his rafters rough-hewn. The next two days saw his house nailed up with ironwood pins set in by a bow-drill and the thatch roof on. Migi stood and regarded his new home with immense pride. A white man would have thought it a mere dog kennel, for it was exactly that shape, perched three feet above the soil on posts, its floor just long enough to lie full length upon and wide enough to sleep two. He could stand up inside —if he stood directly under the ridge! The hut also had a door opening, wide enough to pass Migi's shoulders, just high enough to scrape his back as he crawled within.

A frown crossed Migi's brown features under the bang of blue-black hair as he eyed this door-opening with disfavor. It needed something to close it, for while the cracks between his boards were so narrow that only his war parang could be jabbed through them, the door was plenty large enough to admit a leopard should one get their scent and decide to investigate. He made a stout wooden hatch for it, but knowing nothing about a hinge was at a loss how to make it stay on when once inside. The bow drill finally gave him a brilliant idea. Coaxing it to accept a quart drill much too large for it, Migi finally achieved a hole in between two boards above his lintel. Through this hole he drew his canoe rope, and with this the door could be hauled up like a portcullis and secured with more rope tied to a crooked peg inside.

That night Migi slept in his own house, with a far greater sense of security than when a rude bamboo cot had left him at the mercy of night prowlers and made him doze with every sense on the alert. But a terrific tropical downpour that night showed him that the hut, while a grand little home, was a trifle crowded in rainy weather, for he could neither cook in it nor do anything much else *but* sleep there! He spent the next day in extending the roof out before and behind the hut to make a living-room in front of the house and a cooking-place behind it.

So far not a human soul had visited him. No one cared that the jungle had swallowed him up as utterly as it does the tiger-cat that prowls in the night. It was high time to go for his bride, for their home was done. Migi surveyed his handiwork with immense pride. Not much of an edifice, if you viewed it by Dyak standards; little better than the thatch nests of the sorry Punan savages, who slept in their own campfire ashes. But home, sweet home! A most dangerous home, if Migi had allowed himself to think so! Almost at the mercy of the jungle's big prowling cats, entirely at the mercy of wild elephants and rhino!

But Migi did not permit himself to worry about that now. His ax and his parang and his dexterous fingers had provided a home for Mata-Manis. Now to fetch her to it in triumph! That would be a hazardous step for them to take, he felt with his courage fighting his fears within him as he went down the trail to where his canoe lay hauled up in the brush. Could he risk her here? An elopement, the kampong would view it. They would do more than laugh at his hut; they would come in force to burn it and hale them both back to the village, the outraged father demanding his price for his daughter, Bukit Bruang seeking his head for stealing the girl that he already regarded as his own property.

AT TWILIGHT Migi paddled close under the banks along shore. The river was deserted of canoes, all the fishermen returned to the kampong for the night. After dark he landed a considerable distance upstream and made his way through the jungle, to arrive finally at their old trysting-place on the corner of the rice embankments. The bell-like call of the minah thrush presently whistled out into the night. None of the kampong dogs took alarm as Migi waited, listening. That minahs do not call at night had not penetrated their intelligences.

Presently there came a rush of light feet and Mata-Manis was in his arms: "Take me away! Oh, take me away from here—anywhere, Migi!" The stifled sobs burst from her as Migi let her out of his embrace for the long look that his soul delighted in. "It has been terrible since you've been gone! The whole family saying dreadful things about you—that big bear Bukit Bruang calling on my father with ceremonies — all the girls of the kampong looking wise at me! He has made the offer, and the chief says I must obey."

Migi glowered. "No more is he chief to me!" he exclaimed. "I am head of my own kampong now! Will you come, Sweet-Eyes? I have a home for you now, a poor, sorry thing in the jungle, but I built it with these two hands. I was happy in doing it for you, Sweet-Eyes. But oh, it is but a wretched hovel when I think of the big room in the kampong you should have, the feasts and presents, the merry-making——"

She stopped his mouth with a soft palm. "Boy! *My* boy!" she cooed. "If you built it, it is a palace! Red-flowering vines on our garden fence—oh, I can make it beautiful!"

Migi's heart sank as he wondered what visions she was making of that poor hut of his. "Thou wilt come, Eyes-of-Love?" he asked her.

"Yes!" agreed Mata-Manis impulsively. "What care we for them? A home of my own—it is all I ask, my man!" she said with the woman's nest-hunger in her voice.

"It is not fair to thee, Sweet-Eyes," protested Migi, for the reality of what he was doing was beginning to unnerve him. He risked a terrible retribution for them both by this! Scouts would locate their hut within three days, Bukit Bruang, the war chief, leading them. He would have to be met with weapons, by a mere boy. Nor could the village be brought to listen to the really fine thing he had done, provided a home for his girl since he could not afford to buy her a room. The community spirit among the Dyaks was too strong to listen to that with any patience. They would burn his hut, hale the girl back, and leave him to settle with Bukit Bruang.

But for answer Mata-Manis fled away into the darkness to bring all the personal possessions she herself owned to start this home.

By dawn he had led her to the hut in triumph. Migi thrilled with delight over her cries of pleasure, her raptures, her happy voice as she set about those details of housekeeping so dear to the female of our species. One day of bliss, of peace and jungle plenty, their honeymoon; and then the shadows of night fell.

And the night had eyes, eyes of death, the ruby eyes of the king cobra, the green fires of the leopard, the twin flash of the wild dog in the bush, the little pig eyes of bear and rhino and elephant. They all asked Migi, not what sort of shelter he had built but what kind of fort this home of his was. It was their first night alone in the jungle. Through love and courage they had won the right to each other, but——

A stick cracked in the jungle outside. Migi and Mata-Manis listened warily. They had roped up their door for the night and their tikkar mat was spread. Outside of their board walls the untamed savagery of the jungle was abroad in the night. A prowling Something was out there!

"*Aiee!*" whispered Mata-Manis, shivering, as presently they heard bushes rustle and swish and a rank odor tainted their glade. Migi grinned and felt over his rope fastenings. Then with a stealthy *wheep!* his war parang slid from its scabbard. A deep, animal cough, ferocious in its menace, its savage fury—either leopard or tiger-cat, both deadly.

"*Sayah banyak takut!*—I'm terribly afraid, Migi!" Mata-Manis shivered and shook while Migi watched through the cracks. "Oh, we *can't* live here!"

"Peace, woman!" hissed Migi sternly. "Take thou my sumpitan spear."

He turned again to the cracks while Mata-Manis in terror grabbed for the barrel of *Migi's* sumpitan, the long iron-wood blow-gun with its spear-blade lashed to the muzzle. The grip of it gave her courage. A weapon! Something to fight with, to defend their home, their lives, just as could a man! She was strong; with this in hand she could even kill that brute out there.

She had hardly crouched by to help her man when a hideous shriek rent the jungle night and something big and heavy thudded against their hut. The rasps of claws tearing at their thatch roof mingled with a diabolical crescendo of snarls. Migi jabbed again and again with the war parang, upward through a crack. Mata-Manis thrust blindly in the dark with the sumpitan, driving it through the thatch at this deadly thing that was destroying their home and striving to come at their lives. There was a mortal squall, coughing roars of agony, sounds of the prodigious acrobatics of a wounded animal thrashing around in the jungle outside.

Migi turned to her with a low laugh. "A robe for thee, Sweet-Eyes, against the chills of early morning! We will find him, stiff and cold, tomorrow."

The dying gasps and groans came to their ears sweetly. The tiger-cat—they were sure now it was that fierce lord of the Bornean jungles—was kicking convulsively his last, out there. "And 'twas thy thrust did it, Brave One!" added Migi loyally, though he knew just where his parang had struck. Mata-Manis said nothing but took him fiercely in her arms. "Man!—*My* man!" she cooed in his ear. "Nay, 'twas thou! And our home is strong and safe."

The jungle had still something to say to that, however. It was midnight when they were again awakened, this time by the resounding trumpet-blasts of wild elephants disporting themselves up at the headwaters of their brook. Squeals, neighs, grunts, grumbles, all the inde-scribable noises an elephant makes, mingled with the splash of showering waters and the snap of broken cane in the swamp. The moon had risen high and all the jungle was flooded with silvery light. Black as ink the crisscross of bamboo and tree-branch shadows; cold, silvery, and cruel the green-white light in their open glade. Mata-Manis and Migi listened uneasily. If those great elephants should come downstream, nothing could save their home! The kennel would be a mere box under their tusks, their lives the plaything of wild elephants enraged by man-scent.

For some time the sounds went on. Then they came nearer, the crash and swish of branches more distinct. Migi lowered the door of their hut. Their only safety now lay in immediate flight if these great creatures should get their scent and stampede. Mata-Manis gathered the things she valued most and did them into a bundle in her very best slendang shawl, then took Migi's shield and chopper-parang and waited. Migi crouched at a crack, war parang and sumpitan in hand, whispering her the direction they should fly, uphill to the left where elephants could not follow with any speed.

Ponderously they advanced down the creek. The ground shook and trembled as their huge feet slipped off boulders in the stream; small trees, pushed over in their advance, crashed down. Migi glanced at his girl. She too squatted at a crack, trembling so that the hut shook, but the grip of her hand on his arm told him that she was ready to fly with him to the safety of the upper heights. He thought most upon the lugubrious probability that this home of his that he had built with so much labor, and now loved, was soon to be knocked to splinters by these jungle people. He prayed in an audible whisper to the good *hantus* of the woods to lead them away while there was yet time. Mata-Manis joined her prayer with his as they knelt together on the mat.

A great gray elephant stood motionless in the ravine below their knoll. A huge and nervous female without tusks was she, the leader of the band. Migi held his breath and his heart beat fast as her trunk went up searchingly, the moist fingers of its tip opening and closing as she tested the wind suspiciously. He hoped and prayed that for once the vagrant air-currents of the jungle would be still.

For a full minute the old female stood snorting and grumbling in the moonlight, her big ears flapping out and back, her trunk wavering like some huge searching leech. She stared fixedly at the hut on the knoll above her, asking the sensitive nerves of the proboscis what manner of thing this might be. Migi's hand crept out in the darkness to find Mata-Manis'. Their clasp was of partnership. Come what might, abandon their home and fly, or be delivered from this peril, they were one!

A ponderous and unwieldy swing of her whole body brought the big female sidewise to them. Other trunks searching about over the tops of the lower bamboos disappeared. She lurched on downstream, and after her four others and a calf.

"Allah is good!" Migi breathed a pent-up sigh of relief. "Also are the *hantus* of the forest good! We make an offering, the best thing that we have."

"Even so," agreed Mata-Manis and she unwrapped her precious splendang from the bundle. "This in the fire tomorrow."

"And this," added Migi, taking a prized amulet from his arm.

They performed that ceremony with the sincere piety of children at daybreak, before ever rice was cooked or meat grilled. The tiger-cat was found and skinned for a morning occupation. To Migi it repre-

sented wealth, something valuable, a beginning toward that debt that he owed Mata-Manis' father. This home of theirs had advantages; it was an animal-bait, of sorts. If the village would only let him alone, he could amass skins and rattan enough and soon owe them nothing!

THE day wore on; peace and security once more. And then toward evening an arrow fell into camp. That silent messenger, swishing down out of the sky and sticking with a quivering shock into the soil near their fire, brought a rush of frightened exclamations from Mata-Manis. "*Aiee!*—Already, Migi!—My father!—Bukit Bruang! Oh, let us run!"

Migi had leaped for his sumpitan. Then he noted that a pith collar was tied around the arrow shaft.

"Nay—a friend shot this!" he reassured her. "It is a message."

Together they opened and read it, Mata-Manis leaning fearfully over his shoulder.

"*Djaga!*" was the one word it bore, writ in Arabic by a point of charcoal.

" 'Beware!' " read Migi. "Ho! Now must I fight for thee, Eyes-of-Love! Bukit Bruang comes!"

A piercing shriek from her had drowned his words. She was clinging to him now, her eyes brown wells of terror, her grasp frantic in its intensity. "*Never!* He will kill thee, heart of mine!" she cried, appalled. "Quick! To the trees! What chance hast thou—a mere youth——" she shook him in the agony of her fear.

"*Apa guna?* What avail?" Migi shrugged his brown shoulders. "In the jungle? He tracks us. On the river? Our canoe is seen. And shall we give up our home to the torch? Not for twenty Bruangs!" said Migi sternly. "Nay!" he silenced her protests. "The sumpitan is just. It makes equal the weak and the strong." He tapped the ironwood barrel of his blowgun significantly.

She shook her head violently. "Never shalt thou stay here! He kills thee—and my heart dies within me! To become his woman, his pretty wife-slave — *aagh!*" Her bared white teeth bit the air in a fury of primitive passion. Then she raged at Migi, shaking him frantically. "Up, my man! The trees leave no trail! What is this hut compared to thy *life*—and mine!—Come!"

"It is our home," said Migi somberly. "And here I stay and fight. Go, woman, and by the tree trail!" he commanded her. "This is no place for thee, now. I stay here, in ambush with the sumpitan."

His ferocious countenance and stern eyes awed Mata-Manis. Was this the Migi of the laughing face and boyish ways that had made love to her carefree and joyous this past year? A new kind of admiration for him grew in her eyes, for her man was indeed a man and would hold his own with a strong hand. Then the eternal partnership of male and female prompted her to his side, eyes flashing, small hands clenched.

"And am I to hide in the trees like an ape, leaving thee to fight him alone?" she demanded. "Nay, what Bukit Bruang does to thee he does to me. I stay, Migi!"

"Peace, dear one," said Migi. "It is foolish talk, yet brave; and I love thee the more for it. But between him and me it must be alone, man to man. The sumpitan dart must decide—in that I can not meet him with shield and parang."

Mata-Manis surveyed the slender and unmatured figure of Migi before her with admiration but without confidence. The terror of losing him was in her eyes, a woman's terror that no man can appreciate. Love, dependence on her protector and provider, abhorrence of wife-slavery to Bruang, all spoke eloquently out of her eyes.

"Nay, Migi," she whimpered, "what chance hast thou, even with the sumpitan, against this man's craft and experience? What snares and pitfalls will he not set for thee! Thou art already slain, fallen into his toils, in thy youth and innocence. Some trick of which thou knowest nothing—and thou liest dead of his dart in the jungle. And my heart is desolate and empty, and all my life one long rain. Come! We fly from here through the tree-tops. It is the only way."

"Am I a cowardly Punan savage that lives in the trees for fear?" asked Migi harshly. "This is our home. I love it. If any man seeks me, here am I. And it I defend to the death!"

His tone was so resolute that her heart sank. There was no hope of persuading him to flight, yet it was foolhardy to remain. What chance had he against the great war chief, Bukit Bruang? But then, they two together, with some trick of their own that would equal matters? It was not fair for a man like him to hunt down a boy like her Migi! She would kill him herself if she could!

While Migi was busy poisoning the tips of some of his hunting-darts with the virulent red upas-vine juice, which is pure strychnin, she thought it over; then she came to him with a woman's craft in her eyes.

"So be it, my heart! We stay. But not with those." She pointed at the darts that Migi was twirling in a small bamboo pot filled with sticky gum. "He would outmatch thee, Migi. Nay!"—her voice rose in protest as a fierce light of negation flared up in Migi's eyes—"Thus shall we kill him——"

Migi listened to her idea with a tolerant smile. "*Hai!* perfidious and crafty Little One!" he chided her. "But it would never work with a war-wise veteran like Bukit Bruang! Thinkest thou not he would search everywhere for *me*, first?"

"And he would not find thee, Migi!" laughed Mata-Manis. "Lo, our door is open, our mat spread! And furthermore, he will look neither *at* the hut *nor* the door!" She raised her eyelids and gave him that glimpse into her innermost woman's heart that always set Migi on fire. "When men see that, they have neither wits nor caution, Migi—they see only *me!*" she smiled mischievously. "So greet I Bukit Bruang—alone."

Migi shook his head. There were a thousand chances that her plot might miscarry. But it had one point in its favor: Bukit Bruang might come in with a rush, seeing her here alone and being told that he himself had fled in fear. He agreed at last. His home was a sacred thing; any man who invaded it laid himself open to every trick their two wits could devise.

THE tropical sun set with its usual suddenness. The short twilight came on. Mata-Manis busied herself nervously at household tasks in the kitchen back of their house, peering out now and then, for it was all suspiciously silent, no bird piping his note, no hurried rustling of small creatures in the brush. That meant that men were about. How many? She hoped it would be Bukit Bruang, alone. An attack by the whole village would ruin them!

A stick cracked in the jungle. Mata-Manis went forth in the direction of the sound, her heart pounding with excitement. He was lurking out there, the man who had come to kill her boy!

"It is thou, Migi?" she called out. "*Hai!* but thou hast been long away!— Come! It is late."

The bushes moved and the man she most dreaded rose stealthily out of them —Bukit Bruang! Mata-Manis gave back in fright before him.

"Peace, girl—I will not beat thee," he called after her.

She halted and let him come near; then gave back before him again. The war chief advanced warily, his eyes searching everything. That would never do! She let him come quite close; then looked up at him saucily.

The man took fire and his eyes gleamed upon her rapaciously. Mata-Manis gave back again, coquetry in her glance. Her eyelids raised provokingly. Bukit Bruang threw all caution to the winds at that one glimpse! He looked neither at the hut nor the door, but at *her,* as he came on eagerly, followed her under the brush shelter behind the hut. Before Mata-Manis knew it, she was seized in an embrace that threatened to crush her in its primitive passion.

But she had strength enough and presence of mind enough left to turn him lithely—and with a thrust of her slender foot to push his broad back up against the boards of their home . . . there was an upflinging of the mats within, the rasp of steel through the cracks, the thud of a point driving through bone and flesh. Bukit Bruang went suddenly limp in her arms. He made not a sound, but his grip on her relaxed. Mata-Manis sprang back; shrieked once; stared fascinated at the point of Migi's parang, which jutted out through him red and glistening, where her own head had just been. And the next moment she was in Migi's arms, sobbing with mingled relief and horror—but their home was saved.

Next morning Migi made a raft. On it he sent floating down to the village the head of Bukit Bruang. He would have dearly loved to have kept that head, dried it carefully, hung it over his door and fed it sacrificial rice and cigarettes. But it was his message to the kampong that his home was sacred and inviolable, the place where he meant to stay. The man or beast who invaded it did so at his peril!

"The guide was lowered over the fear-inspiring edge of the precipice."

The Ball of Fire

By S. B. H. HURST

Bugs Sinnat, ace of the Secret Service in India, trails a renegade English captain who turned thief and murderer—the story of the world's largest ruby

HE WAS known as Ben Mohamet, a powerful, fighting Afghan of the stern Durani Clan, and he swaggered, as night fell, along the bank of the river Ganges, sacred to the Hindoos, in the holy city of the Hindoo religion, Benares, which is the oldest city in the world.

He turned along a street leading from the river. With an oath he kicked a sacred cow out of his way, paying no more attention to the shrill cries of Hindoos than he would have paid to the same number of chattering monkeys. He was a tough person with a reputation to sustain, a Mohametan who worshipped one God, and who loudly proclaimed that the other creeds of India were offal. But he was more than this, and while his tough reputation was useful, the stain on his skin and the beard on his face were absolutely necessary—if he wished to live and continue in business. For underneath it all he was the famous Sinnat of the Indian Secret Service, known to a few intimates as "Bugs."

It began to rain as he walked in the general direction of the Bisheswar. He turned to the left from this "central holiness," and walked along another street, of stone, six-story buildings, of riches. This ended among huts of the very poor. Near one of these huts he waited. He had an appointment.

The rain and the dark had driven the wretched population of the district into their crude shelters. There was no one in sight. Then Bugs heard footsteps, and turned, expecting to see Shir Ali, who, though a real Afghan, was Bugs' friend and associate in the Service. Instead, he saw a fat man of criminal appearance, who approached cringingly and began to beg.

"Big man, I am hungry. *Bot garib*, very poor am I, and my poor wife is sick. Help me, I beg of you!"

"You are fat!" sneered Bugs.

The man came closer, his pawing hands waving as he pleaded. Bugs felt like hitting the fellow, who was apparently a professional beggar, but he was waiting for important news from Shir Ali, and he had no wish to start a row in that particular quarter, where Hindoos might pour out like rats to attack one lone Mohametan! So Bugs backed away toward the door of one of the huts, swearing profusely in *Pushtu*. He backed into a puddle of water, and slipped. As he slipped the fat man jumped for him. At the same moment another man jumped out of the darkness of the hut. Bugs had no chance to use the gun under his arm. Before he could attempt to draw it he was struck in the face with a stone. He felt the blinding impact in a flash of agony. He fainted, for the first time in his life.

He recovered consciousness, lying on his back on the floor of the filthy hut, and tightly bound. Some one had just kicked him.

"Outwitted you, eh, Sinnat?" sneered

an English voice. "You traced me all the way from Burma to Benares. Then you disguised yourself as an Afghan. But you are not so clever as you think you are! And now you are at the end of your rope!"

Bugs, gritting his teeth in pain, did not answer. The English voice continued, after another kick:

"You know who this is, don't you? The 'renegade Englishman,' eh? Once an officer and a gentleman in the army! Rather clever, what? To get you, I mean! It has not been done before! . . . You are in a hut owned by professional *thuggee*. The fat beggar and his pal! No god, no honor and no religion—and no pity (particularly that!) is their creed! As you know! Very amusing. They will deftly dispose of you, and by this time tomorrow your corpse will be floating gracefully down the Ganges. . . . I wonder how much you guessed about my activities in Burma. You were after me, I think, for the murder of two Buddhist monks. Did I do that or did I hire some of my friends among the wizards of Burma, who so hate the Buddhists? Guess, Sinnat! You have a few hours to lie here, and nothing to do but guess. You pride yourself on your knowledge of Burma. Perhaps I know it better! Now I can go back there. You are out of the way. And with the help of my wizard friends I shall get what I am after—which with all your fancied intelligence you know nothing about!"

Bugs said nothing. The Englishman, once Captain Armstrong, kicked him again, saying:

"I am going now, leaving you alone with the two thugs."

Armstrong turned away. As an afterthought he kicked Bugs again. This time his foot struck Bugs' head, and Bugs again lost his senses.

BUGS awoke to hands fumbling in his clothing, and the voices of the two thugs.

"There is no money on him," growled one. "Only this little gun under his arm."

"Better not keep that," answered the other. "If we tried to sell it it might be traced to us. This man doubtless has many friends!"

"He has!" another voice shouted.

Into the hut another man literally threw himself, like an enraged grizzly— a grizzly armed with an Afghan knife, and skilled in its quick use. The thugs, taken utterly by surprize, had no chance against Shir Ali. Their lives left them. And Shir Ali, with the same knife, was carefully cutting the ropes that held Bugs.

"Hold steady, sahib! It is dark in here, although the dawn is on its way. . . . You have been here hours. And I waited hours, my soul in my mouth with anxiety. Into many huts did I go growling, seeking thee. But no trace of thee. My heart would beat and then stop. Many excellent husbands have thought I was after their wives this night! It was funny to hear them! . . . Steady, sahib. Just one more bit of rope. Ah, here it is. . . . Yes, I waited, wondering. But so often does our business make one late that for some time I did not worry. Then I began to seek. You had told me to meet you in this street of low people. At last, as I crept cautiously, I heard these dead things making talk concerning thee. Then I knew thee for near dead and helpless. So, I came, and attended to the business of sending two thugs to hell. Now, sahib, I will attend to thee."

Shir Ali lifted Bugs to his feet.

"Come! You are dizzy and sick. Lean on me. I will get thee to the hospital!"

Bugs was able to walk, but he was terribly weak. He leaned on the big Afghan.

"Thanks, friend!" he murmured.

"Nay! Do not try to talk. See, let me lift you. . . . Here is the door of the damned place. And now, the street. See, the night is nearly done. The dawn is lifting. Let's hope we meet no police! Hindoo police in this part of town, thanks to the loving-kindness of the English. Why don't they leave us of Islam to settle with the kissers of sacred cows? . . . Ah, in luck! There comes a *ticka gharri!* We will ride!"

A one-horse hack of decrepit appearance, both as to animal and vehicle, dawdled out of the gloom. The driver slept comfortably. Shir Ali grabbed the horse. The driver woke up. He took one look at his prospective fares and reached for his whip. Shir Ali transferred his grabbing to the driver.

"Be good, heathen," said Shir Ali conversationally, "and drive us to the hospital."

"Na! Na," wept the driver. "I drive no Afghans. Mine is a decent hack! I am a Hindoo!"

"And that," grunted Shir Ali, as Bugs managed to open the door and get inside, "is meant for an insult! A Hindoo, eh? Well, so is a monkey! They are all the same breed! But I won't hurt you!"

As he spoke, Shir Ali climbed to the driver's seat. With one hairy arm he encircled the driver's body, saying, "One little shout for help, Monkey, and you will never shout again! Your ribs will be powder!" With his other hand Shir Ali took the reins. He shook them and the old horse ambled slowly forward.

"Sit steady, sahib—it will not be long!" he bent down and said to Bugs. "This diseased hack is no doubt Hindoo, also, though it seems like another insult to call even such a wreck a name like that. . . . Keep quiet, insulter of hacks," this to the driver again. "You said this was a Hindoo hack! Why revile thine only means of livelihood? Behave, and perhaps I will pay thee for the ride! Who knows?"

The dawn broke over Benares in flashes of splendid crimson. The first rays of the sun made a glittering crown for the minarets of the Mosque of Aurangzeb, which that Mohametan emperor had erected years before as "an insult to all Hindoos." Shir Ali called the outraged driver's attention to this fact.

"Look and weep, Hindoo. Ah, the muezzin calls to prayer! I regret that I am otherwise occupied, Caller of the Faithful! Also that I am in very bad company! Very low company! God help the morals of this poor horse! Corrupt association with a Hindoo has even deprived him of the use of his legs! He tries to trot, though, poor devil! . . . Sit still, driver, lest you fall off! . . . Ah, here is the hospital!"

The driver managed to laugh.

"This is a sahibs' hospital — not for horse-thieves like thee!"

He had observed an English policeman standing at the corner.

"*Shabash!*" exclaimed Shir Ali. "This monkey has guts—when he sees help in uniform! Yet, Hindoo, since thou art poor and no Brahmin, I will pay thee for the ride. We have decided, my friend and I, to patronize the hospital of the sahibs. . . . The sun rises. Here, Hindoo of low caste, is eight annas for thee!"

"The fare is a rupee," wailed the driver, who had received double what he would have asked a co-religionist.

"The fare will be nothing and there will be nobody to drive thee to the dogs' hospital if you holler! One more word and I take back my money. I may even take the horse! And the hack, too—as payment for my outraged feelings which riding with thee has damaged. Drive away!"

The driver obeyed. . . . A young doctor stood at the door of the hospital, watching the wonder of the sunrise.

"Ah," he saw Bugs' eye. "A nasty wound! I can not keep you here, but I will do what I can to help you before sending you to the native hospital."

"Please tell Doctor Walters that Mr. Sinnat wishes to see him immediately," answered Bugs.

"Great Scott!" gasped the intern, startled to hear an educated English voice issuing from such an Afghan apparition.

B UGS came out from the anesthetic to find Doctor Walters smiling.

"You won't lose your eye, Bugs!"

"What! I thought it was gone!"

"So did I at first. But it's going to be all right now. It was a close call, though. Take it easy for a few days, and you'll be all right!"

"In my business," drawled Bugs, who was feeling somewhat like himself again, "one can never take it easy. Where is Shir Ali, that big Afghan who brought me here, and, incidentally, saved me from a nasty death?"

The doctor grinned.

"Just outside this room, and very suspicious of me! I think he wanted to superintend the operation. Had to be awfully diplomatic to get him out of the operating-room. He has been growling ever since, like a big dog."

"Send him in!" laughed Bugs.

Shir Ali was admitted. He looked gravely at Bugs and raised a huge hand in salute. He spoke solemnly.

"Before God, sahib, this is a hell of a place! It's so damned clean! A man is afraid to breathe here, much less spit. But God is good! You will not lose your eye! And now we will go hunting again, you and I. That fellow!"

"As soon as the doctor lets me out of this," answered Bugs.

"*Shabash!* Rest you, sahib!"

Shir Ali left the room. Bugs closed his eyes and thought of Armstrong. Armstrong who had personally captured Thibaw, the last king of Burma, at Mandalay. Who was with Thibaw when he died. Who then, to the surprise of his friends, resigned from the army and disappeared in the mysterious maze of Burma. A series of murders of Buddhist priests had followed. Bugs had got on Armstrong's trail, had chased him across Burma and to Benares. Then Armstrong had outwitted Bugs, as Bugs had never been outwitted before. Armstrong had bragged that the wizards of Burma—who hate the Buddhist priests—were helping him; and he had said that Bugs did not know what he was after. Bugs did know. Armstrong was trying to get the Ball of Fire, known also as "Thibaw's Pet," the greatest ruby in the world. But the wizards? Were they helping Armstrong? There were thousands of them, and at their head was the Devil of the Chin Hills. Bugs had visited this mysterious and powerful person. He was the only white man who had ever done so. He would visit him again, as soon as he could get to him. Five years before he had made a treaty with this black pope of wizardry. Yes, he would use Armstrong's bragging to defeat him.

"A HELL of a country," commented Shir Ali some weeks later. "You say we came here to visit the biggest wizard of them all." Shir Ali shivered slightly. Like all Afghans he was desperately afraid of the occult. "Well, sahib, this is the sort of country that only devils would inhabit!"

"You will go no farther," answered Bugs. "Wait here for me till I return."

"But, sahib?"

"Wait at this camp till I return," repeated Bugs.

Shir Ali saluted.

Bugs went on alone. He had had no word or trace of Armstrong, who of course believed Bugs was dead. No longer disguised as an Afghan, Bugs travelled in the guise of a "gone native," poor white hobo. . . . It was a long trail. No more steamy jungles, thronged by parrots and monkeys, but a desolate region which even the monkeys had abandoned. Rocks that lay scattered as if by the hand of some playful god. Towering hills crested with eternal snow.

It was night and Bugs was very tired when he began to climb out of a defile so narrow and cruel that a horse could not have passed through it. There was no sound but that of the little stones falling and the uncanny, ghost-like whining of the mountain wind. He climbed the walls of a gorge that rose a thousand feet on either side. A few stars showed through the top of the gorge, making it seem like a thin slit cut in the roof of the world.

About two-thirds of the way up this precipice he came to an opening—a tunnel worn by a small river millions of years ago. Bugs entered the tunnel. He rested to regain his breath. Below him the gorge lay black and silent and awful as the bottomless Pit.

Bugs got to his feet, sniffing the smell of smoke. He walked along the tunnel. Presently it showed the dim red glow of a weird inferno. Bugs followed its twisting way until he came to a fire, over which crouched a very old woman, who took no apparent heed of him. Her withered fingers poked at the fire, and she mumbled and muttered to herself. She might have been one of the witches of Macbeth, flung into this far place from the tip of the poet's pen.

"I have come again, Mother," said Bugs in the Shan dialect.

She pretended to see him for the first

time. Her face was the face of a mummy, but it cracked in a smile.

"So I see!" she answered. "It was the day before yesterday when you were here last, wasn't it?"

"It was five years ago!" answered Bugs.

"Was it?" she cackled. "Well, and what are five years to one who has seen more than two hundred—as I have?"

"Just a day and a night, Mother! Just a day and a night! I have come again, Old Wisdom, for a talk with the Devil of the Chin and the Arakan," replied Bugs.

The old woman suddenly "pointed," like a dog scenting game. She was not looking at Bugs, but in the direction he had come. Bugs, startled, could see nothing. Then he heard what the old woman had heard first. The sound was something like that made by a water buffalo—a buffalo climbing a cliff! A grunting, heavy breathing. Dislodged rocks falling into the chasm. An oath in *Pushtu*, half suppressed. And the face of Shir Ali peering round a corner.

"Who is this?" demanded the old witch.

"My man," answered Bugs, who was half laughing, half angry.

"Sahib," grunted Shir Ali, saluting. "I know you will give me hell for this, because it almost amounts to disobeying orders!"

"Almost?" interrogated Bugs.

"Well!" Shir Ali threw back his head. "I have disobeyed thee, then—because, by Allah, I love thee! Could I sit and wait while you went alone into hell? And hell it is—this place and the trail I have followed behind thee! And with the big devil waiting for us. However," Shir Ali coughed to hide his emotion, "however, what matters it so you don't have to die alone. Damn it! Leave it to me, sahib, for I will swiftly investigate the entrails

of that big devil. Have I not kept my knife sharp?"

Bugs slapped him on the shoulder.

"Good man!" he said. "But take thy tongue between thy fingers. Come along! . . . Fare thee well, Mother of Many. When I grow old maybe I will come here again to talk with thee. Then we will sit by the fire together, and tell of what we have seen during our journey down the years!"

"Farewell, King's man," she nodded gravely. Then she laughed shrilly. "And farewell, big dog that follows his master, even when told to stay in the kennel. Good dog! Fine dog! Ha, ha!"

THEY went deeper into the tunnel. It twisted and turned, as the ancient river had worn it. Everywhere was the pungent smoke. As the tunnel became almost too dark for progress another fire gleamed. At the second fire crouched an old man. As they drew near to him, Bugs saw him draw in his head like a turtle and crouch closer to the fire. When they reached the fire he neither looked up nor moved. Shir Ali made no comment, much as he was tempted to shout the stimulating war cry of Islam. For Shir Ali had never been so scared in his life.

Presently they saw a larger fire. Bent figures of men shuffled away into the shadows, until only one crouched by the fire. The firelight flickered on his hideous mask. It was the High Priest of all the wizards of Burma, the Devil of the Chin Hills.

"You know me?" asked Bugs.

The mask nodded. It was not lawful for any one to see the Devil's face.

A smell of unpleasant age permeated the cavern, about which huge bats flickered as if domesticated.

"I made a treaty with you!" said Bugs sternly. "Have you kept it?"

"Yes, King's man!"

"Have your wizards killed any *pon-gyis?*"

"No, King's man!"

"Have they given aid to a white man who is killing them?"

"No, King's man!"

"You know about this white man, and what he is doing. Your words have told me you know. And I know you know all that happens in Burma. Where is this white man?"

"I am glad you came," answered the Devil of the Chin quietly. "I sit here like a spider in his web, and all news comes to me. My wizards have sent me word that this white man is you; using your name and rank! White men look much alike to careless eyes. I was puzzled, because I know you, and know you would not seek my wizards' help to kill *pongyis.* The word has just come in that this white man who is impersonating you is at Powingdaug!"

"Thanks, great Devil," said Bugs quickly. "I must get to Powingdaug at once. You have a secret way out of here which is nearer to Powingdaug than through the chasm. Show me that way. It will remain secret!"

The mask nodded. Out of it came a weird, high-pitched shout. A powerful young hill man, a servant, appeared.

"You will guide my friend and his man," the Devil of the Chin Hills said to the young hill man.

The Devil of the Chin Hills got to his feet.

"Come," he said to Bugs. "I have been troubled. For the Buddhist priests, who have been at war with *us* for centuries, are saying my wizards did the murders. I have kept my treaty with you, King's man, and given you all the information I have. Now I help you with the secret way out of here, and a guide. Be swift, friend, lest the Buddhists persuade the government to make war on my wizards. Be swift, and capture this murderer who is impersonating thee!"

Bugs and Shir Ali followed the Devil of the Shin Hills and the guide up an incline that led to a ledge on the edge of another precipice, where there was nothing but the dark and the stars. The Devil of the Chin Hills shouted again, and more servants appeared. Shir Ali, who had been growing more and more uncomfortable, raised his hand. The battle-cry of Islam was on his lips, but Bugs pulled down the hand.

"Be silent!" he admonished.

"But, sahib, I did not understand a word of thy talk with that Devil. And here is the jumping-off place of the world. Here! And the whimper of a little wind, which may be the breath of the dead! It is better to fight and die like men than to——"

"Be silent!"

The men brought a large basket and a long coil of stout rope. The guide jumped into the basket and was lowered over the fear-inspiring edge of the precipice. Bugs looked out and down. He stepped back hastily, a dizziness assailing him. The wind began to blow cold. It was a dreadful place. Shir Ali could contain himself no longer. His voice rose in the familiar shout. He stood there like a giant of some distant age, a faint starlight glittering on his waving knife. The Devil of the Chin Hills laughed. Shir Ali took a step toward him, but Bugs interposed.

"If he laughs like that again," roared Shir Ali, in *Pushtu,* "God will have one devil less to think about!"

"My man does not understand," said Bugs urbanely to the High Priest of wizardry. "Get into the basket," he ordered Shir Ali, as the men pulled the empty basket on to the ledge again.

"But, sahib, who remains to guard thee!"

And again Shir Ali, in the throes of an

uncontrollable fear of the unseen, sent his voice pealing toward the stars.

"Get in!" said Bugs.

Shir Ali obeyed.

"There is but one God, and here on the brink of hell I proclaim Him!" he shouted as he disappeared in the basket.

The basket came back. Bugs said farewell to the Devil of the Chin Hills, and got into it. It was lowered evenly, but it was a weird sensation. Shir Ali and the young hill man waited at the bottom of the precipice.

"Come on," said Bugs. "We run as we have never run before!"

Powingdaug was two hundred miles away. The secret route would save two days' travel.

THE servant of the Devil of the Chin Hills was young and powerful, and accustomed to heavy travel through a country generally considered impassable, while Shir Ali was also a man of the hills—but Bugs gave them a taste of real going. He allowed hardly a pause through the secret trails. Only four hours' sleep.

Shir Ali kept up gallantly, but when the rocks and barren places gave way to forest and valley the Devil's servant lagged behind. He had no interest in this curiously mad white man, and wanted to leave him.

"Go back to thy devil of a boss, weakling," panted Shir Ali, "and tell him what real men are like. And learn to worship one God, and not to quit as long as your heart beats!"

The Burmese, who did not understand one word of Shir Ali's speech, lagged further behind. Bugs waved him away, and he turned back gladly.

"Come on!" Bugs shouted to the Afghan. "We have neither time nor breath for talk."

They plunged into the mazes of animal trails of the jungle which Bugs knew so well. . . . Bugs was raging. Armstrong impersonating him!

"Quicker! Quicker!"

"At thy heels, sahib! At thy heels! I understand thy haste! You crave *Pukhtunwali!*"

Bugs let out another link of his stride, and the gallant Afghan took it up.

"Faster! Faster! Good man, keep it up!"

"*Atcha,* sahib!"

On and on. The trail seemed endless.

"We make Powingdaug tonight. We do not rest till we get there!"

The monkeys chattered above their heads, the parrots screamed at them. Shafts of torrid sunlight, filtering through the trees, blinded them as does sunlight thrown from a mirror. A touch of jungle fever in Bugs' veins. A picture that grew into a mirage. Wavering and burning. The Ball of Fire.

Armstrong. Cruel, callous. In some way Armstrong had coaxed the dying King Thibaw into telling him that he had entrusted the Ball of Fire to one of his ten attendant Buddhist priests, when the looting British soldiers got out of control of their officers and raged through Mandalay. And now Armstrong, trying to find the one priest among the ten who had the ruby—that priceless gem!—was torturing them one by one to make them give it up; and when he realized that a tortured priest did not have the stone he killed him to prevent him telling those of the other ten who still lived. Thibaw had told him the names of the ten priests, but not the name of the one who had the gem. That was all clear now.

And the Ball of Fire, Thibaw's Pet, seemed to burn and lead the way through the forest before Bugs' feverish eyes.

"Faster! Faster! Good man! Keep it up!"

They panted forward. Their blood

seemed boiling with the terrific strain and heat.

NIGHT fell as they plunged among the village paths—that ancient village of wooden houses, on stilts, with its queer school against the marvelous rock temple where the *pongyis* have taught the children for two thousand years!

Very quiet it was among the fireflies. Bugs and Shir Ali labored like spent horses. They reached the temple in which are five hundred thousand images of Buddha, carved out of solid teak.

At the west entrance the aged head priest was praying—alone. He looked up, staring with feeble old eyes, as Bugs and Shir Ali came up to him. He saw them, he scrambled upright and screamed like an old woman gone mad.

Fear and anger in his screaming. Then a horde of priests, streaming like hornets out of the temple, and the yells of the excited villagers of Powingdaug. . . .

"What the hell?"

Shir Ali, dizzy and worn out, his fighting heart holding beyond his strength, asked the question through parched lips hoarsely, as he gripped his long knife.

Bugs understood. And he knew he faced death. "Shin-byu-sin!" he shouted as loudly as he could. "Shin-byu-sin!"

With a vast effort he scrambled to a ledge in the rock, and helped Shir Ali to his side. His revolver showed in the faint light.

"Shin-byu-sin!" he shouted again.

The villagers, men and women, encouraged by the priests, rushed to the attack. Bugs, who did not want to hurt any one, fired over their heads.

Silence followed the shot. Bugs shouted again.

"Shin-byu-sin! Shin-byu-sin!"

A huge man who had lost his ears pushed roughly through the mob. His name was Shin-byu-sin. Once a highway

O. S.—4

robber, pardoned for service by the British through the instrumentality of Bugs, he had, as he said, sought surer profits and easier work, and—become a priest of Buddha. He saw Bugs on the ledge, and roared.

"What in the name . . . Oh, yes! . . . They say you tortured a priest—he who is dying in the temple. I told them you didn't. . . . Get back, fools!" Thus rudely to the villagers. "Stand aside, brothers in God!" This to the priests. "This man is my friend. I vouch for him!"

Shin-byu-sin put his arms about Bugs and Shir Ali.

"A dying priest, you said?" gasped Bugs. "Take me to him at once!" He addressed the priests. "Priests of the Blessed One, your dying brother shall look into my eyes, and tell you whether I am the man who harmed him. Lead me to him!"

"Yes, brothers, I know and trust this man!" growled Shin-byu-sin.

The head priest nodded gravely.

"It is just!" he said.

Into the innermost recesses of the rock temple—a huge cave, enlarged and shaped by thousands of long-dead priests and monks—lined, as it were a library, with five hundred thousand images of Buddha carved in teak black with age. Three novices lighted the way with ancient lamps, and the procession proceeded in silence along the dim and winding passages, to where the old priest, hideously mangled, waited for death.

He lay in a small chamber, his glazing eyes fixed upon a tiny shrine from where the benevolent features of the Blessed One smiled at him.

Bugs stepped forward quickly and knelt by the priest's side.

"Look at me carefully! In my eyes, friend! And tell all men that it was *not* I who did this to thee!"

The dying priest obeyed. He was in no pain, for Burma has known opium since before the dawn of history. Bugs took one of his frail old hands in his. The priest smiled.

"No," he said. "It was not this man. This man has no guile! He did not do this to me!"

Bugs turned.

"Leave me—every one of you," he commanded. "I have important words for this good man."

The priests withdrew into the gallery, Shin-byu-sin and Shir Ali with them.

"The man who killed thee," Bugs said gently to the dying priest. "What did you tell him? Why did he kill thee?"

The priest tried to smile.

"Thou, also!"

"Nay!" answered Bugs. "I crave not the Pet, but to arrest and punish this creature who killed thee and others!"

The priest looked at the shrine. His entire being yearned toward it. He answered softly.

"In no spirit of revenge do I tell thee, but because my heart leans to thine. That other Englishman wanted to know . . . about the Ball of Fire. He knew a priest had it . . . at Mandalay. He had tortured and killed other priests . . . who did not know. . . . For a long time . . . I did not tell. But I am old and weak. . . . So I told this Englishman. For I am the priest to whom Thibaw entrusted the ruby!"

The dying man paused from weakness.

"Yes," said Bugs gently.

"I almost gloated. That is bad. One might lose Nirvana. But I was thinking of that Englishman . . . trying to bully the Boh Ma-gong!"

Bugs felt a thrill run along his spine.

"Mandalay," murmured the dying priest. "And the king giving me the ruby to care for. He loved it more than life. But I gave it to Ma-gong, a strong man,

and one of the king's generals. He turned his regiment into *dacoits*, and they harried the English until the English sent no more soldiers against him—he killed so many. Ma-gong laughed, and sent a challenge to the English. The English sent one man to Ma-gong. Up that narrow river went this lone, brave Englishman. Oh, a brave man! And he talked to Ma-gong until Ma-gong 'came in,' as they say, and ate the bread of the English king, and took pardon. Ma-gong has the Pet. . . . I can . . . talk no more. . . . Take my blessing. . . . I turn my face to the wall."

W AIT here at Powingdaug," said Bugs to Shir Ali. "I go on alone."

"But, sahib?"

"I go alone," answered Bugs. "A matter of *Pukhtunwali*, a head for a head, as the Rajputs say. Being a Durani, you will understand!"

Shir Ali bowed.

"God go with thee!"

B UGS travelled at top speed, and in five days came to the well-remembered creek. He had been the "brave man" spoken of by the dying priest, who had penetrated through that steamy jungle, run the gauntlet of the robber sentries, and taken the "king's bread" to Ma-gong. The hectic dacoit days.

On the right bank, among the thorns, the ruins of the palisade that had baffled a regiment. And the great teak tree from which a keen-eyed dacoit had kept watch. Bugs hurried. His present mission urged him from the memories. Morning had broken. The parrots and the monkeys waged their eternal quarrel. From the dense treetop came the cry of an old ape that had made its home in the sentry's crow's-nest.

The best trail was the center of the creek, bending and twisting. Myriads of little yellow water-snakes, harmless as minnows. Leeches.

Bugs went on cautiously, his gun ready. At the next bend was the village of Ma-gong, raised above the creek on stilts. At any moment Bugs might see Armstrong. And Armstrong was also a quick shot, and a dangerous and desperate man.

But at the bend Bugs saw only a naked ten-year-old girl who was giving her baby brother a washing, while he bitterly resented the bath. The girl saw Bugs and laughed.

"Were you as hard to keep clean when you were young?" she asked.

Bugs, tense and expecting trouble any moment, smiled.

"I have heard so! . . . Tell me, little lady, is there not another white man, who looks like me, here at the village of Ma-gong?"

She laughed.

"You are pleased to joke with me. Why have you come back so soon? Was it at twilight you left us the day before yesterday?"

Bugs, panting, ran into the village.

Too late! Too late! Was it too late? Armstrong had the Ball of Fire! All Asia was his in which to escape. No use to try to guard the ports of Burma—Armstrong was too clever to use them. . . .

The lazy, smiling people, the familiar chickens, the drifting smell of teak smoke on the pungent morning.

"Ma-gong! Where is Ma-gong?"

The old general—all three hundred pounds of him—laughed from the platform of his house.

"What's wrong?" he asked huskily. "You haven't had time to see old Pagan!" Bugs clambered up on the platform.

"You have been tricked and fooled," he said quietly. "Behold me closely, Ma-gong, and learn that you have not seen me since that day, years ago, when I came through your outposts, and we talked and

became brothers of the Raj. An impostor has fooled you!"

Ma-gong seized Bugs' face and stared into his eyes. He shouted with rage. He seized a club, to strike a gong to rouse his men.

"Fool! I was a fool! An easy fool—to mistake that swine for thee! But Ma-gong is still Ma-gong, and he still has his men. I will get that swine who fooled me. Then I will crucify him to a tree, as we used to do. . . . Rest here, man I honor. Forgive me. I will not be old and fat and careless any longer. I will go out on the trail again with my men, and that liar and impersonator shall scream and bleed from a tree, and——"

"Stay thy hand," exclaimed Bugs. "This is my affair!"

"Thine?"

"Mine! Again has my king sent me! What did you mean by 'old Pagan'?"

Ma-gong laid down the club reluctantly, answering.

"Old Pagan is the other general who stayed with Thibaw until Thibaw bade us save ourselves! I became a dacoit, and feared to lose the Pet, so I gave it to Pagan to keep, until our king should send for it. . . . The king Thibaw died. Two days ago came that thief who impersonated thee, saying that Thibaw had willed the Pet to the King of England, as a gift from one king to another. Believing the tale the swine told me, thinking he was you, I sent him to Pagan!"

"And Pagan is where?" asked Bugs.

"He has lived for many years among the dead and the ghosts and the ruins in the City of the Immortals," replied Ma-gong. That ancient place of ruins. Somewhere between the creek of Ma-gong and the City of the Immortals was Armstrong. Bugs felt he held the winning hand at last. Hurrying through the forest on Armstrong's trail—Armstrong who believed Bugs dead and drifted down the Ganges.

AMARAPURA, the City of the Immortals, built by Bodawpaya-Mentragi, the great conqueror, a place of dead glory where, among the holy men and madmen, lived the old general Pagan, dreaming of other days and heaven. . . . In his care the greatest ruby in the world, for which a ruthless murderer lusted.

Bugs pressed on. No white man could make time through the trackless jungles as he could make it. Armstrong, after years in Burma, was good, but Bugs calculated to catch him before he reached the City of the Immortals.

Day after day, night and little sleep and on again—yet there was no sign of Armstrong. He might have taken a different trail, but Bugs did not think so— for Armstrong, the ex-army officer, would be travelling by compass and map. But there were several trails. No villages. The way was dangerous, beset by wild beasts, but after eight days Bugs had not seen a human being since leaving Ma-gong.

Not until the eighth night when, three hours after the sudden nightfall, Bugs sought a place to camp. Then, suddenly, he smelled smoke. The smoke of a wood fire, perhaps half a mile away.

It was very dark under the trees. Bugs took out his revolver and felt it over carefully. Then he went forward toward the fire, with the stealth and velvet quietness of a tiger.

A change came in the sound of the whispering of the forest. Bugs, standing stock-still, listened. Yes, the change in the sound was . . . or was it a flock of restless monkeys moving their habitation in the night? Bugs went closer. He listened again. A pang of keen disappointment shot through him. The change in the sound was made by human voices—men

talking. Armstrong would hardly be likely to be there—among some Burmese in camp. Yet he might be. Bugs went on again, not a whit of his caution and readiness relaxed. He made no noise with his careful steps. Closer and closer to the voices. Then, from behind a large tree, he saw the fire and the camp. A dozen Burmese men, and, tied to a tree—Armstrong!

Bugs stepped quietly into the clearing. The Burmese leaped to their feet.

"Who are you people?" asked Bugs.

"The men of Ma-gong!" they shouted.

"I see," said Bugs. "And I understand now why Ma-gong took so long to find what he called my 'password'—so you men could get a start of me!"

The leader bowed and laughed.

"Yes, chief! We came through ahead of you!"

Armstrong broke in. He did not recognize Bugs through the smoke of the fire.

"This man is deceiving you! I am the friend of Ma-gong!"

The Burmese took no notice of Armstrong. Bugs showed something that glittered in the firelight. The Burmese saluted. It was the insignia of a general in King Thibaw's army.

"So that Pagan will know me!" said Bugs. "The 'password' of Ma-gong."

The Burmese bowed again.

"What were your orders?" asked Bugs.

"To obey you, chief! . . . If you did not come in ten days we were to nail that thing over there to a tree until he died!"

Bugs nodded.

"Loose him now. He must die according to law. I am on my way to Mandalay. I will take him there. Since the City of the Immortals lies between here and Fort Dufferin I will pass through the City of the Immortals. Loose him, so that he may get some rest and be able to travel to where he will die according to Law!"

Then Bugs walked across the clearing to the tree where Armstrong writhed.

"We are quite a way from a *thuggee* hut in Benares and the dead drifting down the Ganges!" he said quietly.

Armstrong stiffened with the shock, like a man struck by electricity. His swollen eyelids opened so he could see.

"Sinnat!" he gasped.

Bugs turned away.

"Make him comfortable, but guard him closely," he ordered.

BUGS woke in the night. Armstrong was calling across the clearing.

"Sinnat! Sinnat, these chaps don't understand English! I've tried them. Listen! Take the ruby, and let me go! Not a soul will ever know. And I daren't talk! Take it, and lose me. You can get half a million dollars for it in New York. It belongs to nobody. Take it! It's not even stealing—for the army looted Mandalay and thought nothing of it!"

Bugs did not answer. Armstrong began again. Bugs called to the leader of the Burmese.

"Give that fellow some more opium— he's keeping me awake with his crying. If the opium doesn't quiet him, knock him on the head!"

Armstrong, who had not given up hoping to escape, or, if that failed, getting clear at his trial, said no more.

"I won't walk," said Armstrong next morning. "These men must carry me!"

Bugs turned to the Burmese leader.

"I am going on alone," he said. "Take your men back to Ma-gong. But before you go nail this white man to a tree— any tree will do so you nail him so he can not wriggle off!"

The Burmese saluted. Bugs walked away. Armstrong shrieked.

"Sinnat! Sinnat! You can't do that. Could you watch and see another Englishman crucified?"

Then Bugs spoke to the man for the second time.

"I have no time to waste watching! For the rest—I have been called 'Bugs' because I am too easy on such as you. But there is another Sinnat, who is not 'Bugs.' . . . Take your choice. Walk like a man with me to Mandalay and your trial, or stay here and die on the tree!"

Bugs turned away again. Armstrong made no further objection to walking.

GREEN lizards glittering in the sun, mini birds shrieking at the snakes among the ruins of a fallen palace; and a madman who gibbered.

"I seek Pagan, an old man and a general, who lives in this place! Do you know him?" asked Bugs.

The madman laughed. Then he spoke confidentially.

"Yes!" He pointed. "That way. But, remember, Pagan is mad! Be careful. He talks with ghosts and refuses to associate with intelligent people like me!"

Bugs found Pagan sitting on a pile of fallen bricks.

"Ah, good day," greeted the old general. "You see me on fallen bricks. Bricks are like peoples, nations. They stand proudly for years, then fall. All must fall in the end. Some day a conqueror will kick the bricks called England, and they will fall. What can I do for you?"

Bugs showed him the insignia of Ma-gong.

"Ma-gong sent this to vouch for me. He told me that you are the guardian of the Ball of Fire. May I see it?"

The old general looked strangely at Bugs. Then he scrambled down from the heap of bricks.

"I will show you where it *is*," he said quietly.

Bugs followed him through the mystery city of the dead, along ways blocked with ruins, through narrow places between fallen palaces, until they reached that inlet of the Irrawaddy River which was once the bathing-place of Bodawpaya-Matragi and his ladies. But that was long ago. Now it was a snake-infested swamp, overgrown with torturous vegetation, a morass of deep slime and mud. General Pagan stooped and picked up a stone. He raised his weak old arm and threw the stone into the swamp. He shook his head, dissatisfied.

"I was younger and stronger then!" he exclaimed.

"When?" asked Bugs, understanding.

"When I threw the Pet to where never again will the eye of man behold it! They told me my king was dead. I said that no other hand should caress the Ball of Fire. So, with reverence, I threw it into the depths of the swamp. I can not throw so far now!"

The Hopeless Quest at Aissouan

By PAUL ERNST

Arab revolt in North Africa—intrigue and mystery—deadly perils and sublime heroism

"*BARRA!*" growled a surly Arab who was swaying down the narrow, squalid street with a huge skin of water. "Thou son of an evil smell —*barra!* Out of the way."

"The curse of Allah on thee!" responded a tattered bundle of rags that had been groping blindly toward the palace gate. The blind one rubbed an elbow that had been rudely banged against the rough mud of the building wall. Then, shaking his fist, he resumed his tortuous journey, coming at last to the station he had chosen.

This was a huge portal of wood slabs, dotted with large nail heads and decorated, as was the fashion, with an iron knocker in the shape of a hand of Fatma. And here, a stone's throw from the huge pile in which the Sheikh Abdul Kibaba had once ruled, the blind beggar took up his station.

"Give, give, give," he whined. "Alms, for the love of Allah."

Kicks and insults were mainly his lot, with only now and then a French sou piece thrown at him. But the beggar waited with the fatalistic patience of his kind.

"For the love of Allah, alms."

Four men slowly approached. They were richly dressed in burnooses of fine French broadcloth, and one of them wore the turban of a pilgrim to Mecca over

"*A smashing right to the chin sent the guard flying against the wall.*"

his hawk face. They paused a moment by the palace gate, disregarding the whining cries of the beggar.

"I like not the weak-faced jackal, I tell thee," one was saying in a low tone. "The father is a man. *Youh!* But the son is the spawn of feebleness, and the flower of indecision. Yet we give him power here, instead of——" He finished the sentence by running his finger across his throat in a significant gesture.

"Guard thy tongue," advised the hawk-faced one. "The walls see, and the air hath ears."

The first speaker shrugged. "The guards are ours. What need to whisper? I say we should dispose of this son at once, and put one of the four of us in power as ruler of Aissouan."

"That will come soon enough," one of the other two—an older man with the eyes of a fanatic—made answer. "Has not el Hadj said that at the first convenient hour he will act? Meanwhile the people of this accursed spot might rebel if the son followed the father into oblivion so quickly. There are murmurs now, and the murmur of the annoyed lion swells quickly to a roar."

"Bah!" the impatient first one responded.

"But it is so," persisted the elderly man. And the hawk-faced one nodded. "For the space of a breath the son must be allowed to play Sheikh. Then will the old one be killed, whether the stripling falters or not. Then too shall the lad himself be gathered to the bosom of heaven."

"Enough," said the hawk-faced one. "Let us enter and prepare our reports to el Hadj for the meeting tonight."

Casually kicking the beggar out of the

way, he knocked on the heavy wood panel. A square peephole lifted up, and a dark face peered out. The gate was opened promptly.

The four passed in, walking between a heavily armed guard of eight Arabs, and the gate was shut.

"Alms," whined the beggar outside, moving slowly off down the stinking street. "For the love of Allah, give."

Groping his way, he sought an odorous doorway on the fringe of the market square and slumped down in it. There he dozed fitfully, an insignificant figure adding one more blot to a littered, fetid street.

An insignificant figure? Yes. And apparently of no use to itself or any other person that walked under the arch of heaven. And yet four men, one of them high up in the French North African Secret Service, had died that this tattered, disreputable bundle of rags might slump in that doorway and moan in its fitful dozing.

THE opening scene in the train of events that had placed this dirt-encrusted blind beggar in Aïssouan, had taken place in the Café Royale at Constantine in northern Algeria. The players in the drama were two men, one a tall, slow-moving American and the other a stocky, compact son of France.

The American was Bruce Hammond, ex-consular worker in Algiers, expert in all things Arabic, who could speak the three parent Arab dialects like a native, and who had joined the French Secret Service of North Africa after the Armistice *"pour le sport."*

The Frenchman was Lieutenant Reneaux, one of the most capable and trusted operatives in the Service. He was a man with a grave, intent face; and it was gravely, intently, that he was speaking now.

"The plan," he said, "is of a hugeness beyond belief. And it has almost matured, my American brother. When it breaks—if we are not successful in blocking it—hell will blossom on earth."

Bruce drummed his fingers on the marble-topped table and said nothing.

"It is the dreaded confederation of all the tribes that we face, *mon ami,*" went on the lieutenant. "Every Sheikh, every minor Caid from Aissouan to the Isle of Djinn has been approached by el Hadj. All have agreed either to support the confederation or, at least, remain neutral and lift no finger against it. All, that is, save the ancient one, Sheikh Abdul Kibaba."

"Then we have a little time in which to work," said Bruce. "Kibaba controls the thousand kilometers around the Aissouan Range, and the Aissouan Pass is the only gateway through which the hostile harkas can march. With Kibaba faithful the Pass is blocked."

"True enough," said Reneaux. "But— and this is the urgency that has called you here to your signal honor—Kibaba is now not in a position to aid us. Kibaba is proclaimed dead, and Aissouan Pass is open to the fighting harkas of el Hadj."

"What!"

"It is indeed so. The weakling son of Kibaba entered a conspiracy with el Hadj——"

"Death waits for that one," commented Bruce.

"And waits overlong. But to continue: The son of Kibaba conspired with el Hadj to seize Kibaba during the night and make away with him. His people think him dead; but it is my opinion that he is confined in the dungeon under the east wing of the palace. If so, our task is clear. We must get him out, and set him up in power again to close the Pass to el Hadj."

"Yes—that seems to be the point at issue—to free Kibaba, if indeed he still lives, and make him Sheikh again. But it does not appear an easy task to perform."

Truly, it didn't!

Aissouan, City of a Hundred Walls, hung like a crow's nest over the slash in the high Aissouan Range which was the only pass for a thousand or more kilometers through which a large body of men could be marched. Provisioned and well armed, a thousand men placed in that eagle's aerie could block the pass as a cork blocks a bottle neck.

From without, the place was impregnable. From within—well, no city is proof against the kind of treachery that the feebly ferocious son of Kibaba had practised on his father.

An army could not take the place against the son's wish; so the job of restoring Kibaba to power presented itself as one for several wily men alone to achieve. These must somehow contrive to enter the single gate of the city, which would be fiercely guarded now that revolt had seized it; they must pass among the alert rebels as one of them; they must locate the dungeon in which Kibaba was confined, still assuming that he was not already murdered; and then they must overpower the guards and get him out. After that there remained the problem of making him ruler of Aissouan again.

"It does not appear an easy task," repeated Bruce.

"It is an impossible task, an utterly hopeless quest," said Reneaux. "Yet it is one that we must accomplish."

And they had risen from the table to start the journey that might end in that impossible accomplishment.

THE two Service men, accompanied by three Legionnaires, all disguised as Bedouins, started out with a ragged camel caravan with the intention of going first to Shahn. At that far southern spot, Bruce and the lieutenant planned to leave their escorts and go on alone to Aissouan itself.

The Touaregs, those veiled fierce robbers of the Sahara, had changed their plans. Roused by the impending rebellion, they roamed the desert thick as fleas on a cur's back; and the five supposed Bedouins suffered charge after charge from them on their slow southern trip.

At Shahn it was decided that the three Legionnaires should keep on with them at least half-way to Aissouan. With the Touaregs out in such force, the two Service men could never have won all the way through alone.

The five had got almost to the point where they must separate, when that last fatal encounter with the veiled men had come.

Luckily they had reached a point where the first red outcroppings of the Aissouan Range began to show a few feet above the desert sand. And in the center of one such outcropping, shrinking down under the scant protection of the sand-bitten, reddish rocks, they had made a desperate last stand. This Touareg band was fully fifty strong; too powerful by far to be driven away by five men, no matter how resolute and well armed they showed themselves to be. Five against fifty, with the fate of a large portion of French North Africa resting on their shoulders, they had tried to decide what they might do. The decision had been made for them by fate!

The first to fall was Lieutenant Reneaux. And with his dying breath he had commanded the American, begged him, pleaded with him, to try to steal away from the rest of the little band when evening fell, and make his way to Aissouan alone. The Legionnaires had staunchly backed him up in this command.

"You must get through," one had said. "Us—we do not matter. We shall hold off these dogs of Touaregs till night-fall. Then you shall take the one camel left alive and fly from here while we hold the veiled ones from pursuing you——"

"And after?" questioned Bruce. He gazed at the dead Reneaux, the first hero to die a martyr's death in this cause which, even if successful, would be written down in obscure government archives never to be known and lauded by the public at large. "The four of us are barely able to stop them. Three would soon be overwhelmed."

"We shall not be overwhelmed till you are well on your way," the man promised quietly.

There was a renewed attack. "Kill! Kill! Kill!" howled the Touaregs, sweeping toward them in a great half-circle. The four fired till their rifles were hot in their hands. Each shot, aimed with the sure speed that has nothing to do with haste, told on man or camel. The Arabs retreated again.

"I can't go and leave you to die," protested Bruce.

"But you must."

Bruce gazed long at each of the three Legionnaires. Only a little liking he saw in their eyes, for after all he was an alien and fate had spared him instead of their beloved countryman, Reneaux. But he saw respect and confidence, and — although he was their superior—stern command.

"We three must die here," said the Legionnaire without hesitation. "We must die here giving the Touaregs the impression that there are *only* we three. Otherwise they would comb the desert till you too were found. And you must live—you who could exist in Aissouan where any of the three of us would be detected and killed in a day."

"*Encore!*" snapped another Legionnaire, who had been staring out over the fast-darkening desert. And in one more flying charge the Touaregs were on them.

This time they came more slowly, firing as they advanced and firing to better advantage than before. Rock splinters flew over the heads of the four. Bullets splashed against the stone, or glanced, whining, over their heads. One of the men cursed and jerked his leg as though it had been stung by a giant hornet.

That attack was almost the last. On and on they came, with here a man dropping, and there a camel lurching to the sand with a scream of pain. It is probable that they suspected by now that these were no true Bedouins that faced them; their shooting was too good and their courage too unfaltering. Anyway their ferocity seemed to increase instead of diminish with their losses. So near were they, before they finally broke formation and streamed away on either side of the rocks, that the nearest Touareg plunged head first onto the fringe of the outcropping as a careful bullet of Bruce's found his brain.

"There will be but one more rush," prophesied the Frenchman who had been urging Bruce to leave. "We can not stop them again. Go now, while there is yet a chance. The night has fallen enough for the attempt."

And Bruce, feeling like something vile and contemptible, averting his eyes from the eyes of the rest, prodded to its feet the one camel left alive, and faded out into the night. Ghost-like he headed north, hoping to swing around the attackers in a wide circle and point once more for fateful Aissouan.

There was no moon yet, but the stars seemed to his fevered imagination to be as bright as lanterns and close enough to earth to be touched. Surely the Touaregs had been methodical enough to surround the rock defense with scouts! And surely these scouts could see him on his camel half a mile away in that clear low light!

On he rode, taking advantage of every piled sand ridge for cover, fearing at each descent into a miniature valley that he would come head first into a group of Touaregs; and still he was hailed by no guttural voice, heard no quick shots of any far-flung watchers. If there were outposts, he was somehow slipping through their fingers.

Far behind him he heard a renewed outburst of firing. The noise grew imperceptible at last, as his camel stretched its long legs in a franker flight; till at length no sound could be heard in the immense stillness of the desert.

With his chin bowed on his chest, despising himself for his enforced desertion of the three behind him even while he realized that deadly necessity had caused it, he plodded west and north.

All night he traveled in that direction, gradually changing his line until by dawn he was pointing straight west. That day he camped; and next night he traveled west by south till he had picked up the Aissouan route once more. Purposefully he drove his decrepit mount till, a few kilometers from his goal, it dropped to rise no more: a dead camel abandoned on the desert's face would rouse less suspicion than a stranger riding up on a live one!

The dawn saw a ragged blind beggar waiting patiently at the foot of the almost endless steps up whose winding way one must climb to reach at last the high gate of the City of a Hundred Walls.

PROTECTED by his ragged, heavy woolen burnoose from the broiling rays of the sun, Bruce lay for some hours in the sheltering doorway. To all outward appearance he was in the coma suitable to an outcast pauper. His red-rimmed, vacant eyes (made red-rimmed by deliberate inflammation of the membrane of the lids) showed little but the whites. Flies, crawling over his lips and cheeks, were carefully allowed to have their way and swarm unbothered. Now and then a muttered "Alms!" helped to keep up the completeness of his disguise.

But inwardly his mind was keenly at work on the new facets of the problem that had presented themselves by the entrance to the palace courtyard. By one of the strokes of luck that come to those who dare, he had learned a lot.

Old Kibaba was still alive; that was now a definitely established fact. The son was in bad odor with el Hadj and the allied chiefs, but was for the moment being catered to. The people of Aissouan were uneasy and suspicious at their old Sheikh's disappearance; probably el Hadj had circulated some story of his death by natural causes, and the subjects did not quite believe the tale. And—this above all—there was to be a conference that night!

Bruce stirred in his doorway so that he could gaze up at the bulk of the palace, keeping his eyes nearly closed to veil the fact that he was perhaps not as blind as he pretended to be. He must be present at that conference and hear the battle plans discussed; but how he was going to manage it, he hadn't an idea.

He stared at the palace, diagramming it in his mind with what he could see of it, and what he remembered of its topography.

It was a huge affair, about three of our stories in height. The front of it, across which ran the courtyard, faced the street and could only be reached by the one gate which, he had seen, was guarded by eight men. The sides were sheerly walled, with all its windows heavily grilled. As well try to break into a prison. The rear looked down on Aissouan Pass, three hundred feet below. It would seem that nothing could approach that side unless equipped with wings.

Yet it was the rear of the palace Bruce

now concentrated on. The cliff side had open windows. Confident that no one could break in that side, the builder had designed the customary open Moorish window apertures—the double arches with the marble or alabaster columns in the center. Bruce was sure that, if he could manage to scale the cliff, he could enter one of those windows unobserved. But was it possible to scale the cliff?

"Alms," he droned mechanically as a beady-eyed merchant passed by. He studied his mental picture of the cliff. It shot straight up; but it was scribbled with cuts and ridges from the action of sand and wind through the ages. A man *might* be able to scale it; at least the feat was not flatly impossible. But after that . . .

Bruce stirred uneasily. After climbing the cliff, he would be faced with the task of ascending the wall of the building itself. That looked, from the floor of the Pass, at least, to be smooth as glass. He might very well crawl fly-like up the cliff, to find the more difficult descent, and the ascent of the palace wall, alike impossible. Then would he rest on the narrow ledge until seen and leisurely shot to death!

His jaw hardened. Well, that was a chance he must take! Four men had died that he might be here, with this ghost of an opportunity of accomplishing what he had been sent to do. He must not fail those four.

"Give, give," he whined, starting to crawl down the filthy alley toward the interminable stairs that led to the floor of the Pass. "For the love of Allah. . . ."

THE sun had set two hours ago. The night, with its foreshadowing hint of bleak cold that comes in late fall on the desert, pressed down oppressively on the Aissouan Range, with the stars seeming almost to scrape the blunt peaks in their nearness. Up and down the Pass as far as Bruce could see, nothing moved. Cautiously he crawled to a vertical rift in the cliff wall, like a zigzag chute; and, clinging to each small irregularity in the rock, he began to climb.

That ascent, under the dim light of the stars, with bare hands and feet numbed by the cool of night and bleeding from contact with the rough stone, was one long nightmare. It was a drab flirtation with death during every instant of it— not the death of heroic battle, but the inglorious death of sprawling down through thin air to dash against the rocks far below. And as he went higher his peril increased — the rocks grew ever smoother, and the helpful rift in the wall dwindled to nothing.

Forty-five awful minutes had elapsed before he hooked his fingers over the brick ledge of the far window he had marked as his goal. A dozen times he had swayed giddily and been on the point of letting go—when the faces of Reneaux and the three Legionnaires seemed to stare at him in the darkness, reproaching him with the futility of their sacrifice should he give up. The last thirty feet up the rough bricks of the building wall had been accomplished without himself quite knowing how it had been done.

Exhaustedly, he raised his head above the sill of the window to which he clung, and gazed into a room of the palace. It was a small room, bare and evidently not much used. There was no one in it now; and, wearily, Bruce rolled over the ledge and dropped to the floor, to lie for long moments on the cold stone, gasping for breath. Then, after he had recovered some of his strength, he crept to the open arch of the doorway opposite the window, and listened.

In the distance, down a long corridor, he could hear a babble of women's voices, broken now and then by a high-pitched laugh. Cautiously, he began to steal down the corridor toward the sound. He had a pretty fair idea of where he wanted to go, and how he was to get there. . . .

The average Arab palace is constructed along standardized lines. There is what corresponds to a court room, a large chamber in the front center of the building. Off this there is a smaller room which is a sort of private audience chamber. And running around both these rooms, half a story higher, is often a concealed gallery with grilled openings near its floor through which one may look down at the occupants of both. If there were such a gallery here, it would probably be beyond the hareem and down a few steps, where the Sheikh's wives could gain access to it and peep worshipfully at their lord and master as he dispensed justice to his subjects. It was for this probable gallery that Bruce was now making.

He reached the large room which was the hareem proper, and peered cautiously into it. . . .

Eighteen or twenty women of all ages, in the gauzy trousers of hareem dishabille, were sitting around a pool in which a fountain was playing. They were chatting and laughing contentedly enough— all save one. This woman, a tall, beautifully proportioned, Junoesque creature, sat apart with sadness written large on her face. Kibaba had one wife, at least, whose heart was saddened by his sudden disappearance.

The corridor continued along the side of the hareem, separated from the room proper by a line of graceful columns. And along that open space, which was lit only too plainly by the flicker of innumerable perforated brass lamps, Bruce must pass on his way to the place where the listening-gallery ought to be.

He watched the women till it seemed that none of them was glancing in his direction. Then he sprang quickly and noiselessly to the first of the pillars. For a moment he stood behind this, painfully aware that its circumference was a trifle smaller than his own, and that he must be apparent to any who might look directly at him. None did, however, as was proved by the fact that none screamed. He darted for the next pillar.

There were twenty columns along that south wall of the hareem. Bruce took about ten minutes to go from the first to the nineteenth. There he silently congratulated himself that he had managed to traverse the distance unseen. But when he looked out at the group of women again—he saw that he had not gone unobserved after all!

The wife with the sad face was staring straight at him, with unwinking alertness in her eyes. Rigid as stone, Bruce stared back at her, waiting for the shrill outcry that must at any moment apprise the others of his presence there. But the outcry did not come. After a long, comprehending stare, the woman deliberately turned her attention back to the fountain.

With his heart pounding at his inexplicable escape, Bruce accomplished the last step of his journey, and ducked down a low flight of stairs away from danger. For the moment, at least, he was safe. But why had the woman let him go? Why wasn't he at this instant on the way to the death that waits for any trespasser in the intimacy of the hareem? The answer came a moment later; at least it was a logical theory.

She was intelligent enough to reason that any man who prowled in that palace like a thief in the night was pretty surely a friend of the deposed Kibaba—an enemy to those who ruled in his place. On the chance that the prowler might accomplish some purpose, she had let him go. The act argued that she might be an ally; that she was loyal beyond question to her unlucky lord.

THE stairs led to the kind of gallery Bruce had been praying he might find. Crouching low in the scented dimness, he made his way along it till he came to a fretted aperture through which uncertain light beams flickered and voices came. Here he kneeled on the floor and looked down.

Seven men surrounded a magnificently dressed stripling with a weak chin and a cruel mouth who sat on an elaborate stone seat built into the wall. Of the seven, four were those Bruce had seen at the gate that morning. Two of the others were strangers to him. As he looked at the seventh, the blood drummed in his ears. For he was looking at the fountainhead of the impending rebellion, the brains of the whole evil conspiracy—el Hadj.

Piercing light gray eyes; a great, aquiline beak of a nose; a body twisted from some disease of infancy, but none the less majestic in bearing for all that; an air of power and ruthless forcefulness; such were the dominant features of the man who was pitting his cunning and genius for organization against the whole of France.

Even as Bruce recognized him, el Hadj began to speak. He outlined in detail a campaign of bloody invasion of French North Africa so complete, so ingeniously worked out, so infallible-seeming, that Bruce shuddered as he heard it. Thousands of French land-holders were to be slaughtered. The French quarters of a hundred towns and cities were to be sacked and the inhabitants massacred. After first driving a wide wedge up through central Algeria, the Arabs were to sweep the European usurpers into the sea. Arabs would once more rule over Arab land.

"The plan is ready," boomed el Hadj. "The fighting harkas are assembled and wait but the word. Now that our powerful and illustrious brother of Aissouan"—the stripling on the great stone seat smirked fatuously—"has given his consent to our march through Aissouan Pass, all is complete."

"All," murmured one of the others, "save the death of Kibaba. We can not give the word till he dies. For until he passes on to paradise, our plans are as straws to be disarranged by the first careless breath of heaven."

The boy's cruel mouth twisted, but he shifted uneasily in the big stone seat.

"Until Kibaba actually dies," pressed on the objector, "we can do nothing definite. For at any moment some loyal one might learn that the Sheikh is alive and imprisoned. There might be an outbreak that would free him. Then what? Then might our thousands march to the very foot of the Pass, there to be blocked and made impotent at the last moment! For Kibaba, alive and ruling, would never let us by. The dotard is too firmly under French influence."

All looked at Kibaba's son. He snarled at them.

"My father can not possibly escape. Give the word to march whenever you please."

"It is true that, were the worthy Kibaba to die, a chance would be eliminated that we can not afford to take," said el Hadj suavely. "It grieves me to announce it, but so it is."

"Bah! He's afraid to end the old one's life," some one said cunningly.

Kibaba's son straightened. "Who dares to speak so? I? Afraid?"

"They why does not Kibaba die?"

Again all eyes went to the boy's face. He looked down.

"He will die soon. That I promise."

"When? Tomorrow? In a week? A month?" el Hadj drove home the advantage.

"In a month."

"But in a month the accursed French may have learned our plans and have taken steps to block them. That would not stop us, but it might impede our progress."

"In a week, then," said the badgered prince.

"But why wait even that short time? Why not now? At once? Tonight!"

Almost pleadingly, the boy looked from one relentless but smoothly smiling face to another. His vicious mouth and small pale eyes denied that there was a shred of honor in him. But it was obvious that the thought of putting his father to death was distasteful even to him. At length, however, he nodded his head, his will beaten down by the wills of those opposing him.

"Not tonight, worthy comrades. But tomorrow. I swear it. I have hesitated thus far through a natural sentiment——"

"For which we honor thee," murmured el Hadj with a scarcely veiled sneer.

"——but tomorrow he surely dies." He pompously inflated his narrow chest. "And now shall we partake of refreshment? I have obtained some dancers I think will be acceptable—better even than the Ouled Naïls. . . ."

Bruce waited to hear no more. The deliverance of Kibaba, somehow, from his dungeon—and before Kibaba's faithless son could crown his youthful villainy with parricide—was the supreme necessity of the moment.

He went back toward the hareem. He could never find the passage leading down to the tunnel by himself. But the woman who had so surprizingly spared his life might gamble further on the meaning of his skulking visit there, and direct him in his search.

He had just got back to the hareem, and had at last managed to catch the woman's eye, when he heard footsteps in the corridor behind him. Wildly he stared around for some place in which to hide. The corridor was bare. The sound of footsteps drew rapidly nearer.

With no chance to hide, and no chance to run for his life, there was but one course open to him. He must trust to his disguise.

Commending himself to the God of the Christian, Who is after all not so distant a relative of the Allah of the Arab, he slumped down on the stone flagging of the floor, let his head roll back and his mouth sag open, and pretended deep sleep.

There was a startled grunt as some one's foot brought up against his side. Then there was a shrill shout. Blinking in feigned amazement, whining placating sentences, Bruce allowed himself to be dragged down the corridor away from the hareem, after which he submitted docilely to the rough grasp of half a dozen of the retainers of el Hadj. With many kicks and blows, he was led to an arched doorway and thrown into a room where eight men reclined about a cleared space where a dancing girl was contorting her statuesque body.

It was the private audience chamber into which he had looked a few moments before. He was in the presence of the fierce el Hadj, and the sadistic son of Kibaba, with nothing between him and death but a beggar's burnoose.

THERE was a long, hard silence while eight pairs of eyes roamed over the prisoner's ragged, dirty clothing and stared piercingly at his vacant orbs.

"Well," said el Hadj at length, his voice terrifyingly silky, "what have we here?"

"A skulker who was found within the hareem, beloved of Allah," responded one of the guards respectfully. "A descendant of carrion who wishes to hasten death by gazing on the beauties of the Sheikh's wives."

"Not so," whined the captive. "I gaze on nothing. I am blind, my masters, as can be plainly seen. Blind and old and helpless. I beg for alms on the streets——"

"Indeed?" sneered el Hadj, his gimlet eyes never ceasing to scrutinize the tattered figure. "And what is an aged, helpless, blind beggar doing here in the palace?"

"Sleeping, most illustrious one. Merely sleeping. This evening, just after muezzin call, I went to find a hole in which to hide my unworthy body from the chill of night. I felt a gate open, and crept in, not knowing whose gate it was nor where it might lead. I went through some sort of courtyard, as I could feel by the paving, entered a door, and went down a corridor. I found a warm, attractive spot, and there I went to sleep, thanking Allah for His goodness in leading me to comfort. That is all, Magnificent One."

El Hadj's long fingers caressed the sparse beard on his chin.

"Old and blind and helpless," he reflected aloud. "Yet thy face looks not like the face of an old man, studied closely. And thy shoulders are broad for one who is helpless. Blind? We shall see."

He drew from his sash a long slender dagger, and approached the prisoner. The dagger was levelled at one of the vacant eyes, and slowly thrust toward it.

Not a muscle of the intruder's face moved. The vacant eyes continued to stare sightlessly at a spot a trifle over el Hadj's head. The needle point of the knife came nearer, within an inch of the right eyeball. . . .

"In the name of Allah," whined Bruce next instant, "torture me not."

He clapped his hand to his eye. The point of the knife had pierced the eye-lid enough to draw blood. But not till it actually touched his flesh had Bruce so much as blinked.

"Enough," said Kibaba's renegade son pompously. "Are we men of no importance that we trifle with such dung? Let us finish the matter in this beggar's death."

"With your permission," said el Hadj, "I think it would be wise to order him held for questioning. His story is that of a fool! Is it likely a blind beggar could creep through a gateway we have given express orders always to keep locked? Is it likely such an one could crawl past eight men, and enter the palace arch unseen by any one? Could he walk openly through many rooms to the hareem corridor without being observed and stopped? And regard his feet and hands. Mingled with the dirt that doubtless exudes from his very soul, is blood. What is there in the traversing of the palace flooring to gash his feet and hands thus? Nay, Great One of Aissouan, let us keep this interesting blind beggar alive. In the morning he may be persuaded to speak, after experiencing red-hot iron, or the stake. But first"—he advanced again with the slender dagger poised—"first let us make sure he is really blind. With his two eyeballs impaled on this blade of mine we shall know that his tale of the blindness, at least, is true."

Bruce's face drained white under the stain of his disguise. But again he didn't shrink a fraction of an inch from the other's venomous approach. Only, under the tatters of his burnoose, every muscle in his body tensed with preparation for his last fight in life.

Then the dancing girl screamed as the dagger swept closer to the beggar's contorted face. She had been cowering beside the stone seat of Kibaba's son, shuddering at the threatened violence of el Hadj. She was a slim young thing, surely not more than fourteen years old; and at her outbreak she shrank into herself and stared at the men, fearful that she had displeased them to the point of a flogging.

"Hold thy knife, Leader of Hosts," commanded the boy arrogantly. "Do as thou wilt in the morning. But for tonight, let us return to our entertainment. It will be spoilt if blood is spilt—won't it, little Vision?" His hand went to caress the girl's head, and he leered at her.

"Is entertainment more important than the plan of empires?" growled el Hadj. But he stayed his hand, though his lips hardened at the imperious tone of the weakling on the Sheikh's throne.

"To the dungeon with him," he said to the guards. "And see that he is safely caged, or his fate shall be thine on the morrow."

Still whining dolorously, and droning of his innocence, the "helpless, aged, blind beggar" was dragged from the room and propelled roughly down a long flight of stairs and through a heavily barred doorway. This opened onto a down-sloping tunnel, which ended at last in another great door. A key a foot in length and weighing at least five pounds opened this; the hinges grated; and Bruce was thrown into a hole of blackness that stank so that his hair crawled on his scalp.

The eight-inch door thudded shut. With its closing, the last dim flicker of light disappeared. A silence as profound as that of the tomb settled over the place; and the mad American who had joined the North African Secret Service *"pour le sport"* sank to the chill rock of the floor to wait for morning and the dread questioning he was to undergo.

A FAINT rustle sounded in the darkness. There was a sound as of some one —or, perhaps, some Thing—crawling closer. Bruce crouched in his corner, star-

O. S.—**5**

ing vainly into the blanket of darkness to see what made the noise. He might as well have been blind.

"Who's there?" he heard a harsh, cracked voice at last.

He hesitated a moment before replying. Could this unseen one be a spy of el Hadj's, placed here to trick him into some damning admission?

"A helpless, blind beggar," he whined. "A helpless old one, forsaken of Allah and thrust in here to rot."

"Bah!" was the weary, muttered reply. "And I had thought perhaps my son——"

Bruce straightened tensely. In the stress of his own sudden capture and what it portended, he had for a time forgotten the reason for his being in that black hole.

"Thy son?" he repeated. "Art thou, then, the great Sheikh, Kibaba?"

"I am, spawn of filth," was the reply, arrogant in spite of tribulation.

"And I, son of stars," said Bruce in rapid French, speaking softly for fear there was a listening-post behind some wall, "am come to rescue thee if possible."

"What sayest thou?" was the quick, eager exclamation. "Thou art of the French?"

"I am American, Great One. But I am sent by the French. We had news of the confederation of tribes under el Hadj. We heard that thou wert imprisoned here, and that, under thy son, the Aissouan Pass was opened to the rebels. The all-powerful French government sent me to release thee—their friend—and set thee in power again."

"Friend," brooded the voice sourly. "Friend! The French government is my ally—not my 'friend.' I but aid them because I am old enough to know that my race is born for subjection, and the French are as good masters as any."

Bruce maintained a diplomatic silence.

"And now that thou are here, 'friend,' how is my escape to be effected?" The strong old voice was slightly sardonic. "We are in the heart of a mountain of stone. The door could not be battered down by a hundred such as we; and there are two picked guards outside it."

"Nevertheless, with the help of Allah, we may somehow win free." Bruce was silent for a moment. Then: "How often do they bring thee food?"

"Twice a day," said the old Sheikh. "At noon, and at nightfall—though there is no noon or nightfall in this darkness here."

Bruce frowned. Of course! The evening meal had been brought hours before. And long before the noon meal should be carried in next day, he would be on the rack—or the stake. The faint hope he had entertained of overpowering the guard that brought in the meals died out.

"What visitors come to see thee?" he asked.

"My son comes occasionally," said the Sheikh, his voice shaking with bitter grief. "My dutiful son!"

"And that is all, Illustrious?"

"Now and then my wife, Khatma, is allowed to come. Khatma." The harsh voice softened. "She alone of all my wives is faithful to me now."

Bruce shook his head. The only possible way out of that dungeon was through the door. The door was opened only for the admission of food, or for visitors. Neither meals nor visitors would be forthcoming at this late hour. And in the morning . . .

There was silence in the pitch darkness for a long time. Bruce concentrated fruitlessly on various plans of escape, none of which seemed even remotely feasible. Then there was the sound of the great key in the door-lock.

"What can that be?" whispered Bruce.

"I know not — unless it be Death," answered the Sheikh dully.

Bruce glared through the darkness at the spot where he judged the door was. And then it was opened and a feeble gleam of light—seeming almost dazzling bright after the blackness—outlined a tall, shrouded form. The figure stepped inside, the door was closed behind it. With rusty creaking, the lock was clicked shut by the huge key; and a woman's voice broke the stillness.

"My lord, art thou still here? In this dark I can not see thee."

"Khatma!" gasped the Sheikh Kibaba. "Khatma! How art thou here at this late hour? And why?"

"I had to visit thee once again in life," said Khatma. "I, thy slave, overheard them plan—in the council room when a curious blind beggar was being questioned—to put thee to death on the morrow. So did I steal away to see thee once again. A ruby to one of the guards, and thy diamond-hilted dagger to the other, gained me entrance here."

"Keep thy veil securely before thy countenance, child. Thy 'curious blind beggar' is here with me now, and he is not at all blind. But he said nothing of my planned execution."

"I saw no reason to disturb thy last night," muttered Bruce. His tone was absent. He was thinking. Hard! The guards, after admitting this woman here, would of course expect her to leave again. They would be used to her presence, and would not look at her too closely. . . .

He broke in abruptly on the sorrowful conversation of the Sheikh and his favorite. "Thy wife, Great One, is a tall woman. Nearly as tall as myself——"

"Dog!" was the blazing interjection. "How dost thou know that?"

It was on the tip of Bruce's tongue to say artlessly that he had observed her in the hareem. But he stopped himself in time. "I saw her outline, very vaguely, as she entered the door. I saw that she was of noble height. And it occurred to me that her presence here might be our salvation."

"Say on," commanded the Sheikh, after a silence that bristled with suspicion.

"My thought is this, favored of Allah: Suppose I should don the garments of Khatma, and leave the dungeon in her place. Then could I surprize the men who guard us, who would look only for a woman and be unprepared for the sinews of a man. I could fell them, open the door for thee, and we could fly from the death that waits us with the rising sun. How think thou?"

"The plan of a fool!" spat out Kibaba promptly.

But the woman, with quicker, more practical wit, ventured a respectful objection. "Perhaps, lord, there is wisdom in the stranger's words."

"Hold thy tongue. And draw thy veil more closely about thy face. I feel it loosening in thy grasp. Hast thou forgot all modesty?"

Bruce smiled in the darkness. He couldn't see his hand before his eyes—yet Kibaba fretted like an old woman over the possibility of his seeing Khatma's face.

"The plan may seem a hopeless one," he urged, "but it is all we have left to try."

"Never!" said the old Sheikh stubbornly. "Allow my wife to expose her body—even her face!—to another man? Impossible!"

Bruce swore to himself. "But in this darkness I might as well be the blind one I claimed to be. I can not see thy Khatma."

A sullen, stubborn mumble was the only answer. But suddenly he heard the rustle of fabric, and sensed that Khatma, taking command on her own initiative, was starting to disrobe. Promptly he began to take off his beggar's garments.

"I forbid thee——" said Kibaba, but a note of irresolution in his harsh voice told of his indecision.

"My Lord, it means thy death if I don't. And, as the stranger says, the darkness veils me as well as any silks or woolens could. Wilt thou draw near and allow me to adjust this habit of mine upon thy body?" she continued, speaking in Bruce's direction.

"For the last time——" croaked Kibaba.

"Thou canst place thy two hands over my face to veil it," said Khatma. And the Sheikh drew near and did so. Thus was modesty preserved.

Bruce, stripped to the skin, approached the corner where the two were huddled. "Thou art ready?" murmured the woman.

"Ready," replied Bruce. "And hasten! At any moment the guard may come to terminate thy visit here."

Khatma hastened. In the dark, Bruce felt soft, lovely hands fasten feminine garments about him. The dressing seemed to go on interminably, partly because of his feverish apprehension that at any moment the guard might come prematurely, partly because of the number of things that went to make up his new disguise. But at length he was clothed; and a fine wool haik was thrown across his shoulders and draped over his face to complete the process. The lovely hands left him.

"And now thou art a woman," said Khatma, with a hint of tremulous laughter in her voice.

Almost with the words the heavy dungeon door was opened. A guttural voice insolently bade the wife of the Sheikh that she must leave.

Bruce walked toward the door, stooping as much as he could to hide his tallness. Through the rough-hewn doorway he went, and into the dimly lighted passageway outside. The Arab who had opened the door—and who had stood at vigilant attention lest the two men within should try to overpower him—closed it securely and lolled against it. Bruce shuffled slowly toward the upper end of the passageway, where was the second guard. There was almost a right angle bend in the tunnel between the guard at the palace entrance, and the one at the dungeon door. On this bend depended the success of his desperate plan.

He rounded the turn without rousing the suspicion of the first Arab; and went slowly toward the barred door that led up into the palace. As he approached this, the second guard, a big man with a slashing scar running down his cheek, left his post and came toward him.

"This ruby," he grumbled insolently, "is smaller than I thought. I would not have taken the risk of admitting thee here had I looked at it more closely." He rolled a glittering red stone in his greasy palm. "Thou must give me another gem, or I will not let thee pass."

Bruce held his breath. He dared not speak, of course. And the fellow was evidently expecting an answer of some sort—either a protest, or frightened submission to his banditry.

"Hast lost thy tongue?" the guard demanded. He stopped his approach, and Bruce groaned to himself. Somehow he must get the man within reach before he became alarmed at his obstinate silence.

"By Allah," said the man, tilting his head, "thou must have grown. At least it seems thou art taller than I thought. I'll see thy face, perfume of paradise."

Bruce shook his head, and drew the haik closer across the bridge of his nose. "No? Then shall I tear the veil from thee——"

The words ended in a startled grunt. For, in coming near to tear aside the veil,

he had at last got close enough for Bruce to spring.

Savagely the American locked his fingers about the Arab's throat to cut off any cry for help. The Arab caught at his wrists to loose the murderous grip, and kicked wildly with his slippered feet. Chest to chest, shoulder to shoulder, they swayed and struggled in the dimly lighted tunnel.

For one instant the guard loosened Bruce's hands and opened his mouth for a ringing yell. Bruce's fist, smashing against his lips, stopped the sound before it could issue forth. His clutching hands found their former stranglehold. And, still in deadly silence, the struggle went on.

The Arab seemed to gain strength instead of losing it as the fight wore on. His fingers tore at Bruce's wrists in a frenzy of effort. He writhed and twisted, and once his teeth, exposed in a snarl of animal fury, sank deep into the American's arm.

But finally the iron grip around his windpipe was tightened. He gasped, and flecks of white appeared on his battered lips. His face turned purplish-gray, and his struggles weakened. After a last convulsion of effort, he sagged forward.

Long after he had ceased to move, Bruce kept that death grip on his throat, panting for breath, with the sweat pouring down his face and neck to mingle with the blood on his arm where the Arab's teeth had met. At length he laid the inert body down on the floor of the tunnel and prepared for the next move.

He approached the bend in the passageway and cautiously peered around the corner. The Arab at the dungeon door was still lolling carelessly back against the massive panel. Evidently no sound of the fight had reached him.

Bruce drew back out of sight—and

moaned, as though he were in deadly agony.

"Achmet?" came the guttural voice of the guard, after a moment's silence. "Achmet?"

In answer, Bruce moaned again; and there was a pad of feet as the man came to see what was wrong with his comrade.

"Achmet. What is it? Art thou in pain?"

He was quite near the turn now. Bruce gathered himself to leap. . . .

The guard's turbaned head was thrust around the corner. His eyes rested on Bruce, who, bloody and dishevelled, with the haik ripped back to show his cropped hair, bore no resemblance whatever to the ostensible Khatma who had passed a few minutes before.

"Allah!" the guard ejaculated, staring at the American. Then he reached for the revolver at his waist. Before he could grasp it, Bruce was upon him.

There was little necessity for preserving silence now—no sound could be heard around the bend of the passage and through the great door leading into the palace. He slashed out with his fists to down the Arab in the shortest possible time.

A smashing right to the thinly bearded chin sent the guard flying against the wall. He howled, plucked out a dagger with a diamond hilt, and charged.

The blade ripped at an angle into Bruce's side. For an instant he felt the shock of it, as though a thin wedge of ice had been driven into his flesh and left there to melt. Then the sensation was numbed by the concentration of the fray.

Quick as panthers the two clutched and battered at each other, whirling about in the flickering beams of the brass lamp that hung from the low roof. But the fight, though fierce, was short: the Arab's ignorance of fist-fighting lost for him.

He lunged for the American with all his strength, leaving an opening to the face that a child could not have missed. Bruce brought up his right fist through a full arc — and landed his knuckles with crashing force on the point of the guard's jaw. Without a sound the man slumped to the floor and lay there like a run-down mechanical doll.

Bruce bent over him and searched for his keys. Then he whirled to unlock the massive door.

"Kibaba," he shouted, bruskly waiving formalities of titles, "Khatma—come out. The way is clear."

The Sheikh—now seen to be a gaunt, white-haired, grim eagle of a man— emerged into the corridor. Behind him came the woman, tall and lovely, clad in Bruce's rags and hiding her face behind her upraised arm.

Quickly Bruce seized the still unconscious guard and dragged him into the cell, after which he closed and locked the door. Then he turned to the Sheikh.

"Do thou lead. The way out of the palace is known to thee—and some place where we may possibly hide till day dawns, if we live that long."

WITH a nod, the tall old man took the lead; and the three filed up the sloping passage to the palace. The big door at the tunnel entrance was unlocked, and they stepped cautiously into the great room beyond. It was empty. El Hadj had evidently thought the prisoners too well caged to bother with a guard there.

Tiptoeing over a profusion of deep-piled rugs and through fretted, Moorish archways, from one deserted room to another, they followed the Sheikh toward the front of the palace. At last they reached the small audience chamber, and here they saw the first person they had encountered in their soundless flight.

Sitting slumped on the great stone chair that jutted from the wall was a young man with weak features that contrasted with a cruel, self-willed mouth. His chin was sagged on his chest, from the left side of which protruded the hilt of a knife.

For a long time Kibaba gazed at the lifeless body of his eldest child. No expression of any kind showed on his face; but his thoughts must have been the bitterest a man can have. Then he turned away — as though the dead youth had meant nothing whatever to him—and beckoned to Khatma.

"Leave us, my flower," he commanded. "Steal up the stairs to the hareem, and through it to thy chamber. If Allah wills, I shall see thee again soon."

With an obedient inclination of the head—and with a flash of admiring black eyes at Bruce over her upraised forearm —the woman left. The two men continued their stealthy journey toward the palace gate.

As they came to the great door that gave onto the courtyard, they drew back in the shadows and held a whispered consultation. In front of the portal leading to the street were the customary eight guards el Hadj had seen fit to station there since the overthrow of Kibaba.

"We are blocked hopelessly," murmured the old Sheikh. Into his voice crept a hint of the fatalism that corrodes all the East: what is written, is written; only a fool fights against destiny. "Two men are helpless against eight."

But Bruce was the kind of a fool that does fight against destiny; he had come of a nation of similar fighting fools.

"There'll be something we can do," he whispered back. "We'll find a way to get past them."

Kibaba shrugged resignedly. "Only the spirits of the departed could slip through that gateway without rousing the dogs in front of it."

Bruce caught his breath as the fatalistic sentence suggested something to him —a plan so tenuous, so bizarre that it did not seem possible it could succeed. And yet, the Arab is as superstitious as any other man; and moonlight such as that which flooded the courtyard before them distorts all objects and gives them unearthly outlines in its refraction. . . .

Quickly he began to smear blood from the shallow gash in his side onto the white haik wound around his shoulders. Then he slit a hole through the bloodied fabric, and thrust his thumb up into it.

"Follow me," he said.

He raised his arm, bending the elbow in a right angle, with the thumb stuck upright over his head, and began deliberately to walk into the moonlight courtyard toward the eight Arabs by the gate!

"Thou art mad!" gasped Kibaba, catching his arm and trying to hold him back.

"Follow, I said!" Bruce wrenched his arm free. And with wonder and doubt in his eyes, the Sheikh walked after him toward the gate.

Afterward, in their report to the furious el Hadj, the eight men of the guard varied their incredible accounts very little. All claimed fearfully to have seen about the same thing—the grim ghost of the Sheikh Kibaba, whom they had been assured was dead; and a very tall woman, a giantess of a woman, whose head seemed to have been hacked off, but from between whose gory shoulders rose the severed stump of her backbone—a bloody, grisly projection about the size of a man's thumb. Naturally the men had all fallen on knees and elbows, faces east, and called on Allah to aid them. The two fearsome apparitions had then disappeared.

"Disappeared!" raved el Hadj. "Disappeared! They walked through the gateway and down the street. That's how they disappeared. Dogs! Unnamable vilenesses! Thou shalt kiss the feet of Death this day, and return, if thou art able, to tell me if what thine eyes saw at the gate were truth or not!"

But it was not till the second hour after dawn that el Hadj decreed this death sentence on, and held this converse with, the tricked guards. And at that hour, up under the mud roof of a mean hovel about a quarter of a mile away, the two fugitives were hidden in a coffin-like storage space among strings of red peppers and bags of date seeds.

SOMBERLY, silently, the old Sheikh sat in the airless cubicle under the roof and stared unseeingly at the rough walls. Huddled in this fetid niche, his burnoose smeared with the filth of the cell in which he had lain for so many weeks, he was yet a palpable leader—an eagle among men. But he was a draggled, heartsick, well-nigh broken eagle.

He was hollow-eyed from weariness. He was tortured by the memory of his treacherous son. All his sixty years weighed on his bowed shoulders at that moment when he squatted in so un-Sheikhlike a manner in the Arab equivalent of an attic.

"We might well have waited in our prison for the death that was written for us this morning," he muttered at length. "I shall never rule in Aissouan again. And thou wilt never leave the city to go north to thine own people. Both of us will die here in this squalid hole."

"The hell we will!" said Bruce to himself, in English.

"It appears to me that all has gone most propitiously," he addressed Kibaba. "We have escaped the talons of el Hadj, for the moment at least. We have reached this spot, in the heart of thy city, in safety. There remains now only for thee to let thy people know that thou art still alive, and to take up again the reins of power."

"But how is that possible?" brooded the Sheikh. "Long before I could send messengers here and there, we shall be hunted down and killed. I have no chance to address them. Ah, well . . . what Allah wills. . . ." He sighed despairingly.

A hot reply surged to Bruce's lips. The dead weight of Kibaba's fatalism, which he had been forced to bear in addition to the strain of engineering their whole escape, had worn his nerves to the snapping-point. But before he could give vent to the words, there was an interruption.

Their host, a dull-eyed worker in brass who still seemed fuddled with wonder that here in his humble house he was sheltering the great Sheikh Kibaba who had been proclaimed dead, climbed up the rude ladder made of sticks in the mud wall, and poked his head into the tiny storage chamber.

The town, the two gathered from his words, was in an uproar. El Hadj's entire military escort, a picked band of about fifty men that Kibaba had trustfully allowed to accompany him into the city on his arrival, had been combing the streets for two escaped prisoners from the palace dungeon. El Hadj had not disclosed the identities of the two, but had announced that they were infidels from the north—men whom it was his duty as a loyal friend of Aissouan, and as a sort of informal regent since the sad death of Kibaba, to hunt out and kill.

Thus far the strictest search had not turned them up. So el Hadj had commanded that every man in Aissouan appear at noon at the market square. There, one by one, they would be examined and questioned by el Hadj himself. In the event that even this measure did not result in the fugitives' recapture, el Hadj's band would search every house in the city till their hiding-place was found.

There was much angry talk among the people of Aissouan at this. It was unbearably dictatorial for this visiting Sheikh from the south to talk of searching homes with his warriors. It presented ominous possibilities for loot and rape, though el Hadj had sworn not to enter any hareem and not to allow his men to touch a sou's worth of property.

However, only a few firebrands were talking openly. In the main, the people seemed to think they must submit. They were leaderless, bewildered, with Kibaba dead and a new rumor starting that the son had also died.

"It is as I told thee," said Kibaba to Bruce, shaking his white head sadly. "Either hiding here in this vegetable bin, or later in the market place, we shall be caught and killed. It is inevitable. That order for every man in the city to report at the market square will be our doom."

"On the contrary," said Bruce, his eyes blazing, "it will be our salvation! It is the command of a fool—a blunder I would never have dreamed a leader like el Hadj could make!"

The Sheikh stared at him perplexedly.

"Seest thou not how we shall profit by that blunder?" Bruce hurried on. "A general assembly! All thy subjects that live within the city walls congregated in one spot! Could any better opportunity be made for thee to address the loyal ones of Aissouan?"

"As Allah lives!" The Sheikh lifted his head. "Thou art right! There is a chance. . . ." He turned to the brassworker and spoke, with some of his old spirit stirring in his voice. "Mingle with those on the streets and spread the word that the Sheikh Kibiba lives, and will present himself to his people in the market square at noon. Go!"

IT LACKED but half an hour of noon when Bruce and Kibaba slipped from the door of the brass-worker's hut and mingled with the excited crowds that surged toward the market square. They had waited till the last possible moment to lessen the risk of their being prematurely discovered by el Hadj's men; and now they moved in the center of the throng, and kept the hoods of their burnooses—which their host had supplied them to take the place of Kibaba's draggled finery and Bruce's woman's clothing—pulled low over their foreheads.

There were more than hints of rebellion in the expressions and exclamations of the pushing crowds of men around them. El Hadj must have acted in desperation when he so high-handedly defied the rights of the people he was ostensibly only visiting.

"This image of evil from the south—who is he to lord it over Aissouan?"

"Who are these prisoners he is so eager to recapture? Why does he not inform us of their names?"

"Yea—perhaps they are the great Kibaba, and his son! Who knows?"

"Never shall I permit el Hadj's vermin to enter *my* house!"

These, and similar hot words, rose on all sides. But, as the milling procession neared the market square, the voices gradually were stilled. El Hadj had only fifty men against the thousands of Aissouan; but these fifty were picked fighters, splendidly armed and competently led — while the thousands, without a Sheikh, were a body without a head.

At the entrance to the market square each man was halted and cursorily searched for weapons. One of el Hadj's warriors ran his hands over the bodies of the citizens; and any knife or gun that was felt under the folds of his burnoose was taken; "to be returned to thee later," was the appeasing statement. But the angry looks grew blacker at this indication of dictatorship.

It was a trying moment when Bruce and Kibaba filed toward this search. The Sheikh was not an ordinary-looking man; and his nobility of aspect was heightened, rather than decreased, by the poor man's outfit he wore.

But they passed the ordeal safely. The guard ran his hands lightly over Bruce's body, and wordlessly motioned him into the square. He did the same to Kibaba —stared for one long, intent moment at the tall, straight old man—then turned his harassed attention on the man in line behind him.

In the huge market place all was milling confusion. Pallid youths who spent their long days from dawn to dark in sewing endlessly on sewing machines, those incongruous bits of modernity that have been so universally adopted by Arab fabric-workers; merchants with soft dark eyes and tight hard mouths; water-carriers and petty nobles; sand-diviners and cripples; camel-drivers and teachers of the Koran—every type of Arab was there, treading the dusty, hard packed ground resentfully and muttering at the tyranny that had made them convene in the broiling heat.

Near the center of the square, with hoods still pulled low as though to guard their heads from the sun, stood Bruce and the Sheikh. They could not see around them in any direction: as it happened they were standing in a slight depression which kept them from gazing over the heads of the crowd, though both were taller than the average.

The name el Hadj was on every one's lips; and they assumed that he was in the market place too, though they could not place him. Of course he would be—to no one else would he delegate the important task of scrutinizing in turn each citizen of Aissouan in his effort to recapture Kibaba.

In each alley-like street leading into the market square, the streams of men slowed to trickles, then stopped altogether. The guards of el Hadj swung across the entrances to keep any one from trying to slip back before the examination started.

Bruce could feel the old Sheikh tremble with the importance of the moment that was almost at hand. A hush settled over the waiting throng that stirred restlessly among the bales of fabric and piles of date seeds that perpetually littered the hard ground.

"Now," whispered Bruce, as an agitation in the crowd indicated that the search had already begun. "Now!"

BESIDE them — the reason for their standing in that particular spot— was an ancient stone water trough. With a shout to command attention, Kibaba mounted this and loomed head and shoulders above the mob. Bruce followed him up, and the two stood looking about at the startled, gaping Arabs.

"Men of Aissouan," shrieked Kibaba, "the liar, el Hadj, told you I was dead. It was but in an attempt to seize our city that he so lied. And in that treacherous attempt, he has murdered my son and would have murdered me, also, had I not escaped. I call on all to rise——"

That was as far as he got.

Standing low in the crowd before they ascended the water trough, he and Bruce had been unable to see the terrible sight that now met their eyes: they had unwittingly taken up a position within twenty feet of el Hadj's main band of men, and of el Hadj himself. And now, at sight of these two he was straining every nerve to capture and kill before his plans went hopelessly awry, el Hadj screamed a command and led a hacking charge through the crowd.

A thunderous tumult arose in the square. To the hundreds packed there that momentary glimpse of the Sheikh they had been told was dead, seemed like the short visit of an apparition. Yet the apparition had spoken, had accused the man who had already fired their bitter enmity—el Hadj. And now, where the apparition had appeared, a furious fight was being waged. All pressed savagely, vindictively forward.

In the immediate vicinity of the Sheikh the men of Aissouan were desperately struggling with the band of el Hadj. And the dust of the market square was turning to a red quagmire as the fifty men, armed to the teeth, shot and cut down the scores of unarmed citizens.

In a moment Bruce and Kibaba were surrounded by el Hadj's escort. And in the forefront, glaring murderous hate at the two who were such a menace to his dreams of empire, was el Hadj himself.

"Kill them!" he screeched. "Kill! Kill!" With his own hand he directed a volley of shots at the tall old man and the equally tall figure of the one he recognized as the "helpless, aged, blind beggar."

"The Sheikh! The Sheikh!" roared the mob in answer. And by tens and dozens they swarmed against the solid line of armed men that ringed their leader.

A bullet caught Kibaba in the shoulder and whirled him half around, but still he loomed fearlessly above the fighters. A hand clutched him; he beat the hand away. Then some unseen citizen—who had managed to smuggle in a simitar—tossed him the deadly weapon. He caught it deftly and began to thrust and parry, wounded shoulder and all, as though he were a youth of twenty instead of a man of sixty-odd. Here a skull was split to the ears, there an arm was lopped nearly off as the whirling blued blade wove figures of death around him.

Meanwhile Bruce had wrenched a carbine away from one of the attackers and was clubbing right and left with it. A stabbing pain in his leg marked where a bullet had torn its way through the calf. Another stinging pain in his left arm testified to a well-thrown knife. But savagely he swung his improvised club at heads and faces that ringed around them. There was no more shooting—el Hadj's men had formed a circle and could not have shot without killing each other.

The odds were too great for the terrific battle to continue long. Rapidly it drew to a close. . . .

Bruce swung his club with arms that seemed made of soft rubber. He sobbed for breath. The leg with the bullet-hole in it buckled under him in spite of all his efforts to remain upright. He fell to one knee on the broad stone rim of the trough. Of its own volition, it seemed, his carbine thrust itself against the face of an Arab who was about to stab the Sheikh. He saw the man's nose crumple with the blow — saw his carbine crash down on the turbaned head with stunning force.

The world was reeling before his eyes, now, but he saw one thing more. El Hadj had leaped up on the rim of the trough and swung his sword back to impale Kibaba. But the old man was too quick for him. Like a darting snake, appearing magically from thin air, his simitar flashed up and sideways—to slice half through the rebel chieftain's neck.

"That for the corruption of my son!" he grated, his old eyes flashing vengeance. "And that"—the blued blade hacked again—"for his death!"

El Hadj sank to the stone rim, dead before he touched it, and slumped face down in the reddened water of the trough.

Bruce felt a blow on his head. The

carbine was wrenched from his feeble hands. Then a roar as though the world had been torn asunder, a blinding shower of lights—and he knew no more.

WEAKLY, Bruce opened his eyes. Bending over him with a look of concern on his morose old face was the Sheikh, Kibaba. Over his bandaged shoulder, Bruce saw—wonder of wonders that she should be allowed in his presence —the favorite, Khatma; heavily veiled, of course, but with her black eyes flashing anxiously behind the sheerest of silk gauze that propriety would allow her to drape over her narrow eye-slit.

"Allah be praised, thou regainest consciousness," said the Sheikh. "Three days hast thou lain like one dead. My physician feared thy brain had crumpled under that blow on the head, but now thine eyes appear to show the light of reason."

"Oh, it'd take a harder crack than that to send me silly," murmured Bruce with an attempt at a grin. Then, at the Sheikh's uncomprehending stare, he added in Arabic: "The heads of my people, the Americans, are proverbial for their hardness, Illustrious One. But tell me, how is it that thou and I are not at this moment blissful in heaven?"

"The death of el Hadj caused his men to grow spiritless," responded Kibaba. "My people, inspired by thine example —truly thou art a man in battle—and by the sight of me, rushed them from all sides. Unarmed as they were, they overcame el Hadj's escort and killed them barehanded. Their death—was satisfying."

Which meant, Bruce supposed, that el Hadj's followers had been literally torn to pieces. No less a fate would have sent so ferocious a glare to the old Sheikh's brooding eyes.

"Then all is well?" whispered Bruce, feeling the drowsiness of convalescence stealing over him. "My mission has been accomplished successfully?"

"With eminent success!" said the old Sheikh gently. "Now that el Hadj is dead, the backbone of the confederation of tribes is broken. And Aissouan Pass, under my rule, shall remain blocked to help the French, my allies. I pledge myself anew to that. And now sleep, my brother, to gain strength for thy triumphal journey north to report thine entire victory."

Bruce closed his eyes and slept; and he dreamed that over him wavered the shadowy, sternly approving faces of Lieutenant Reneaux and the three heroic Legionnaires. . . .

Up from Earth's Center through the Seventh Gate
I rose, and on the Throne of Saturn sate,
    And many a Knot unravel'd by the Road;
But not the Master-knot of Human Fate.

There was the Door to which I found no Key;
There was the Veil through which I might not see;
    Some little talk awhile of ME and THEE
There was—and then no more of THEE and ME.
              —Rubáiyát of Omar Khayyam.

Thirty Pieces of Silver

By G. G. PENDARVES

*A grim story of the desert stronghold of Askia Ibn Askia, who ruled as
a tyrant over the Zangali people*

1. An Explorer Disappears

"*ARFI!* Something moves there in the shadow of the high dune to the left."

Joseph Deland—the famous intrepid little explorer, whose caravan was heading southward across the Sahara for the Ahaggar Plateau—peered sharply from under bushy white eyebrows at the spot indicated by his head camel-man.

"I see nothing yet, Muraiche," he replied quietly. "Let us go forward."

A pale moon had climbed the eastern horizon, and the desert glimmered in a blue-green light that was balm to the travellers after long hours of intolerable sun.

Ali and Mohammed, the other two camel-men of the tiny *garfla*, hesitated, showing the whites of their eyes as they gazed in sudden fear at the heavy shadow which lay beneath the dune.

"It is the *Ahl-el-Trab!*" muttered Ali. "Here is the very place and hour for this evil one to lie in wait. It is surely the demon who drags both men and beasts by their feet down to Gehenna, *Arfi!* Let us turn back before it is too late."

Ali's outspoken fears put the last touch to Mohammed's wavering courage. He turned in his tracks, and next moment both he and Ali were making off at a smart pace away from the fatal dune, their indignant beasts roaring in protest at such haste, and swinging long necks in the endeavor to bite their agitated drivers.

Deland's bright dark eyes gleamed with amusement.

"Go after them, Muraiche! Bring them back while I investigate. All right, I'll be careful."

His beautiful white *mehari* knelt at his reiterated "Kh! Kh! Kh!" and he dismounted. Muraiche watched him for a moment, his gaze following the small spare figure with dog-like devotion, before he turned to follow Ali and Mohammed.

"*Imsh'llah!*" he muttered angrily in his beard. "Is my master to be seized by a *djinnee* while they escape? Well indeed could they be spared—miserable ticks of an ass's tail!"

Deland tramped briskly toward the high-crested dune on his left. There was certainly something stirring at its base; a huddled figure became visible, and the sound of a deep groan reached Deland's ears.

"You are hurt?" he said, a moment later, bending over a man's writhing form.

The Arab at his feet made a painful effort to raise himself, his face in the moonlight showed horribly contorted—gray and glistening with sweat.

"Poison!" he gasped, as Deland knelt beside him. "The well . . . Touaregg scum . . . ah-h-h-h!"

The sufferer bit his own finger almost to the bone as a fresh spasm twisted him.

Deland rose quickly and ran back to his kneeling camel. With hasty hands he unstrapped the pack, and extracted his precious medicine chest. He was a fully qualified doctor, but a private fortune and a passion for exploring kept

"Even as his eyes linked with theirs, some words came dimly to his mind."

him from settling down to the usual routine of a medical man. His knowledge, however, was invaluable to him on his travels, and he kept it up to date with the greatest keenness.

Back again by his patient, he put a few pertinent questions, made an examination, and opened his case, his hands moving deftly among the beautifully arranged contents. The Arab drank from the phial held to his lips, his brilliant, fevered eyes on the other's absorbed face.

"If it be Life . . . or Death, I give thanks in Allah's name!" he murmured with cracked, blackened lips.

For an hour Deland worked over him, assisted by Muraiche and the two whom he had retrieved. The latter officiously bustled about in the background, making a fire, heating water, putting up the tent,

ostentatiously trying to make amends for their lapse. At last a faint smile touched the patient's lips, and he looked long and steadily into Deland's face.

"May Allah reward thee . . . a thousandfold! May thy life be long . . . and . . . thy——" His voice trailed off into exhausted silence, his head fell back against Deland's supporting arms as he plunged into a sudden deep oblivion of sleep.

"HM-M-M-M!" remarked Deland to himself a few days later, as he watched his patient ride off from the oasis where his *garfla* had rested, restocked its larder and waterskins, and where he had acquired the necessary baggage camels for the long trek south. "So that's the famous bandit, Ben Seghir! I suppose the government wouldn't thank me for saving his life and letting him go free. Fine man—very fine type! Bandit, eh? Well—well!"

His bright eyes twinkled at his own thoughts as he urged his camel on in the wake of his *garfla*, which was forging on ahead in the first and best hours of the very early morning to the cheerful singing of the Arabs. The caravan was about a mile away, the line of camels stretched like a frieze against the pale sky, as they went in single file along a ridge of dunes.

Deland's *mehari* plunged down an incline, sinking to the knees at every step in the loose soft sand. With a grunt, the fine beast prepared to climb up the opposite slope, when Deland was suddenly surrounded by a group of swarthy savage men who seemed to have sprung up from the earth itself, so carefully had they concealed themselves behind grassy hummocks and the tufts of cacti that grew profusely in that neighborhood.

Deland's first and only shot sent one of the ruffians to the ground, but he was quickly overpowered.

"If you cry out, your body will lie here for the vultures to pick!" A pock-marked villainous face was thrust up against his, while the speaker bound his hands, and attached a length of rope from Deland's *mehari* to his own camel.

Two ahead, two behind their prisoner, the little company rode hard and long almost due west, finally coming to a region quite unknown to the explorer. On and on and on they rode until the sea went down in a red-gold sea of light before them; on and on until the mysterious night received them, and Deland vanished utterly in that world of space and great silence—leaving no more trace of his going than a little pebble pushed over the rim of some fathomless sea.

2. *Plans Are Made in El Kidja*

BRADLEY GLEAVE woke from a prolonged doze and blinked, bewildered for a minute. He had come home in a vile temper from his office, tried to drown the memory of his latest unfortunate deal in several stiff pegs of brandy, and had finally forgotten his troubles in a half-drunken sleep.

From his broad veranda he could see the lights of El Kidja beginning to illumine the blue dusk of the Algerian evening. Glancing behind him he saw the rosy glimmer of lamplight in the sitting-room, and heard a low murmur of voices.

His wife and that cousin of hers—Philip Mace!

Bradley scowled. Confounded young puppy, always on the doorstep, always interfering and tacitly encouraging Muriel to be independent! Curse the young fool! Muriel would have been wax in his hands if it had not been for this everlasting cousin!

He'd show her though! Now that her father was dead and gone, he would have a freer hand. When proofs were finally established that Joseph Deland had made his last fool trip into the desert, the money would all come to Muriel. And he needed that money—only he himself knew how badly he needed it.

He'd have to hurry things up a bit. His servant, Hamid, was like all Arabs, slow and wary, and all for the subtleties of the game. But he couldn't stall off his creditors indefinitely—within the month some positively irrefutable proof of Deland's death must be produced. He'd promise Hamid another hundred pounds to produce the necessary proof and witnesses, and get the thing through without more delay. After all, it was no real crime! Deland certainly must be dead by now, and why wait for the law to come to this conclusion when all that was needed was a good watertight proof? Hamid and he could attend to that little thing most competently.

He heaved his big over-pampered body from his chair, and prepared to interrupt the *tête-à-tête* within doors, when a few words startled him into immobility. He listened intently, his open mouth like a cod-fish, his bloodshot eyes intent and wary.

"Phil, I hate to have you go! It will be so long—so dangerous!"

"Not half as dangerous for me as for most men, Muriel. You know what a tough nut I am, and used to these expeditions. I know a good deal of native lingo, and quite a bit about medicine, thanks to your father. That helps tremendously in the desert."

"If any one can find him, you will," the woman's voice vibrated softly. "I can't believe he's not still alive . . . I simply can't believe it. Oh, if you find him, Phil!"

"I agree with you in not having given up hope." The man hesitated. "It's always struck me as rather strange that all the reports have been so unvarying. As a rule, in a case like this, you get dozens of different tales from as many different sources. All we have heard has been so positively and uniformly bad news, that I doubt its authenticity. It's unlike the natives to be so unanimous."

There was a queer little silence. The eavesdropper experienced a sudden shortness of breath as he waited.

"Yes, I know, Phil." Muriel's answering voice was tuned to a flat calm. "I've thought and thought about it, too! Some one wants the inquiries to stop, to prevent any big effort being made to find Dad."

"It looks rather like it to me," was the reply.

Another pregnant pause. Bradley's open mouth closed, his nails dug into the palms of his hands.

"The very fact that efforts are being made to convince people he's dead, makes me hopeful. Either the one who is at the back of this knows that he is still alive, or at least thinks he may be."

"Some one who wants him dead!" the woman's voice was suddenly bitter, and after a pause continued recklessly: "Oh, why pretend any longer? You know as well as I do, Phil, that there is only one person who could conceivably be at the back of this . . . this conspiracy against my father!"

There was no reply. Bradley edged along until he caught a glimpse of the two within the lamplit room. Philip was standing with hands thrust into the pockets of his white linen coat, his gray eyes frowning and troubled under an untidy thatch of rough fair hair, as he stared into the white face of the woman who confronted him.

"I've stood everything up to now. But this—*this!*" She choked a little, then went on vehemently. "Dad of all people, who's done so much for Bradley! And Bradley wants him dead—*dead!*"

The next moment she was at Philip's side, his hand in both of hers, as she clung, crying, "Phil, Phil, what shall I do? I can't bear it any longer—and now you're going to leave me too. If I could get away—hide somewhere from him!"

Philip's other hand went out, his arm curved to clasp her. Then he stiffened with a visible effort, and drew back.

"I've got the support of the government, and the Sennusis are more than favorable to my expedition. Uncle Joseph was well known amongst them, of course. But if I took you with me——"

"No! no! I never dreamed of that—it would make things infinitely more complicated — quite impossible! I know there's nothing to be done now until you come back. Bradley would never let me go away, and he can prevent it so easily in this isolated place that it's no use thinking of it."

Bradley's eyes narrowed viciously as he listened.

"It's all right, Phil!" Her voice steadied. "It was just the thought of losing you for so long."

For a moment the two looked at one another—a strange expression—as if they saw each other across an impassable chasm instead of a few feet of polished flooring.

"When do you start?"

"In a month's time. I only got the government permit today. I start for Algiers early tomororw morning to get my personal kit, ammunition, and drugs. From there I shall be scouring in all directions to round up men and camels."

Bradley's face grew blacker as he listened to Philip outlining his plans, discussing alternative routes to the Ahaggar region which had been Deland's objective. His castles in the air began to totter. Once this expedition started, it was good-bye to his hopes. Public interest would flare up again, and the hope of finding Deland be revived. Whether successful or not, months and months must pass before the return of this rescue force. He could not hope to tide over such an interval. Unless something stopped Philip he was ruined, smashed, utterly down and out.

Unless something stopped Philip!

The words repeated themselves in Bradley's mind. His eyes grew cold and crafty as his thoughts traveled on a new road. Minutes passed, and still he stood there thinking . . . thinking! At last he crept away down the veranda steps to the shadowy garden.

"Hamid! Where the deuce is Hamid?" he asked himself, as he went.

3. Philip Is Surprized

PHILIP MACE rode south with abstracted gaze, his thoughts intent on the many problems inseparable from his undertaking. Mentally he reviewed his preparations, trying to discover things forgotten, visualizing for the hundredth time all possible and probable eventualities for which he must make provision.

He was travelling for the moment with a couple of servants, and the man he had yesterday selected as guide for his expedition. His main *garfla* was assembled, and waiting at a *fonduk* two days' journey from the village of Kebr, which he had left at sunrise that morning.

He had made a special journey to Kebr to secure the services of this guide, the man on whom the safety of his whole caravan must depend for months to come across the trackless desert. Unexpected obstacles had arisen in this matter of a guide. One after another of those whom he knew by experience, or repute, to be first-rate men were unwilling to be hired, or else they had just been engaged by some other *garfla*.

The man he had finally chosen had been recommended in El Kidja, and also at many of the towns and villages which he had visited in the course of his preparations. Harassed by repeated disappointments he engaged Ali, although he would have preferred an older man; for age, and the vast experience of graybeards who had tracked across the desert all their lives, put youth and strength completely at a discount when a guide was in question.

The four men were not returning to the *fonduk* by the well-marked frequented route which Philip had taken to Kebr in the first place. This way was of Ali's choosing, and so abstracted was Philip that he scarcely noticed the wild desolation of the region, with its spiny cacti, withered camel thorn, and the boulder-strewn ground which made the camels' progress slow and difficult.

He did not see the furtive meaning looks exchanged by his two servants, nor the malice that gleamed under Ali's dark brows. When the midday halt was made, and the camels barracked, Philip chose a large boulder to support his back, lighted a cigarette, and drew out a notebook.

But his pen fell from his hand, the cigarette from his lips, as two sinewy brown hands closed round his neck from behind. In a few minutes, with Ali's murderous grip still at his throat, his two servants bound his arms and legs, and he lay stretched out on the hot dusty earth, his gray eyes blazing into the dark face of Ali, the guide.

"So that's the sort of ruffian you are!" Philip's mind was working furiously as he spoke. He felt, in the first bewildered readjustment of his ideas, more astonishment than anger. He had neither gold nor merchandise with him; what reason had Ali for his assault?

"Lift me up so that I can talk properly," he ordered. "I suppose this is a question of ransom? Well, you win the first trick! Now, loosen these ropes and I'll hear what you've got to say."

"*Billah!* Rather is it I—Ben Seghir—that will listen to what thou wilt say when the Black Camel [death] approaches!"

Philip stiffened in his bonds—a sudden constriction at his throat—the blood singing in his ears. Ben Seghir! Ben Seghir, whose evil fame was a byword along the desert routes from Tripoli to the Sudan—the bandit who had led all the most daring and successful raids on

O. S.—**6**

the big trans-Saharan *garflas* during the last two years!

He twisted about to glance at his servants. No hope from them. Their eyes were fixed expectantly on Ben Seghir, their hands itching to obey his orders. No hope of rescue in this barren unfrequented region—all around the gray monotony of the desert stretched to every horizon. The desert—ready to number him among the vast multitude of her dead; equally ready to let him go. Impassive, remote, giving welcome and farewell to none.

"But the *effendi* would talk?" Ben Seghir asked mockingly.

He turned to the waiting men, and gave them an order. They grinned, and going to the bandit's camel-pack, took from it a couple of spades. With these they began to dig with most unusual vigor, jesting under their breath as they worked, showing the whites of their eyes as they glanced maliciously at Philip.

Deftly Ben Seghir ran his hands over his captive, taking from the pockets all he found, including a wallet containing letters and snapshots. He examined everything leisurely, with the naive interest of a child.

"It is sad that these letters are in thy barbarous language. It would have been interesting to read them to thee when thou art in there." He nodded to the deepening hole. "I will leave thy head above ground, for thou wilt have need of eyes and ears on thy road to hell . . . the way is dark . . . and long!"

Painfully Philip raised his head a few inches from the ground. His thick hair was rough and wild, a streak of dust and blood across his cheek where the stones had cut him as he struggled, but his clear steady eyes met those of his enemy unafraid.

"I have heard much of you, Ben Seghir," he said, "but not that you were a coward."

The bandit's teeth flashed in a scornful grin.

"Thou dost think to taunt me into giving thee a swift death. *Maleish!* Thou dost come to conquer my people—infidel dog! Thou dost make maps and pictures and books of my country and go away! Then dost thou return with soldiers and armies and many guns to make new laws, and taxes, and to put a yoke upon the chosen of Allah!" He turned aside. "Put him in—and may his accursed soul be tormented by every *shaitan* [devil] of this evil place when I have set it free at last!"

The two diggers dragged Philip over the rough ground to the hole they had made. They dropped him in feet first, and began to shovel the sand and stones in around him.

"Ugurrah! What is this?" Ben Seghir was looking earnestly at the contents of the wallet. He strode over to Philip, his *burnous* swinging widely about him.

"Who is this . . . who is this man?" and he thrust one or two pictures before Philip's nose.

The latter's mouth tightened and he shook his head.

"Take me out of this and untie me, and I'll talk—not before!"

To his astonishment Ben Seghir himself began to dig away the sand already packed about his body. The other two men also dug furiously, spurred on by the bandit's kicks and curses. In a few minutes Philip was sitting unbound, Ben Seghir holding a flask of palm wine to his lips, while the two servants chafed his ankles and wrists.

Philip strove to preserve a calm front, but he had an uncontrollable desire to burst into loud prolonged laughter. The relief was so sudden and unexpected, and as inexplicable as the first attack on him. Was he at the mercy of a madman here in the wilderness, or was this merely Ben Seghir's idea of prolonging his torture? He drank deeply of the strong fermented liquor, and got a grip on himself with an immense effort.

"Who is this man?"

Again Ben Seghir held the pictures out to Philip. The latter glanced down, to see that they were all of his uncle, Joseph Deland. They were particularly good ones taken on the eve of his last fatal journey into the desert.

Philip looked at Ben Seghir's changed eager face with dawning hope. He knew the extraordinary influence the missing man had exercised amongst the desert tribes. Was it possible that even this ruffian——?

"That is my uncle, Joseph Deland, a famous scientist who has been lost in the desert for many months. I am leading an expedition to find him. At least, I was until you interrupted me," concluded Philip lightly, lighting a cigarette with hands that shook only very imperceptibly.

He received another shock when Ben Seghir abruptly took his hand in both of his, and lifted it to his lips and brow.

"Blessed be Allah, who hath opened my eyes before it was too late. I have sworn to serve Deland *effendi* while life burns within me. He, and all that are of his blood, are sacred to me. May his enemies perish from the earth!"

Ben Seghir's eyes filled suddenly with fierce anger, as he stared out across the wide desert.

"Tell me more," he asked suddenly. "Tell me more, *effendi*. Much is dark and clouded in my mind."

Ben Seghir listened with absorbed interest, putting shrewd questions at intervals, as Philip recounted the events which had led up to his expedition, and everything connected with it.

"There is a story told concerning thy great prophet, Jesus!" the bandit said, after a long silence at the conclusion of Philip's tale. "The story of a traitor. For thirty pieces of silver he sold his Master to the Jews. A traitor called Es Kariot."

The bandit, who had been a student at the famous *medersa* of Kairween, nodded complacently as he produced this evidence of his learning.

"He who gave me this to kill thee"— Ben Seghir indicated a bag of money he had drawn from beneath his robe—"he also should be named Es Kariot. A traitor and a great liar! No word hath he spoken of Deland *effendi*, or that thou wert of his blood, and went to seek him! He hath tricked and deceived me as to the purpose of this journey of thine. Almost he hath made of me a traitor like himself. Almost had I betrayed unwittingly one who brought me back from the gates of hell—one whose wisdom and compassion are greater than I have known in any man."

"There are few like my uncle," the other agreed. "I owe everything to him."

Ben Seghir took the bag of money, untied the string threaded through the leather, and looked at the heap of coins. Gold and silver of the various currencies used in the desert lay glinting in the sun.

Slowly the Arab's long brown fingers sorted the coins, selecting only the silver Turkish *mejedies* until thirty were counted out, and put carefully away in his broad leather girdle. Taking the remainder, with a dramatic gesture natural to his race, he flung it out over the stones and sand.

"May Allah strengthen my arm against him!" he said, and gravely resumed his place at Philip's side. "I will go with thee on thy search. But it must be other-wise than the way thou hast chosen, *effendi*. It must be said that I have killed thee, that Es Kariot may be deceived. We will not travel with the *garfla*. Two or three men can travel swiftly and safely where a great caravan would perish. Where we go, we go alone and very secretly. These two worthless ones we can take to serve us, unless thou dost desire that they should die!"

He turned upon these last, who stood uncertain as to what was required of them now. Ben Seghir abruptly solved their difficulties.

"You lumps of swine's flesh! Bring food—bring water—bring rugs that the *effendi* may ease the limbs thou hast bruised! By Allah, must I cut off the hands and feet you have forgotten how to use?"

4. In the Desert

Six months—ten months—a year of intolerable suns hung in skies of molten brass, of magic dawns and flaming sunsets, of lost wells and mirages, of hunger and torturing thirst, of heart-breaking monotony, nerve-racking danger, pain, weariness, and toil beyond belief.

A year over the limitless rolling dunes stretching in nightmare endless seas of sand. Over arid naked plains where not even a stick or a stone relieved the straining vision. Across bleak tablelands where the great winds howled and whistled with cutting devilish ferocity.

A year of threads picked up and lost again, of chasing shadows and will-o'-the-wisps. A year of stern unceasing conflict with unfriendly tribes, with fevers and agues, with superstition and prejudice that blocked the way.

A year of this, and Ben Seghir and Philip still struggled doggedly southward, lured by elusive persistent rumors picked up here and there—rumors of a white man—a Healer. Southward . . . southward was the invariable answer to their diplomatic questionings. And southward the two followed the shadowy trail.

Lean and weather-beaten as old Sinbad the Sailor himself, the two men came at last to the foot-hills of the rocky fast-nesses south of Timbuktu. They pos-sessed two thin mangy camels which they had purchased with their last ounces of tobacco and salt that morning at an oasis; they had two precious *fanatis* filled with water and a small skinful of dates each. That was all.

Their *hamlas*, tent, sleeping-bags, in-struments—all had been lost or stolen or bartered for food long since. One of the camel-men had lost his life in a hand-to-hand fight at Zem-Zem, where he had been ill-advised enough to exhibit a piece of money. The other servant succumbed to the effects of a great thirst engendered by thirteen days over a practically water-less way, followed by immoderate drafts of *lakby* with which he celebrated his ar-rival at a *douar*.

At the foot of a narrow winding pass hemmed in by tall cliffs, Philip looked about him with red-rimmed, sunken eyes.

"This is the pass through the moun-tains of which the old Shekh spoke. This must be the Diabi Ridge."

"Even so," agreed Ben Seghir. "Be-yond that opening in the cliff-face the great valley must lie, where dwell the Zangali tribe. And in the hills at the farther side of that valley Askia Ibn Askia has his palace. I recognize this place, *effendi*, from the tales my father told me when I was a child. He took a wife of the Zangali people and lived in that valley until she died—very young and very fair she was, and my father fled this place and its memories when she left him."

"If half the reports we have heard have any truth in them, this ruler of the Zangalis, this Askia Ibn Askia, is going to be a very tough nut," Philip ruminated half to himself. "We've had fairly defi-nite accounts of him these last weeks— he doesn't seem to hide his light under a bushel. First of all, he's stricken with some deadly disease. Secondly, he's a tyrant who would make the Roman em-perors, at their most decadent, look dull and uninventive. Thirdly, there is some white magician at his court who makes great spells, and who appears to be a fairly new star on Ibn Askia's horizon."

"Thou hast spoken," was the other's reply. "Let us cross these mountains and seek out this Shekh in his palace."

"We're running into the greatest dan-ger, remember," Philip reminded his com-panion. "And there may be no more truth in these reports than in all the others we heard, and proved false."

"It is as Allah wills," was the grave response. "Let us therefore find this Askia Ibn Askia. If it is written that we die at his hand, wherefore should we seek to escape? What is written—is writ-ten."

Philip extended a thin grimy hand. "My sentiments down to the ground," he answered warmly. "I wanted to make sure you felt as I did about this. I've the strongest presentiment we've come to the end of our search. We'll camp here tonight. It's sheltered and there's good grazing for the camels; we can hobble them and leave them here until our re-turn—we can't get them across this ridge. Tomorrow for the lion's den, my brother Daniel!"

5. The Hospitality of Askia Ibn Askia

AN ORANGE moon lifted slowly over the long spine of the Diabi Ridge, throwing fantastic shadows across deep chasms and beetling crags. The moonlight fell serenely over the huts and hovels of Askia Ibn Askia's dominion in the Zangali valley beyond, and its full orb discovered two figures toiling up the range of hills on the farther side of the plain.

A jackal howled a greeting to the travellers as they approached the summit; the terrific roar of a mountain lion echoed and reverberated in the hollow hills. But within the great barrier of cactus-hedge, crowning the slopes above the two men, all was dark and silent as a tomb.

"It seems peaceful," said Philip at last, as they cautiously approached. "At least we shall be allowed to pass the barricade. There seems no guard."

"They wait within," was Ben Seghir's gloomy reply. "The Singing Mountain never lies, and long ere we left the valley its voice would warn them of our approach. As soon as we pass the opening in the wall of cactus, it will sing no more."

Both men glanced back at the dark forbidding crag which towered over the plain they had left below; the low eery song of the wind piping in its crevices reached their ears. But as they reached the gap in the tall hedge, Philip noticed with a shock that the strange note of the Singing Mountain ceased abruptly.

"All is as my father said," murmured Ben Seghir, as they walked the narrow streets, their long black shadows at their heels. "And here should be the Place of Speaking."

They halted before a pretentious building, a painted massive temple of an earlier civilization, which had been adapted to the needs of the Shekhs of the Zangali tribe.

No slightest sound of life or movement reached the straining ears of the two as they climbed the stone steps, and passed through a vast pillared entrance.

Philip felt his pulses racing as he and Ben Seghir walked down one long corridor after another and paused at last before a Moorish arch, hung with a heavy curtain of marvelous hue and fabric.

As they hesitated, the curtain was swung back by some swift invisible hand, and Philip gasped involuntarily. Even the stolid fatalism of the Arab was shaken, and he muttered:

"*Imsh'llah!* Here is the end!"

Philip stood taut—the shock of what confronted him, momentarily held him, brain and body, in a vise of paralyzing emotion. Then his stubborn fighting spirit reasserted itself. His courage rose to meet the danger. A strange, desperate fury seized him that anything so atrocious, so bestial, so inimical to sane human life could live.

At the extreme end of a great hall was a throne carved from teakwood inlaid with ivory. On it sat a creature who Philip rightly supposed was the Shekh Askia Ibn Askia himself—a small wizened figure wrapped in gorgeous cloth of gold, and wearing a silver turban in which ruby and emerald, diamond and pearl gleamed and flashed above the withered face of the wearer.

The face of a demon—old and evil beyond belief. The dark wrinkled skin was scored by a thousand lines, and in the sunken eyes a red gleam smoldered, that was a reflection of the very fires of hell.

In Philip's eyes an answering light responded, cold and clear as a winter star, and he strode forward with the Arab at his elbow. A long cackling peal of laughter burst from Ibn Askia's lips as the two approached his throne.

They passed between a double rank of warriors, whose extended spears glowed white-hot within a few inches of their thinly-clad bodies, and each warrior in turn laid his spear-tip upon that of his opposite neighbor behind the two, as they passed up that fiery lane.

"Thou canst not complain of the warmth of thy welcome, white man! It shall not be said that the people of Zangali can not entertain their guests worthily."

His malicious cackle broke out again, and a huge gray ape, fastened to a pillar in a recess behind the throne, chattered and shook its chain savagely. Meeting the disdain in Philip's steady gaze, the Shekh's laughing mouth shut up like a trap.

"Dog! Thine eyes are too bold—my vultures shall pick them from their sockets ere tomorrow's sun has set! Thou, and this accursed spawn of Eblis at thy side! Who are ye that do not shrink from my fiery spears? Who are ye that enter my palace clad like beggars, and with the pride of kings? Ye shall die . . . die, I say!"

The self-possession and calm poise of the two infuriated the Shekh to a gibbering rage that made him uglier and more inhuman than the gray ape itself; and the two who stared at him did so not altogether from bravado, but in a kind of frozen wonder that such a thing could dwell in human flesh.

Like a tree blasted by lightning, like a mummy risen from its centuries of sleep, like a soul escaped from hell in a borrowed outworn body, the Shekh half rose from his throne, shaking with passion, barely able to articulate:

"Die . . . die!" The voice cracked on a sudden squeal of laughter again. "Nay, ye shall live . . . live in . . . torment . . . live till ye crawl to me . . . to beg for death!"

Suddenly, like a corpse-candle extinguished by the wind, the evil light behind his eyes went out; the jaw dropped; the figure collapsed and crumpled back on the throne.

"The Healer . . . the Healer! Ah-h-h!" he gasped.

One of the immense slaves, who formed the bodyguard around the throne, vanished swiftly, to return almost immediately with a man wrapped in a dark *burnous*. The face which looked out from beneath the hood almost forced an exclamation from Philip's lips; beside him Ben Seghir stood like a carven statue, but deep in his brooding eyes a look of almost fanatical devotion suddenly dawned.

It was the missing man—Joseph Deland. Except for the deep bronze of his skin, and the new lines which danger and hardships had drawn on his wonderfully chiselled face, he was unchanged. Humor and patient understanding still lit the deep-set eyes, the same thoughtful watching intelligence furrowed the wide brow, the same peculiarly tender compassion curved the strong mouth.

His keen glance fell at once on his nephew and the Arab at his side, but not by the flicker of an eyelash did he acknowledge them. Calmly he gave them the glance he might have bestowed on any stranger, and turned to minister to the stricken man on the throne.

In a few minutes Ibn Askia recovered sufficiently to sit upright and beckon to Philip and his companion:

"Tomorrow"—his voice was the rattle of dry leaves in an east wind—"tomorrow my sorcerers shall work terrible magic! They and their devils shall chase your souls to hell . . . and bring them back again, that I may laugh . . . and mock at your entreaties!"

Exhausted by pain and fury he collapsed limply once more; and two slaves, in long woolen robes of red and blue, lifted him into a sort of sedan-chair and bore him from the hall.

6. In an Ancient Granary

IN THE ancient granary built into the foundation of the temple-palace of the Shekh, Philip and Ben Seghir spent long sleepless hours that night. Momentarily they hoped and expected to see, or at least receive some message from Deland.

In the thick darkness there was the sound of intermittent rustlings, the scurryings of little creatures over the stone and straw of the granary pavements, the squeak and chirp of many small night-things on their hunting, and faint and far off, through the slits in the massive walls, came the sighing breath of the desert wind to the ears of the two prisoners.

But no stealthy footstep, no welcome cautious whisper greeted their straining ears. At last the dense blackness began to be streaked with gray, and the outlines of the huge earthen pots for storing grain became visible. It was a vast granary, built for year-long sieges in olden times, when the Zangalis were but a handful of wandering nomads on the desert, and the palace was a temple devoted to strange and long-forgotten gods.

In the gray dawn both men secretly admitted to themselves that they might expect nothing but the vengeance of the demented Shekh. Defeat was doubly bitter now. To have seen Deland again, and to be butchered for Ibn Askia's amusement without ever joining forces with the man they had tracked so far and so long! Not even to have the chance of one good fight with the enemy, and die side by side with the man they had found at last!

Philip cursed aloud that he had not used his weapon to kill the devil-haunted ruler when he was face to face with him, and unbound, the previous night.

"*Effendi*, it is the wisdom of the unwise thus to heap mud upon thine own head. It was not written that the Shekh should die by thy hand. Neither dost thou reckon on the price we should have paid for that killing. We—and also Deland *effendi*, may Allah protect him!"

"With my weapon gone, and my hands shackled, I can only remember the chance I missed. And we are going to pay anyhow. We've gained nothing—nothing! Not even a word or a look from my uncle. I should have shot Ibn Askia between his eyes when I had the chance."

"All is as Allah wills!" was the imperturbable reply. "We live still, and here is another day. Who can say what good and evil lie between sunrise and its setting?"

Lacking the Arab's profound fatalism, Philip continued to gird at himself, while the gray light grew clearer in their prison. Not until a strong shaft struck through an opening in the walls, and fell on a vast jar towering above its fellows, did Philip notice the marking on it.

Idly at first, his mind still preoccupied, his eyes saw the uneven clumsy lettering without attaching any significance to it. Quite suddenly, however, he scrambled to his feet, the chains clanking about his wrists and ankles. With stiff awkward movements he stumbled over to the jar.

Yes, it *was* lettering, traced hastily and almost illegibly across the pot's immense girth:

J. D.

Philip gave a hoarse shaky laugh as he turned to Ben Seghir.

"My uncle's initials! Now what do you suppose——"

He broke off and stared about, peering at every jar, looking in all directions for some other clue or message. After the first thrill of the discovery, his heart sank. Evidently there had not been time to complete the message. Or perhaps his uncle had once been a prisoner in the granary, and written that. Perhaps it was no clue at all.

He kicked about in the dust and moldy grain around the jar in vain. He made a new tour of inspection, gazing at the huge grain receptacle from every angle. Then he turned to Ben Seghir eagerly.

"Inside—inside, of course!"

With a spurt of new vigor he ran against the jar, and sent it crashing. The brittle clay broke and splintered in every direction, and after a few minutes of eager search among the pieces, the Arab's desert-trained eagle vision discerned the tiny folded paper in the dust.

"Am a prisoner," Philip read aloud. "Am doing all in my power—it is very little. Askia suspects you came for me. He may die any hour, but will sting to the last. Don't give up hope. It's a miracle that you have found me. Another may save the three of us even yet. Askia will set his devilish Tibetan sorcerers on you. They are inhuman, possessed of extraordinary occult powers. Fight with your mind, your will, your whole soul! Above all—*do not look into their eyes!* Let them blind you first! Fight—*fight*—you're up against a most devilish thing. J. D."

Ben Seghir listened intently, sitting cross-legged in the dust, his worn face and undimmed eyes fixed on the dancing motes in a long sunbeam.

"Why has not Allah, in his wisdom, permitted that Es Kariot should be destroyed by these yellow devils?" he ruminated sadly. "For the soul of Es Kariot is soft and fat as the body that contains it, and would suffer very greatly, seeing that it can not fight."

The other's stern troubled look softened as he looked down at his companion.

"You're not the first to feel that Justice is unnecessarily blind," he remarked, running his fingers through his dusty bleached hair.

"For me it will be the fire and the knife, *effendi*," pursued the Arab evenly. "Wert thou a true Believer—a son of Islam—Allah's hand would shield thy soul. But thou dost not believe, therefore these yellow devils may have power over thee. For me, however, the fire and the knife!"

Philip saw nothing incongruous in the bandit's profound religious convictions. He had met these seeming discrepancies of character in the desert too often to wonder at them. He envied the Arab's calm faith, and the fortitude with which he contemplated a hideous death.

For himself . . . a long shudder ran through him at the images that rose in his overtired brain.

He thrust the little note deep into a pocket; the touch of it might bring comfort and strength during the hours of the coming day. Then, subsiding limply by the Arab, he leaned back against the rough walls. Exhaustion of mind and body drugged him to a semi-consciousness, and in half-waking dreams he followed a phantom Muriel over dark lonely wastes — wandering hopelessly — never able to reach that wraith-like figure just beyond his grasp.

7. Terror

IT WAS full noon; the round patch of sky, visible through the open dome of the roof, was white-hot, when, in the great hall where the two prisoners had first seen Askia Ibn Askia, they faced him again.

The place was crowded from wall to wall with naked figures, rank with the odor of the oiled perspiring bodies of warriors and slaves, who squatted shoulder to shoulder, knee to knee, their sullen faces stirred to a faint animation by the promised spectacle, but the dominant emotion on every brooding face was fear. Fear of their mad cruel ruler, fear that a glance, a movement, an unconscious gesture would bring Ibn Askia's beast-like fury upon any one of them.

Philip and Ben Seghir stood in their tattered soiled *barracans*, the chains still about their feet and hands. After one glance at the Shekh's venomous face, Philip looked at the two figures standing on the raised dais which supported the throne. In spite of his courage, he knew the taste of deadly fear as he looked.

Yellow-clad, yellow-skinned, approaching the gigantic in stature, with flat expressionless faces, their small oblique almond-shaped eyes under bristling tufts of eyebrows showed a cold remote hate beside which the Shekh's mad fury seemed an almost friendly quality.

Tibetans—renegade priests—who for good reasons had been obliged to flee from the sanctuaries of their monasteries, and had smuggled themselves as pilgrims to Mecca, and from thence with the great *Haj* had journeyed across Arabia to Africa, where the silent desert had received them, hidden them from the pursuing vengeance of their terrible Order.

Philip had read of these dehumanized creatures, who turned the occult and mystic splendor of their priestly knowledge to uses vile and degraded beyond all thought. He recalled, with a cold sickness in his breast, the words of a man he had once met at the famous Teng-Su Club in London, a man who had made daring explorations across unknown Tibet. This explorer had given Philip a vivid account of much he had seen and heard.

At their highest, these Lama priests lived like gods among men, so high and strange and mystic was their rule, so absolute their obedience to their lofty code, so terrible and inexplicable the supernatural powers they commanded. But the renegade priests! Like Lucifer, they sank from highest heaven to lowest hell.

Philip gave credence to all he had heard, and taken as travellers' tales, when he met the frozen evil in the depths of those slanting eyes that stared unwinking into his.

Their eyes! Even as his look locked with theirs, some words came dimly to his mind—some urgent command he could not for the moment recollect. He would recall it in a minute . . . in a minute! How curiously light his tired body felt suddenly . . . what was that sound of wild bees in his ears? . . . how did this great smooth gray sea suddenly appear before his eyes? . . . eyes . . . what was that about eyes? . . . there were no eyes, only sea . . . deep—fathomless—undulating—pulling him down . . . down . . . down!

Depth after depth he plumbed, until he knew that he could not return, for he had fallen off the margin of the world into the vast uncharted ether. Once, from some far-distant star he heard a voice and knew it called him:

"*Effendi!* Do not look into their eyes! Do not look into their eyes!"

He could not make sense of that. There were no eyes, but the urgent warning seemed to check his swift descent, and he began to swing in great whirling circles, and both voice and star vanished and went out.

Then Terror met him!

Terror, that with slow and dreadful ease severed the soul from his shrinking body and pursued his naked and defenseless spirit with a silent menacing calm—like the calm at the heart of a raging typhoon.

Through hell after deeper hell, Philip fled before it. Overtaken, tortured, he escaped, to flee through the vast spaces that cradle the universe.

He perished by fire and in the green depths of the sea, he was torn asunder by wild beasts, he died of plague and famine. He was crushed in the great folds of monstrous serpents, he writhed with the bitter taste of poison on his tongue. He lived a thousand lives of shame and violence and sin—he died a thousand hideous and lingering deaths.

And on the threshold of each death the vast evil waited for him—and he fled past sun, moon, and stars—through great seas—on the wings of howling winds. Through time and space he flung himself, only to meet the Terror face to face in the end . . . to be plucked back to new abominations . . . live out another life to its bitter death!

Quite abruptly he was back on this earth again. On the verge of madness, weak as a man after long fever and delirium, his face gray, his breath whistling through his clenched teeth, he lay at the foot of Ibn Askia's dais. The Shekh was laughing until his withered frame threatened to shake to pieces. The two Tibetans had withdrawn to the shadows behind the throne, where even the savage ape whimpered, and cowered from their proximity.

Ben Seghir stood in his chains, his eyes full of reproach and anxiety as he looked at Philip. To him, Ibn Askia turned suddenly:

"Thou hast no mind to torment! *Ugurrah!* Thou hast a body, however." He struck his hands together, and slaves came running. "The fire—the torturers—in haste, in haste, you crawling things of dust!"

Philip closed his eyes. A deadly faintness threatened to snatch him back to oblivion, and he fought with all his will to retain consciousness. The Shekh prolonged the preparations, watching Philip meanwhile. When all was ready, and the white-hot irons but a few inches from Ben Seghir's proud face, Ibn Askia turned to the white man.

"Thou wouldst save this desert scum? *Billah,* that is in thy power to do! Crawl to me, dog, down on thy hands and knees —bow thy stiff head to my feet and swear that there is none greater than Askia Ibn Askia—ruler of the Zangalis. Also, that my people and I shall not forego some small amusement, my sorcerers shall once more work magic with thee."

"Promise nothing, *effendi!*" came Ben Seghir's urgent murmur. "I can but die! Worse than death awaits thee if thou dost look once more into the eyes of the yellow devils!"

Ben Seghir was cruelly silenced, and the Shekh leant forward to look into Philip's agonized face. Ibn Askia was drunk with the sense of power—his madness rose like a tide within him, the fierce exultant pounding of his heart shook his withered body until his ugly head rolled on his shoulders. Stamping his feet, beating his fists upon the arms of his great carved throne, he laughed and cursed and screamed at this proud white man whom he had brought so low.

Philip tried to speak, tried to command his limp useless muscles to wave the torturers away from Ben Seghir, strove to curse the gibbering Shekh. But the swooning weakness came over him in waves, and he could neither speak nor move.

Ibn Askia's maniacal laugh threatened to choke him. He rose, clutching at the gold-embroidered robe around his throat. His voice shrilled to a squeal, and died in his throat with a strange abrupt bubble of sound. His arms thrashed impotently in blind arrested movements. His eyes glared and grew fixed, and the dark skin of his face turned gray.

As before, one of his bodyguard vanished, to return in a few minutes with Deland. He walked in quietly and looked about him, comprehending the horrible drama he was entering upon, with bright penetrating eyes . . . the breathless sweating audience, the two prisoners, the Tibetan sorcerers, the ape that shook in a palsy of fear beside them, and the staring unnatural quiet of the master of the ceremonies himself.

The hiss of indrawn excited breathing, the rattle of the gray ape's chain alone broke the silence, as the Healer bent over the throne and made a brief examination.

With slow precision Deland presently folded the golden robe again about the motionless Shekh, deftly drawing a corner of the rich fabric across the staring sightless eyes. Then he turned to face the assembly.

"People of Zangali!" he began. "Your Shekh, Askia Ibn Askia, is dead!"

The quietly uttered words shocked the dense crowd into a frozen silence. Each man sat like stone, afraid even now that the silent thing beneath its golden pall might strike to kill.

The prisoners exchanged glances, while Deland surveyed the serried ranks of slaves and warriors intently. All three were thinking the same thought. How would this event affect them? How could they mold this crisis to their own advantage?

And in the shadows behind the throne, the two Tibetans stood like statues, their slanting eyes agleam.

Abruptly one of the tallest of the warriors sprang to his feet, tossing his spear above his head. "Imsh'llah!" he cried. "We are free men at last! The great devil whom Allah sent to torment us is dead!"

He broke into a strong rhythmic chant, stamping his feet and swaying his great shoulders; and in a few moments the vast hall was full of stamping feet, while the shouting and chanting rose wilder and wilder. Curtains were torn from the lofty arches and trampled underfoot, as the mob burst out in all directions to call the tidings to the four winds of heaven.

The roll of drums echoed through the streets to the plain below, giving the news to the tribe; soon the rocky ascent to the palace was alive with men, women, and children scaling the rough ways like monkeys and shouting as they came.

No one took any notice of the prisoners. No one except the two tall Tibetans.

As the crowd rose in its first confusion, Deland took a swift stride to his nephew and kneeling to support his head, put a flask to his ashen lips. But even as Philip drank, the two ex-priests were upon him, one dashing the cup from his lips, the other plucking the older man from his side, as one might pick up a twig from the earth.

Philip fought with his last ounce of strength; the few drops of the cordial he had drunk, and the brief glimpse of escape gave him abnormal strength for the moment. He dashed his fist into the malevolent yellow mask that leered into his face, but he was clasped like a child in the gigantic arms of the Tibetan.

He fought in vain to turn away his eyes — he couldn't m o v e his head — couldn't even close his eyes . . . nearer . . . nearer that nameless gray cloud of evil descended on him.

But Ben Seghir, maimed and tortured, was yet free! His tormentors had fled with the rest, and he stooped to the hot irons. The sight of Deland, as well as Philip, in the hands of the yellow devils, transformed him into a madder and more dangerous thing than Ibn Askia himself had been. Gripping a hideous weapon in each torn bleeding hand, he sprang like a tiger, and with all the wary cunning of the jungle beast.

The Tibetan who held Deland prisoner

in his grasp, dropped him, and fell like a great tree cut down; and where his wicked slanting eyes had been, there remained only two dreadful empty sockets, burned deep into his brain.

The other Tibetan saw, and as Ben Seghir leaped for him, he held Philip before him as a shield, circling to face the Arab.

Deland made a spring, his small lean body clinging to the massive yellow shoulders from behind. In a flash he unloosed the turban wound about the ex-priest's head, and passed a thick fold across his face, muffling him completely.

The yellow giant, like some great snake, stood circling swiftly on his own axis, swinging Philip like a club. But, blinded and encumbered, the Tibetan was caught at last, receiving one jagged sizzling iron deep in his body.

Mad with agony, the giant dropped his human weapon, tore the bandage from his eyes, flung Deland from his back to the floor, and staggered toward the Arab. Ben Seghir ducked under the two huge arms and thrust his weapon under the outthrust chin of his enemy. As the latter tottered backward from the impact, Ben Seghir flung himself upon him, bearing him backward to the ground.

And what he had done to the first, he did also to this second assailant, piercing him to his evil brain.

No one noticed the Healer, with two others wrapped close in burnouses, walk slowly away when evening came. No one remarked them crossing the valley, and toiling painfully up the steeps of the Diabi Ridge.

The Zangali were drunk with freedom and palm wine, and if they had noticed, they would not have cared. The plain and hillside blazed with bonfires. The roll of drums, the shrill strange music of reed-pipes, the rhythmic stamping of countless feet in the red firelight beside the cooking-pots, the fragrant blue clouds of tobacco, the sound of hundreds of chattering voices, laughter and song, and, at intervals the long-drawn exultant tribal cry of the Zangali people rose to the starlit splendor of the heavens.

8. Thirty Pieces of Silver

THE great yearly garfla from Timbuktu had almost reached the borders of Algeria. Philip, with Deland and Ben Seghir, joining it in that desert city, had journeyed north under its protection. The irony of the bandit's being befriended by the merchants of that richly laden caravan was appreciated only by the three themselves, however, for Ben Seghir was too much disfigured to be recognizable.

During the long months of the return journey Philip's mind grew more and more despondent. What was there for him at the end of this great adventure? he asked himself.

His youth was gone, the last spark stamped out under the iron heel of suffering. He looked ten years older, and felt more than that. It would be hard to take up the thread of his old civilized life again. His value, his ambitions, his whole philosophy of life—all were radically altered.

And Muriel! Ah, it was she who was at the core of his problems! More than ever he loved her—needed her—felt existence barren and purposeless without her. Could she free herself from Bradley? Would she come to him if not?

How would Bradley face the situation on his return with Deland? Should he feign ignorance of Bradley's treachery—or not? What would be the best for Muriel—the best for all concerned in the long run?

Ben Seghir voiced this question when

he came to take farewell of Philip, two days before they were due at El Kidja.

"And Es Kariot? What of him, *effendi?* *Billah*, what greeting hast thou for him who sent me to slay thee? Es Kariot, whose heart is evil even toward the Wise One—the Healer! By the life of this moon, I would know what is in thy thoughts concerning him."

Gray eyes met black—Ben Seghir's unfathomable as some dark mountain tarn in that long silent interchange. He put Philip's hand to his lips and brow, and bent forward to kiss his shoulder in farewell salute.

"What is written, is written," he remarked. "May Allah make smooth the way for thy feet."

SHORTLY before dawn, two days later, Philip and Deland arrived at the gates of El Kidja. They made their way through the sleeping city like ghosts returning to some ancient haunt. Swift messengers had been sent ahead to break the news of their coming to Muriel; but, nothing definite regarding time being connected with desert-journeys, the two arrived alone and unheralded at the house with the big veranda, where Bradley had played the part of eavesdropper almost two years ago.

Deland went in alone, leaving Philip to saunter about under the shade of bamboos and palm-trees. For long the latter waited there, wondering at the unnatural air of quiet that reigned, even after Deland had disappeared indoors.

Not a servant was to be seen, or even heard. No voice, or step, or cry of greeting came to his ears. He began to get uneasy. Was anything wrong? Any one ill? At last—as he was on the point of entering the house to investigate—Deland appeared on the veranda. The latter's face was very grave, and his voice, always quiet, was more deliberate than usual.

"I was coming for you, my boy. A terrible thing has just been discovered here —a ghastly occurrence!"

"Muriel! Not Muriel!"

"No—no!" Deland patted the other's arm reassuringly. "No — it's Bradley. He's been murdered. They've only just discovered the body."

Philip followed the other through the dim quiet house to a spacious room upstairs. Muriel was standing there by the open shutters, her dazed eyes enormous in a thin white face. She put a cold hand into Philip's without a word, her eyes reverting to the silent figure on the bed.

Bradley Gleave lay there, the handle of a dagger protruding from his breast— achieving a dignity in death, that in life he had never attained.

Philip's gaze travelled from the still face to something which gleamed on the white sheet folded across the dead man's body. He stared, incredulous. He took a few swift strides to look more closely.

Yes—it was money! Silver money! Something began to take shape in the depths of his whirling thoughts.

He stared down at the little pattern of coins. They were Turkish *mejedies* laid neatly in three little rows, one below the other. Three little rows—ten coins in each!

"Good God!" he whispered, with fascinated eyes fixed on the glinting coins. *"Thirty pieces of silver!"*

Four Doomed Men

By GEOFFREY VACE

*A strange murder mystery in Delhi—four men saw the great ruby,
and one after another they died*

A SCREAM, rending the stillness of an India night, is not unusual. The scream which stopped Chowkander King on that mysterious by-street of Delhi, where a man is wise to move on, and mind his own business; that turned his face toward a forbidding-looking doorway, and sent his feet, a second later, flying up a narrow winding staircase more forbidding than the doorway—that scream pulsed with mortal pain and terror.

At the top of the staircase, King stopped. The scream had passed. He waited an instant for it to be repeated, but there was no sound. Only an oppressing feeling that he was being watched; that, foolishly, he was walking into a net.

He turned to the door—and stopped. It was not the door at all. It did not move under his hand. The knob was fast; it was not made to turn. With a swift intake of breath, King turned completely around, and faced the door again. He was doubly sure now, that he was being peered at through some hidden opening. He laughed suddenly, deep in himself. Of course!—he had tried the wrong panel in the square hall. He looked about again. Cunningly placed mirrors reflected each other, making it impossible at first glance to tell which were real and which were not.

King waited, his eyes becoming more accustomed to the half-light. After a moment of careful thought, he stepped forward and seized the handle of the right door. It yielded under his touch, and swung inward. A light curtain, swaying slowly under a faint breeze, brushed into his face. Without stopping

670

he pushed it aside, and took five steps into a pitch-black room.

At the fifth step, King halted. He seemed to sense other beings in the room, whether behind him or before him he had no means of telling. His finger sought the butt of his service revolver, and clutched it warmly. From far away came the sound of a door closing softly. A soft green light suddenly broke the gloom. With the light came the unmistakable odor of musk.

King felt a slight movement at his side, and turned his head. A door had appeared in the wall. A tall figure in the native dress of a Sikh leaned gracefully in the opening. His body was completely enveloped in a long silken robe which swept the floor and revealed only a pair of turned-up, pointed shoes. His head was swathed in a great turban, at the side of which flashed the jewelled hilt of a small dagger.

"The sahib is perhaps in the wrong house?" he suggested, meditatively. His eyes glowed, his voice was soft. He strode into the room with a dignity and grace that perhaps, some day, the West will master.

Chowkander King watched him closely. He was beginning to feel that perhaps he had been too hasty. Perhaps it would be wise to pretend that he *had* got the wrong house, and make a safe getaway. But something caused him to change his mind.

"I heard a scream," he said, watching the Sikh carefully, yet not appearing to. The robed figure raised a deprecating hand, and a shoulder.

"Walk slowly and pull back that curtain."

"Sahib—this is India. This is Delhi. Screams are not uncommon."

"This scream was most uncommon. It was the cry of a man who is being murdered, and knows it, yet can not prevent it. I believe it was the cry of that man who lies behind that curtain."

"Sahib!" The Sikh was startled out of his calm. He stepped quickly to King's side. The faint smile of condescension had left his face. His eyes burned.

"Sahib, no man lies behind that curtain. You have made a mistake. The door is immediately behind you!"

King could still have withdrawn—but King seldom withdrew.

"No mistake has been made," he replied, not taking his eyes from the Sikh's for an instant now, "unless you have made it. I rather think you have. You neglected to make sure that the man's feet were as carefully concealed as his dead body!"

The Sikh moved quickly—but Chow-kander King was quicker. His revolver came level with the man's eyes.

"Too late now, my friend. You can see the telltale foot from here. Walk slowly, and pull back that curtain. Then stand behind the body. And remember, I could shoot you with ease, and I should not hesitate for one moment to do so."

The Sikh bowed low, folding his arms across his chest.

"The sahib errs," he said with dignity. "But having no choice, I shall do as the sahib says."

He turned his back on King's leveled weapon, and strode slowly to the portière. With a swish of his arm, he threw it aside, and stood behind it.

"Who is that man?" King said, sharply.

The figure lay half on its side, half on its back. Its long arms were flung wide, its slant eyes closed. The silk robe, three-colored, which covered it could belong only to an Oriental of high caste.

The Sikh raised his head a trifle, sending scintillating lights from the jewels of his dagger.

"I could tell the sahib who the China-man is; yet once again, I make the suggestion that the sahib is in the wrong house. Perhaps it was the house next door that the sahib wished?"

"Perhaps it was," King replied. "Then again, perhaps it wasn't. Answer my question!"

The Sikh shrugged again.

"I do not know the man's name, sahib. I have forgotten it."

"Then you shall come with me to the police. I understand they have ways of their own of refreshing the memories of men who have a convenient habit of forgetting. Who killed the man?"

KING did not expect a direct reply from the Sikh, but the answer he got was hardly the evasion he anticipated.

"I could not be sure, sahib. It was one of three men."

King eyed the man steadily for a full minute without speaking. Then: "He has been dead perhaps five minutes—not more than ten. You are alone in this house. Yet one of three men killed him. Are you one of those three?"

"But no, sahib. I had no hand in the murder of this unfortunate Oriental. It is no affair of mine."

King kept his temper. Years of service with the British Indian Intelligence had taught him the wisdom of that trick. He smiled slightly, intending to disarm the Sikh.

"Perhaps you would be so kind as to tell me how this man came to be stabbed in your house?"

The smile had the intended effect. The Sikh bowed again. He raised his silken arm and pointed to a long table in the middle of the room.

"I had visitors tonight, sahib. Four men—I do not remember their names. I was showing the gentlemen a stone—a pigeon's-blood ruby from Burma. It is pure, sahib, and precious. It rested on the table in that case you see there. Of a sudden, the lights were put out, mysteriously. It was minutes before I could get them on again. And the ruby was gone. One of my gentlemen had stolen it. There could be no other conclusion. I moved them to shame. I scorned them, and told them that I would put out the lights again, and when they were again put on, I should expect to find my stone in its case on the table. It was dark—there was the sudden sound of a scuffle; a scream, sahib. I had the lights on in an instant——"

"Yes?"

"The stone was still gone, sahib. And this man—was stabbed."

King watched the man closely. His revolver never wavered from its target. No man yet had caught Chowkander King asleep.

"And the other three men vanished into smoke, I take it?" he said, sarcastically.

The Sikh was not the least offended by King's tone. He merely smiled and stretched his hand again.

"The sahib was not quiet coming up the stairs. The hall of the mirrors confused him, as was intended. Meantime, the three left by other ways. There are ways—and ways—out of this house, sahib!"

King nodded.

"Your story may be the truth," he said shortly. "Nevertheless, you shall come with me. You have refused me your name. That is enough for me—and the police. Come along!"

The Sikh brushed past the curtain, and passed in front of King without a word. He walked straight to the door which led into the deceptive hall, and opened it. King glanced at the body of the murdered Chinaman—and what followed was too sudden for the eye to register.

With a swiftness, beside which the recoil of a snake is sluggard, the Sikh snatched the jewelled dagger from his turban and leaped at King. The muzzle of King's revolver came round in an instant, but to have shot would have brought half of Delhi clamoring at the door—and that was something King wished to avoid; he was on the track of something that certainly was not the business of half of Delhi.

He darted back, raising his arm and taking the knife slash across his sleeve. He seemed to lose his balance, and fall to the floor. The Sikh laughed triumphantly, and his knife flashed up again. But if the Sikh was fast—King was lightning. His left hand clenched at the floor and swung up in a wide arc. The arc ended abruptly at the point of the Sikh's black beard. Without a sound, the great form slipped down and lay motionless.

King stood over him, staring at the closed eyes and heavy beard. He fingered the tear on his own sleeve where the knife had struck him, dusted imaginary dust from both sleeves; then dug into the pocket of his tunic and produced a small notebook and pencil.

King was a methodical man; he never wasted a moment. Nor did he ever change his direction. He had decided to take the tall Sikh to police officials and hold him in connection with the death of the Chinaman in the fine silk robe. The fact that the Sikh lay unconscious on the floor caused no change in King's plans. It simply meant that they would be delayed. There would be time to kill. And

King went about it in his usual manner.

His pencil scrawled over the page of his notebook. He wrote a few lines, then stopped to read them.

"Moy Dong," he read, "the Chinaman of the High Dynasty, who has been spending so much time among the Sikh troops —is dead. He was killed in the house of Rahman Singh, the Sikh, who has also been seen too often at the native barracks. Was Moy Dong killed by Rahman Singh?"

King read the note twice, and shook his head. He looked again at the form on the floor at his feet. No—he did not believe that the Sikh had actually wielded the knife. But——

With the "but" King stopped, and touched the Sikh with the toe of his boot. The big native groaned and raised his head.

"As soon as you can walk," King said slowly, "we will go to the police office."

I T WAS ten minutes later before the man was sufficiently revived to get to his feet. He walked unsteadily to the hall, King's revolver pressed to his back.

They passed down the stairs thus. In the street hardly a man was visible. Delhi had long since gone to sleep.

"Walk straight, and remember, just because I didn't shoot you down like a dog the first time, doesn't mean that I would hesitate a second," King said softly. The Sikh nodded, but did not speak. A slight smile curved his mouth—a smile that King could not see.

If King had thought that police headquarters of Delhi would welcome him, he was disappointed. The native officer in charge refused to accept the complaint of murder against the tall Sikh. He simply opened his mouth and goggled at the thought. He cowered when King threatened, but it was no use. He insisted upon calling the captain from his bed. King argued and cajoled. He simply wanted the Sikh held until morning—but he finally gave in. Captain Kirby was awakened and summoned.

He appeared in the room ten minutes later, still apparently drugged with sleep, outwardly cursing all men who disturbed his night's rest.

"By Gad, King!" he exploded, when he caught sight of the Secret Service man. There was no love wasted between the police and the Secret Service. "If I'd known it was one of you bally interferers, I damn well should have told you to go to the devil! Can't you chaps ever mind your own business? I've been four solid hours getting to sleep, only to be pulled from my bed to be told that some poor chap has been clouting his wife; or has war been declared, and you're going back to England tomorrow? Gad! I hope it's the latter!"

King brought his gaze down from the ceiling, and allowed his heels to drop back to the floor. He seemed to be controlling his impatience with an effort.

"Now, if you're all done, Kirby, let me tell you why I did come," King said quietly. "I have unearthed a nice little murder case. The suspect is in the next room. Your lunkhead assistant refused to take him into custody."

Kirby snorted.

"A murderer! A mere murderer! India's full of 'em, King. And the less we have to do with them, the better off we are. That is, unless the murderer was a white man. Then—things are different. Let's have a look at him anyway. I'm awake now—and I probably won't get to sleep again for another four hours, so I might as well make the most of it."

Still fuming Kirby threw open the door of the adjoining room. He stood for a moment on the sill. King could not see his face, but he heard an almost inaudible gasp. And as he heard the gasp, he saw something else that nearly made him repeat the gesture of the police captain. He stared long at Kirby's feet, and then passed through the door behind the captain.

The Sikh stood motionless. Kirby turned hurriedly to King.

"Is this the prisoner?" he cried excitedly.

King nodded, not taking his eyes from the Sikh's face.

"This is the man suspected of murder, Kirby."

Kirby groaned. His shoulders seemed to loosen, allowing his gaunt frame to sag.

"Good God!" he said, breathlessly. "What mare's-nests you S. S. chaps do dig up! Take this man out, and send him home. Apologize to him! Anything—only don't anger him."

"This man is accused of murder, Kirby. It makes no difference to me if he's the god Shiva himself, I intend to prefer a charge against him, and investigate a neat little plot. Don't be a fool, Kirby."

Kirby groaned again.

"Fool? I, a fool, King? No!—you're the only fool here. You have arrested a man who practically controls the Sikh movement in Delhi. With a turn of his hand he could cause every loyal Sikh regiment to mutiny, and shout for Germany! Loose him, I say, for heaven's sake!"

King turned to where the Sikh was watching the white men argue about him. They were not speaking his tongue, but he understood—and he still smiled.

"For some unknown reason, you were right," King said to him. "I made a mistake. I got the wrong house. That scream I heard was a myth, and you couldn't possibly have killed that man who is dead in your house. Go!"

The Sikh smiled until his teeth gleamed. He looked straight at the eyes of Captain Kirby, and turned to the door. In an instant the night had swallowed him up.

"You chaps are always getting our necks into a sling——"

But Kirby was talking to himself. King, too, had gone.

KING walked slowly down the narrow street. Two things bothered him. One was the fact that the Sikh and Kirby had had a mutual understanding. The second was that Kirby had lied about having been in bed for four hours; for beneath the bottoms of Kirby's pajama legs, King had plainly seen the ends of a pair of regulation leather leggins. Captain Kirby would be most unlikely to go to bed for four hours, and forget to remove his leggins.

King did a dangerous thing—dangerous because he was undoubtedly a marked man. He had caused the arrest of a Sikh of importance; he had angered the police captain, for some reason which he was racking his brain to find out. As for the dangerous thing that King did — he stopped under a lamp in a small street, and, heedless of the target he made for unfriendly bullets, he pulled out his notebook.

"Kirby mentioned twice that he had been in bed for four hours," he wrote, "yet he had not taken off his leggins. Moreover, he was stunned at the sight of the Sikh. Could it be possible that Kirby was one of *the four?*"

Having made the note, King ripped the page out and made tiny fragments of it. On the next new page, he made another note:

"Kirby of the police was one of the four who saw Rahman Singh's ruby."

The doubt had left him suddenly. Then King ran true to form. He had been warned to leave the Sikh alone. But if a man reputed to control the wills of the thousands of Sikh troops had for some reason killed another man—and if the trusted captain of Delhi's police was in the plot—that certainly was the business of the Secret Service.

So, contrary to the wishes of Captain Kirby, and contrary to his own good judgment, Chowkander King once more climbed the mysterious staircase, and found himself in the hall of mirrors. This time, he made no mistake about the door. Nor did he care whether the tall Sikh was before him or behind him. He entered the murder room with his gun in his hand, and his eyes wide open.

He walked straight to the shimmering curtain—and then stopped. The body had gone.

"Sahib!"

The voice startled King into turning more quickly than he had intended to. A babu—a native Hindoo of considerable learning, naked but for a loin-cloth and cloak—confronted him.

"Well?" King snapped, assuming anger to hide his surprize.

"Take warning, sahib, from a person whose name I shall not mention. Go no further into the death of Moy Dong. He was a marked man. The sahib would be wise to heed the warning."

King would have answered, but the fat babu waddled out of hearing through an unexpected door.

King swore softly, and followed the babu. A few steps took him down a small corridor which turned sharply to the right. There were no entering doors; the babu must have come this way—and King wanted to talk earnestly with that half-naked man of learning.

At the foot of a flight of stairs, he stopped. There were three doors, all of them closed. King's eyes fastened on the middle one. It seemed to him that that one had just shut the instant he got there.

There was no light inside at all; only pitch blackness, and the uncanny feeling that he was not alone—that he was being watched. He walked slowly across the floor. His foot suddenly collided with something soft. In a second he had reached down and felt it, and pulled his hand back with a shudder.

At least, he had discovered the body of Moy Dong. He would have a chance to examine it. With a package of matches in his hand he knelt to the floor. The first flame flared up and smoked out. But in the second of light, King had seen something that made the hair prickle at the nape of his neck.

The body was not Moy Dong's; not a Chinaman, but a Hindoo priest, wrapped in his filthy white robe. And in the Hindoo's clenched fist was a small dagger—the same that had protruded from the shoulders of Moy Dong on the floor above. King had to light a second match to make sure of the brown stain on the blade of the knife.

Once King was sure of that stain, and knew it to be the blood of a man not long dead—knew it almost certainly to be the blood of Moy Dong—he turned the body of the Hindoo over and held up another match.

There was no doubt as to the way the priest had met his death. The blue mouth and goggling eyes shouted their tale of strangulation, and King gave his attention to the man's throat. He was surprized to find no mark — but then he turned the body back again, and discovered the two deep thumb marks at the back of the neck, and he immediately visualized an enormous pair of hands—a pair of hands that King had seen not long ago. If he could have seen to write, he would have pulled out his notebook and made an entry. That entry would have read:

"Found a Hindoo priest—undoubtedly Krishna, the man interested in the Sikh movement for freedom. He was killed by severe pressure applied to the base of his skull. His hand kept hold of a bloody knife, even in death. Did he kill Moy Dong? If he did—who killed *him?*"

Since it was impossible for King to see to write without holding the match, and impossible for him to hold the match and write at the same time, he merely thought the entry, and made his way from the room as swiftly as he could move.

He couldn't tell where he was going, but the general direction was down—and away from that awful room. He went along another passage, and up a flight of steps. At least he was out of the cellars, and on the level of the street.

The faint odor of perfume came to him again, and he followed it; back to the room where he had first encountered Rahman Singh.

"Sahib!"

King stopped, listening. It was the same voice, undoubtedly. The voice of the fat babu. King listened.

"Heed that warning, sahib. Go no further into the death of Moy Dong, the Chinese. Let the death of Krishna the Hindoo remain a mystery. Go, sahib, while you are yet safe. The sahib will not be warned again!"

King toyed with the butt of his revolver. He still had the feeling that he was being watched from behind—yet the babu was most certainly behind the curtain in front of him. He waited. Then:

"Babu, there are two men dead—murdered—in this house. Both those men were interested in the movement to free the Sikhs. Who killed those men?"

"Sahib——"

King whirled about. The voice had spoken at his elbow. The tall Sikh had come up noiselessly behind him. That explained his uncanny feeling of being watched. Rahman Singh folded his arms across his chest, and lowered his head until the great black beard rested on his silk robe.

King watched him, and watched the

curtain from behind which the babu had spoken. It no longer swayed. The babu seemed to have gone.

"The babu is right," Rahman Singh said, in a deep voice. "Leave the house, sahib. Heed the warning of Kirby sahib at the police office. The sahib is playing with fire; fire of white heat."

King smiled grimly. He swung his revolver loosely by the guard. He noticed that Rahman Singh's eyes seldom left the weapon. He noticed, too, that the dagger of the Sikh's turban had gone.

"Two men are dead in this house, my friend. I have seen both bodies, thanks to the babu. One, a Chinaman high in the Dynasty; the other a Hindoo priest. The first was stabbed. The knife which stabbed the first was in the hand of the second. The second was killed by breaking his neck——"

"The door is once more opened for the sahib. Do not come back!"

The smile had gone from Rahman Singh's eyes; his last words were as the crack of a whip. King did not move. Their eyes clashed like crossed rapiers, feeling out the strength behind them.

A minute passed, only their breathing breaking the stillness.

"Rahman Singh," King said softly, a peculiar gleam of triumph in his eyes, "there were four men at the table, looking at the Burma Ruby. How many of those four are still alive?"

Only Rahman Singh's lips moved. The curtain seemed to sway. It might have been King's imagination, but he was ready for attack from any side. He remembered plainly the speed with which that jewelled dagger could be whisked from the Sikh's turban.

"Two!"

The Sikh spat the word, then slowly raised his arm and pointed to the door.

"Go—sahib!"

King grinned.

"All right, my friend," he said slowly. "I am not quite right; and I am not far wrong. Salaam, sahib!" With a mock bow, King closed the door behind him and ran down the steps to the street.

IF KING were asked where he walked in the next hour, he would be unable to tell. He traversed most of the narrow streets of Delhi. He went through every passage of his mind in an effort to link the murders of two men interested in a rebellion of the Sikh cavalry, by a third man interested in the same thing. But he was practically certain that the third man did not murder the first two! Besides, there was the police captain who wore his leggins to bed. He——

Chowkander King stopped his walk abruptly, and turned on his heel. He snapped his finger in a gesture of disgust —disgust at his own stupidity—and went charging full speed along the small street in the direction of the police office.

As he rounded the last corner, he put on an additional burst of speed. There was a crowd of curiosity-mad natives packed thickly about the door. King pushed through, sweating, impatient. A gaunt arm seized his shoulder. He looked into a pair of hard gray eyes above a sandy beard. Commander Carron had evidently dressed in a hurry; his tunic was unbuttoned half down the front.

"King! Thank God you've come! We've been looking over half Delhi for you. There's the devil's own mess here. Come inside——"

King interrupted him, striding past into the room.

"How was he killed?"

"Killed? How——?"

"Kirby—how was Kirby killed, Carron? Knifed—or strangled? Don't stand there gawking, Carron! For heaven's sake, speak up. You've been searching half Delhi for me; I'm here. Tell me what I want to know."

Carron told him.

"Poisoned, King. Bite of a tarantula. Got it in a box in the next room. But how the devil you knew——"

"I didn't know, Carron. I guessed—when I was half a mile away in Chadni Chowk. I ran into a little play-acting to-night. Four men viewed a particularly famous Burma Ruby, in the house of Rahman Singh, the chap who has been influencing the Sikh troops against British rule. Two of those four men are dead. I took Rahman Singh into custody, and Kirby refused to book him; told me I was crazy to play with the man who held the destinies of the Sikhs in the palm of his hand. And Kirby pretended that I had got him out of bed, where he had been four hours getting to sleep. But I noticed that he had his leggins on under his pajamas. Fool that I was, I have only just ten minutes ago realized why Kirby had his leggins on! How do you know it was the tarantula?"

Carron had regained some of his dignity.

"No doubt of it, King. The guard heard a sort of thump, and pushed open the door of Kirby's room. Kirby was lying on the floor, with the great hairy spider on his cheek. It must have bitten him while he was asleep, and the poison worked slowly. We have caught the man who did it, so there is no mystery there. The fellow evidently had the spider, and wanted to put Kirby out of the way. He simply went into Kirby's room when Kirby was asleep, and loosed the insect. He waited a little too long——"

"Who was it?" King snapped the words.

Carron smiled a smile of satisfaction. At least there was one thing King didn't know!

"A babu——"

"A fat babu? Nearly naked? Waddles when he walks?"

The smile went from Carron's face again. He nodded.

"He's in the guard room. Know him?"

"Of course. He's the fourth man who saw the Burma Ruby at Rahman Singh's."

"The fourth! Who the devil were the other three?"

King extended three fingers of his right hand and took hold of the first.

"One—the first—was Moy Dong, the Chinaman. The second was Krishna, the Hindoo priest. The third—was Kirby! The fourth, the babu. The only thing I don't quite understand, is how Rahman Singh fits into the picture. Also, where is the Burma Ruby? Get the babu. Bring him to this room and leave him here with me. I have a few questions I want to ask him; then you can do what you like with him. Get him up here right away."

CARRON went to the door and gave an order. A minute later, the half-naked babu came in. At sight of King, he shrank back, a look of genuine fear on his oily face.

"Sahib—I know nothing, nothing at all. I only came with a message—a message from Rahman Singh to Kirby sahib —and Kirby sahib was dead. I know nothing, sahib!"

"Sit down, babu," King said sharply. The babu slumped heavily into a straight-backed chair, and King turned to Carron.

"He won't talk if you're here, Carron. Go out; see those curtains over there?" King whispered now, and indicated the swinging portières with a nod of his head. "Go through the next room, and get behind those curtains from the other side. Listen — but don't move. Don't even breathe if it makes a noise! And don't come out under any circumstances until I call you. Plain?"

Carron understood. He went through

the door without even glancing at the babu.

"Now," King started, drawing a chair to the table. *"Babuji,* the time when you knew nothing is past. This is the time when you know something; just how much you know, I'm going to find out."

A faint rustle of silk told King that Carron was in his place.

"Sahib, I know nothing!"

"What was the message you brought from Rahman Singh to Kirby? Hand it over to me!"

"I have lost it, sahib. I do not know where it is!"

King rapped sharply on the table. The door opened; a tall Sikh guard stood at salute.

"Guard! Take this man out. Have that filthy loin-cloth stripped from him. I'm looking for a message to Kirby. Turn him inside out!"

The big Sikh grinned; he hated babus. In two strides he was at the naked man's side. The babu shrank back. The thought of losing his loin-cloth appalled him.

"Nay, sahib!" he wailed. "There wasn't any message. Do not let him touch me. Do not! There wasn't any message!"

King nodded, his lips compressed in a thin line.

"I thought as much. You came here to put the spider in Kirby's room; not to deliver a message for Rahman Singh at all?"

The babu squirmed, and held out his hands, palms up to the ceiling.

"No, sahib! I did not come to put the spider in the room of Kirby sahib. I came to deliver a message for Rahman Singh."

"You just said there wasn't any message."

"There wasn't, sahib. None that I could hand over to you. It was what you call by word of mouth. A verbal message."

"Then what was it?" King demanded. "Repeat it!"

"That I can not do, sahib. So much has happened since that I can not even remember the first word of it. I swear it, sahib!"

King leaned forward, and thrust a finger under the babu's nose.

"If there was a message, babu, repeat it. If there was no message, you came here to murder Kirby, as you murdered Moy Dong the Chinaman, and as you murdered Krishna, the Hindoo. What was that message that Rahman Singh sent to Captain Kirby? Answer me!"

"Sahib! You are mistaken; I did not murder Moy Dong. The death of Krishna was unfortunate, but I did not kill him. The sahib——"

"What was that message?"

The babu looked into King's eyes, and his red face blanched.

"Only this, sahib," he said, looking at the floor. "Rahman Singh wished me to say to Kirby sahib—'If you have it, give it up. It is not worth the price you will have to pay.' That was the message."

"And did Kirby give it up, when you came for it?" King asked quickly.

"But no, sahib. He——"

The babu stopped abruptly. His face was the color of chalk. He gripped the table edge, and watched the grin of triumph spread over King's face.

"Ah!" King said softly. "Kirby refused to give it up. So you simply loosed the spider—waited until the deadly poison had taken its effect on him—then took it from him! And since you couldn't find it at once, you had no opportunity to make a getaway. If you found what you were looking for, it is on you now—or else it is in Kirby's room. Guard!"

The big Sikh was still near the door.

"Rip that rag from his carcass. Whatever he took from Kirby will be there, unless he's swallowed it!"

"No-no-no-no-sahib!" The babu seemed to shrivel into a mere mass of flesh. "I will tell everything—everything. Only send away the other sahib. I will tell you alone. I promise!"

King signaled the guard to leave the room, and waited until he had closed the door behind him. He glanced at the swaying curtain, and it was with some satisfaction that he realized Carron was still there.

"Now, *babuji* — everything! Starting with the death of Moy Dong, and ending with the death of Kirby."

"I know nothing of the death of Moy Dong——"

"Starting with the death of Moy Dong," King repeated, paying no attention to the babu's words. "At the time of the showing of the Burma Ruby at Rahman Singh's house, there were four men present, besides the Sikh himself. The stone was on the table in a case. The lights went out. What happened next?"

The babu shook his round head.

"I do not know, sahib. It was so long ago; my memory on such things is poor. I can not remember——"

"See if you can remember this." King's finger went under the babu's nose again. "You'll tell all you know, and tell it quickly, or you'll go to the scaffold for the death of Captain Kirby. I'll give you just one minute to tell what took place the instant the lights were turned out. One minute!"

The babu held his stomach, and shook with fright, either real or assumed.

"I'll tell, sahib—everything—immediately. But I must have water. My throat is parched."

KING called for drinks. The guard came in with two glasses of native wine, and placed them on the table. King watched the babu carefully, and thought he saw just the slightest sign of triumph on the fat face.

"What happened, babu," he repeated, when the native had sipped his wine and replaced his glass on the table.

"There was a slight movement near me, sahib. When the lights went on again, the ruby was gone. Rahman Singh was angry. He had the lights darkened again, in order that the thief should replace the jewel. This time, there was a scuffle. There was the blow of a knife—a scream —and the sahib's footbeats on the stairs. There are many ways from Rahman Singh's house. The others escaped, leaving the Chinaman on the floor."

The babu stopped, and sipped his wine. King stared straight at the swaying curtain, and thought.

"Moy Dong was killed by one of four men. Which one, babu?"

"That I do not know, sahib. The lights were out. It was pitch-black. I sensed only the movement at my side."

King stood up. He walked around the babu's back and past the curtain to the door. As he passed the hangings, he mouthed the words, "Don't move!" At the door, he whispered into the ear of the Sikh guard, then walked slowly back to his seat.

Behind the curtain, Carron's heart beat faster. He had seen something King had not seen. The instant King's back had turned, the native had snatched a tiny phial from his belt, and emptied it into King's glass. In a moment, he had replaced the tube, and resumed his expression of innocence and ignorance.

"Now," King went on, as though there had been no interruption, "one of those five took the ruby. Moy Dong took it first from the table. He was killed——"

The explosion of a rifle just outside the door stopped him. The babu jumped, swung around, half got up, then slumped back.

King was lighting a cigarette.

"It is nothing," he said evenly. "The guard ordered the crowd from the door, and shot over their heads to frighten them. I was saying—Moy Dong must have taken the ruby from the table. Whoever knifed him wanted the stone. Who wanted the stone? Or rather, babu, who *didn't* want the stone?"

King picked up his glass. The eyes of the babu grew wide. He watched every movement of King's hand from the table to his mouth. He watched King drink, with only a slight stiffening of his muscles. He sat back and waited.

"Who didn't want the ruby, babu? Who—didn't—want—babu! You—killer!"

King's voice trailed away. His eyes were opened, but only a trifle. His chest heaved; he seemed to stop breathing, and his head fell on to his breast. The babu got up, and stood leaning on the table edge, grinning maliciously.

"Ah—the sahib was so clever! So utterly clever! But he forgot that others were clever too. Moy Dong *did* take the Burma Ruby. He *was* killed for it. Krishna killed him, with one blow of his knife. He ran to the cellars in an effort to escape, but Kirby sahib was too quick for him. With a twist of his powerful hands he broke the Hindoo's neck! Broke it, sahib!"

The babu seemed to grow taller. He had lost his hesitating manner of speech. The uncertainty of words had gone. His voice boomed a deep bass. King's head had sagged. Only the table leg kept him from sliding to the floor.

"That was two, sahib. But there was the other. Krishna—who was trying to make himself an independent ruler; Moy Dong, who would have made the Sikhs many promises on behalf of his Chinese ruler; Kirby, a traitor to his country. He wanted gold only. He was a puppet; they were all puppets. But they all interfered with my plans. And my plans, sahib,

were the biggest of all. I will tell you; in the event of this world war we hear about, the great cavalry troops would have rebelled, and fought for Germany! For Germany, sahib. I could not fail!"

The babu stopped. He seemed to be out of breath. King never moved. The babu might have been talking to an empty room. He went on. His eyes gleamed; his voice grew softer.

"Look at me, sahib. But you can't! No matter. Think of me—think of me with this filthy grease washed from my body; with shoes whose soles are four inches thick, to give me height; with my head swathed in fifty yards of finest silks; with my body draped in a flowing robe, and my face hidden behind a black beard! Think, sahib. I will tell you, for you will never use the knowledge. I am Rahman Singh, the Sikh! As the Sikh, I played upon the sympathies of the regiments. As Rahman Singh I invited my enemies — my greedy enemies—to my house. I showed them a piece of worthless red glass — worthless, sahib — gave them a chance to steal it, and stood back while they threw aside everything for greed; watched them kill each other for possession of what was not worth the life of an infidel!

"The clever sahib! You were warned —twice warned. You thought you could match wits with Rahman Singh. You had the wine brought in, and drank it. Be careful, sahib, in this land where the art of poisoning is as old as the god of death himself. Never drink with an enemy—unless he be a dead one, or nearly dead. To you, sahib, who will be dead in a few minutes from poison—to you, I shall drink. To you—and to Germany's success!"

The babu—still the babu in looks, with his fat stomach and rounded face—but with the carriage and bearing of the tall Sikh, picked his glass from the table and balanced it neatly in his hand. He threw back his head, with a deep laugh.

"To the careless sahib!" he said, and drained the glass.

For an instant, he stood as still as a stone image. His eyes looked straight ahead; the eyes of a man suddenly gone blind. The smile faded from his round face. His head jerked back; the glass clattered to the floor.

Rahman Singh tried to shout, but the words stuck in his throat. With a quick rush, the poison seized him. He fell across the table, his head not a foot from King's face.

"You—devil!" he gasped, and quivered.

Chowkander King got up, and rubbed his arms.

"Never drink with an enemy unless you are sure he is dead, Rahman Singh," he said slowly. Then:

"All right, Carron. Come out!"

The curtain parted. The commander's face glistened with sweat. He walked across the room unsteadily.

"Good God, King! What an ordeal! If I hadn't *seen* you go to the door, and tell the sentry to shoot his gun—if I hadn't *seen* you switch the glasses when the babu turned around to see what was happening—if it hadn't been for those two things, King, I should have thought you were a goner sure, and I should have put a bullet right through that greasy head. How the devil did you know he had poisoned the wine? You were over at the door when he dropped the stuff from his phial."

King stooped and picked the glass from the floor, sniffed it and put it down.

"There is only one person in the world who likes water less than an Indian babu

of this one's class; and that is an Indian fakir who thinks it most unholy to touch the stuff. When a pure, unadulterated babu asks you for a glass of water—watch out. I was only guessing—and guessing wildly. But my suspicion was that he wanted it for that particular purpose. Then, he was terrified every time I threatened to have him searched. He had something he was deathly afraid to let us find on him. You will find, when you investigate, that Kirby was killed with the same poison. The scent of almonds was strong in his room, and that meant—prussic acid. The spider was merely to make it look natural. The bite of the tarantula would have made him deathly sick, and killed him slowly. Death from prussic acid in its native state is nearly instantaneous."

Carron made no reply. He watched Chowkander King lift Rahman Singh's lifeless form from the table, and place it gently on the floor. Then he said:

"For a moment, I nearly rushed out and spoiled your party, King. When your eyes began to stick out, and you got blue in the face, I had my gun pointing right at his chest."

King grinned, and fingered his throat tenderly.

"Don't think for a minute, Carron," he said seriously, "that any half-baked imitation of a man dying would have gone over with an arch-fiend like Rahman Singh—a man who would so cunningly get rid of his competitors by showing them a worthless ruby, telling them a fabulous tale of its value—and then standing by to watch them kill one another for the possession of it. I held my breath until I nearly choked. I'm afraid I was nearly as dead as Rahman Singh thought I was!"

"Yu Lon listened to him and sighed softly."

Song of the Indian Night

By FRANK OWEN

The story of the burning love of an old Chinese fisherman for the lovely lady Yu Lon

THE fragile loveliness of the little lady Yu Lon was of such perfection she seemed almost to be made of porcelain, as though a chance knock would shatter her to pieces. Her clear olive-yellow skin was without a blemish. Even the soft rice powder, scented with lotus fragrance, which she used upon it was merely a gesture. One does not try to improve upon a sunset, the bloom of a nectarine, the glow of a flower, or the gold-rising moon.

Yu Lon was very rich. Her parents had journeyed on to be reunited with spirits of countless ancestors. She lived in a vast house in Canton, faithfully watched over by her old Amah, whose body was forced to creep along upon the earth but whose soul was in the stars. The Amah believed that man can no more control his own destiny than he can control the course of the moon.

She was small of stature and so gaunt that the skin of her face seemed drawn over the bones without any intervening layer of flesh. She went through life perpetually cold, always in search of warmth. There was no warmth in her body except the fire in her eyes. It was as though the Amah herself were dead and only her

683

eyes were still living. Yet their power and force was strong enough to motivate her frigid body.

The old Amah was supremely satisfied with her lot in life. She loved to sit beneath a cherry tree in the garden and bask in the sun. She wooed the sun as ardently as though it were a living person. The sun could give her heat. The sun was the mother of all living. Heat was life.

Now and then she muttered a bit as she drowsed in the garden. She could hear strange voices in the air. Sometimes she paused, scarcely breathing, imagining that very faintly she could hear the music of the stars.

"No man really lives," she told Yu Lon, "until he has truly learned how to listen. Any one can talk. Even parrots and monkeys talk gibberish. But to listen is a gracious art. Happiness, lasting happiness is often found in the wind. To gain complete tranquillity it is necessary to hear the particular music in the wind that is for your ears alone. Some day into your life will come the song for which your ears are attuned. When it does, nor mountains nor chains will keep you from it. Music, gentle music, is the greatest force in the world. It is food for the starving, drink for the thirsty. The material world is a selfish place of crime, deceit and vile pretending. The spiritual world alone is of importance. And music, divine music, is the bridge over which dwellers in this material life pass for a few moments into spiritual realms of color, light and song. There is no age to music. There is no age to any spiritual thing. And for each of us there is a song that is fashioned for our ears alone. The tragedy is that so few of earth ever hear its notes. Heed then the warning of an old woman who has meditated for many years under moons of Cathay. Some day into your life will come a note in music.

It will surge into your soul as tempestuous billows break in foam on the shores of the sea. It will sweep everything before it. It will flood your life. For one brief moment you will cross the melody bridge into realms of poetry and flowers. The course of your life will be changed. But what matter? For you will have found a song worth singing."

NATURALLY the teachings of the old Amah filled up a great part of the life of Yu Lon. To her they were not absurd fantasies, vague wanderings of a dreamer's mind, they were real, more real than the winding alleys, the filth, the poverty of the Chinese city into which she seldom walked. A broken flower to Yu Lon was a vast tragedy in the rose garden. She was unacquainted with the sad fact that thousands of gaunt, stunted children were dying of starvation every day throughout the Celestial Empire. She dwelt in a mystic world of perfume and music.

Frequently she slept all night long in the garden. She removed all her clothes and lay upon the soft grass lush with dew. In the moonlight her little breasts shone like alabaster. The beautiful contours of her body were like those of an ivory statue. No wonder the softest perfumes of the garden drifted to her that they might lave her sweet body. And always the old Amah sat beside her.

"Hark! do you not hear?" she would say in an awe-struck voice. "It is the music of the stars, the same elusive melody which drifted to the new-born earth as it emerged from the womb of the sun. That song is ageless. Nor has it ever been improved upon. What is death? What is life? What has the future in store for any one of us? And when the shell of man dies what comes afterward? Do we go back once more, when our souls are freed, to the warm sun which is the mother of all life?"

Thus time wore on in that Chinese garden and the beauty of Yu Lon increased with the cycle of the years. She was a veritable jewel-maiden, ebony hair splashed with a jade-blue sheen, amber skin, a suggestion of red poppies in her cheeks, teeth like Ceylonese pearls, eyes black opals that burned with a scorching fire. Her figure was of such glory that even the sun trembled. Sometimes when she cast aside her clothes and bathed at the river's edge, small waves formed in the usually still river as the water struggled to touch her soft warm flesh. Her breath was more fragrant than the perfume of red roses. A veritable love-lady she was, made for love and rapture. One glance of her eyes would have sent a man off on any quest of her choosing. But the garden remained silent. No lovers were welcomed there. The old Amah, servant though she was, was the real ruler. She had reared a mystic world about her little mistress. Men who came to woo must exist only in an imagined world of fantasy.

Yu Lon did not rebel at the old Amah's attitude. She had never had many friends in the garden. Those that had come were usually not human. A white heron that circled each morning over the river and paused for a moment at the water's edge to gaze upon her glowing golden body as she bathed. A frog that lived in the lotus pond and croaked dismally as it blinked in the warm sunlight. A tiny bird, chirping for awhile in the early dawn on her window-ledge. A rose that peeped through the casement while she was sleeping. But there were few human visitors except an occasional trader or merchant who sought audience with the Amah.

ONE evening as Yu Lon walked by the river's edge she heard the voice of a fisherman singing. The song was like nothing she had ever heard. The warm blood rushed to her cheeks. Her eyes glowed more brightly than ever. Who was this strange unknown fisherman who sang so wondrously that everything merged into a dream-like haze? There was only the night and the stars and that grand chanting voice from the river. She assumed it belonged to a fisherman, though had he been a prince he could not have devastated the calm even flow of her life more completely. Love had come at last to the garden, perhaps in the guise of a youth strong of limb, straight as an elm, with a face as round and glowing as a pearl moon.

And now a small boat hove into view. It glided along with tiny white sail set, cleaving the blackness of the night like a white moth wooing a star. As the boat was about to glide gently past, out of her life forever, Yu Lon let out a little cry. Here at last was a song worth singing, the song that had been carved for her ears alone, a note in music to complete the glorious symphony of her life.

"Don't go," she pleaded. "Please tarry here with me awhile."

Instantly the fisherman ceased his singing. He lowered the sail and guided his small boat to the bank. In a moment he stood beside Yu Lon. And then suddenly she was in his arms and once more divinely he was singing of nightingales, of love and laughter, of the glory of her lips and her body, of the blue canopy of the sky which is really a quilt of blue velvet to warm the heart of man. Yu Lon, listening, was drugged by the wonder of it. The Amah had been right. All of her teaching culminated now in one gorgeous blossom of love.

The night was dark; the moon, casting

the fronds of the trees into grotesque silhouette, had not yet risen sufficiently to disperse the night shadows of the garden. Yu Lon could not see the face of the fisherman, but she made no complaint. It sufficed that his arm encircled her and her head was against his breast.

"Where," she asked breathlessly at length, "where did you learn such marvelous music?"

And he replied, "In India. That melody is really 'The Song of the Indian Night.' It is the voice of India. I learned it in 'The Vale of Kashmir,' where the very air is impregnated with poetry. I had been working that summer as a servant on a houseboat. What urge it was that forced me to forsake my native China to wander to India I can not tell. It was a force beyond my control. Kashmir dragged me to it as though I were a bit of steel and it a mountain of lodestone. But I never regretted my going, for the Vale of Kashmir, eulogized though it has been by poets for centuries, has yet not been overpraised. It is as though Nature spreads out all her varied carpets of flowers in this spot, making of it a great rug bazar from which the floral grandeur of all countries is chosen. Sometimes the snow-tipped peaks stand out against the sky like a mighty hand of God beckoning to his children. Night after night I used to sit on the deck of the houseboat after my European master and his family had retired. I was stirred by queer emotions. The night was poignant with hidden forces. For thousands of years India has been a land of mystery. When nights are black and a vast net of shadows swoops down over city and jungle, the voice of India still goes on murmuring, chanting, whispering, moaning and occasionally rising into an anthem of love. All of the imagery and sorcery of that strange land, the countless smells and perfumes, the hatreds and intrigues, the restlessness, abhorrent caste bondage, the breath of lovely sensuous women, seem to swirl up into the air in a mighty flood. Each country has a voice, a song made up of the cries and struggles of its people. That was the voice I heard during the hush of the evening on that houseboat in Kashmir. It was 'The Song of the Indian Night.' And though many moods went into its making, it was love that predominated. The love of a man for a woman, of a flower for the sun. It was the most majestic chant to which I had ever listened. It swept into my heart, and now as I journey down the rivers of China, I sing once more 'The Song of the Indian Night.' And I am never poor. Within the song is wealth enough to bring happiness to a thousand kings. Men of earth are fools. They gloat over gold, money, bonds, not placing any value whatever on the perfume of a garden, the song of the night wind, or the laughter of children. Fools! Fools! Rather would I be a beggar and have heard 'The Song of the Indian Night' than a king and be deaf to the countless symphonies which haunt the wind."

Yu Lon listened to him and sighed softly. Here was love such as she had never dreamed existed. Love and complete contentment. And once more the fisherman sang and her senses reeled. She felt as though she had been transported. The old Amah was right. Music was the golden bridge that connected the material world with the spiritual. It was the avenue of man's escape from reality.

All through the night they lingered in the garden. They walked through perfumed paths, rested for awhile on a marble bench beside the lotus pond. The breeze played softly in the treetops, harmonizing with the voice of the fisherman, whose name was Jui Vung. What was time in the rhapsody of music and love? Does one count the hours in eternity? The moon rose like an orange window into the blue-jade sky. It was like a mirror in which all the joys which life affords were reflected.

Yu Lon scarcely breathed, so deeply stirred was she by the witchery of the night. No longer was she in a prosaic garden. The fisherman was a magician. He had snatched her up and carried her off to the hills of dream where "the slumber shadows dwell." She had succumbed to the drug of "The Indian Night."

So the night passed until the dawn leaped up in the eastern sky. Then for the first time she turned and gazed into the face of the fisherman. As she did so she recoiled with horror. The fisherman was an old, old man. His skin was like parchment, lined and wrinkled, scarred by the ravages of the wind and the sea. He was as ugly as the frog who dwelt in the lotus pond. But his eyes were beautiful. Yet they seemed the saddest eyes she had ever looked into. And this was the man with whose voice she had fallen in love, the man who had sung that wondrous song that was for her ears alone.

He noticed her expression and waved his hands in despair. When he spoke his voice was utterly hopeless.

"Do not recoil from me," he murmured wistfully. "I knew that with the dawn all our dreams of the night would vanish. Still for a few hours we lived like gods. We breathed the essence of love, real love. For that we should be thankful. To so few in life this rare opportunity is given. Yes, I am old, if you view my body. But my soul is young. I was born on that occasion of which I told you when I heard the love songs of the Indian Night on the houseboat in The Vale of Kashmir. Our age should not be measured by the years but by the amount of beauty we absorb. Some men live till they are eighty, yet intellectually they die without being born, without once having their souls awakened. You and I were made for each other, despite the great difference in our ages. I do not ask you to marry me now. First I shall go away in search of my lost youth. That youth should have been spent with you. Somewhere I shall find it, for youth can never die. When I do, then I'll come back to you. And here we will live in a harmony so perfect that forever after it will be told about in legend."

The fisherman did not attempt to take her in his arms. Nor did he bid her adieu. Like an amber statue she stood and watched him as he pushed his boat into the river and clambered in. A few moments later the small sail had been set and, as it caught the wind, the boat floated out into the river. As it disappeared from view the fisherman was singing, and even though she knew he was ugly and old she was still thrilled to her very soul by that strange wistful "Song of the Indian Night."

DURING the days that followed life went on much as usual in that Chinese garden. The old Amah sat everlastingly drowsing in the sun, muttering and murmuring from time to time as though she were conversing with transparent forms and wraiths about her. The Amah was obsessed by the glory of the sun. She loved it passionately.

Yu Lon continued living in a world that was of fairy texture. There was little to disturb the tranquillity of her existence. The garden was large and there were no discordant noises from the street outside to drift to that sweet retreat. Yu Lon thought much about Jui Vung the fisherman and that unforgettable song with which he had wooed her. Not for a moment did she expect him to return. He was old. Soon death would claim him. Gone was he from her life but his song was in her heart. Sometimes she had the strange feeling that she was nourishing his child in her womb, so poignant, so alive was that love-song. But of course it was merely weird imagining. It was a dream, even as the old fisherman himself had been a dream. For him there would be no returning. Age can not retrace its steps to youth again. Still the garden was more beautiful because Jui Vung had passed through it. There was softer music in the treetops. Even the perfume of the flowers echoed his songs. One night of love had been given to Yu Lon. It was a night to cherish in memory. It had been a night of spiritual perfection.

So the life of Yu Lon drifted on languidly in complete repose. She did not mourn for the fisherman, for was he not old? He was not of her age but a shadow creeping back from the distant past. Only his song was young, and the echo of his song still lingered in the treetops.

Now there came a time when into the garden entered Dien Daung, a jade merchant who had come at the request of the Amah to display his wares. Of all stones, jade is the most pleasing to the touch. It is the only jewel that is pleasurable to fondle. The Amah believed, as do most of the Taoists, that jade has a spiritual significance. There is something magical about it. That is why a bit of it is buried with every corpse, so that the spirit may more easily secure entrance to the Jade City of the Celestial Paradise.

Frequently the Amah walked through Jade Street, where trinkets of quartz and amber, of amethyst and cornelian were sold beside nephrite and jade, the most comforting of all precious stones. She loved to listen to the tinkle of jade gongs.

She tried to match their notes with the music of the wind. But of all the countless tones and colors, her favorites were rust, mauve and carved green jade against a background of pink quartz.

So Dien Daung came to the garden with his jewels, and while the old Amah muttered to herself and gloated over them, he walked with Yu Lon down near the Lotus Pond and along the shaded paths of the garden. Yu Lon studied his face with interest. Dien Daung was by far the handsomest youth she had ever encountered. Like the full moon was his face, serene, satisfied, not lacking in pomp or splendor. He was tall and well built, like a young god of the mountains, fit to be a prince. No wonder women worshipped him as he rode pompously in his ricksha through the crowded streets and alleys of Canton. As Yu Lon gazed upon him, once more love crept into her heart. If only the fisherman with his golden voice could have had a face and form like the jade merchant! Still, why complain? It was fate. Jui Vung, the fisherman, was gone. Despite his noble promises he would never come back. The leaf can not return to the branch after it has once fallen to the loam of the forest.

Yu Lon was drawn to Dien Daung because of his beauty. But where speech was concerned he was almost inarticulate. He was a dull talker. He never made an original observation, nor a remark which was worth remembering. Even though he was a jewel merchant, he was not even slightly poetical. To him the jewels were merely objects for barter. He was more interested in fine cooking and rich foods. Dien Daung had no song for the night, but he was young and handsome. His youth could make up for many things. Besides, the song of Jui Vung the fisherman still lingered in the fragrant air.

What need had Yu Lon for another singer?

THEY were married just prior to the Moon Festival, which takes place the fifteenth day of the eighth moon, either September or October, when the moon is at the full. At this time there is great rejoicing and feasting. "Moon Cakes" are made and crunched by every one. Peddlers sell them in the streets, singing jolly songs to draw the attention of passers-by to their tasty wares. Yu Lon chose the date for the wedding. It took place in the evening when the moon hung like a sunflower in the sky. The Amah shook her head and murmured dolefully. Tears streamed from her weak old eyes. No good could come of any wedding that was not consummated beneath the warm rays of the sun. But Yu Lon laughed at all dire forebodings. Nothing could happen to mar the festivities. The ceremony was performed by an American missionary, for Dien Daung was a Christian. This, too, worried the old Amah. Were the countless sages of old China thus to be defied?

Yu Lon was extremely happy that night. The garden was more fragrant than ever. The blue sky was like the vaulted dome of a temple. Was it only imagination or was there a barely perceptible note of sadness in the song which the wind played in the treetops? It reminded her of the old fisherman. She was sorry to have the calm of her thoughts so disturbed. Of course she was supremely happy, but she would have been far happier if there had been no music in the garden that night.

As for Dien Daung, his happiness could not have been improved. His round face vied with the moon in its glowing. He was securing one of the most fragilely beautiful women in all

O. S.—8

China for his wife. When the ceremony was over, which had taken place in the garden in the presence of a few friends of Dien Daung especially invited for the occasion, they repaired to where a vast banquet had been set in one of the rooms. As many courses were in that meal as there are beads in the necklace of a Buddhist monk. Dien Daung gazed at the sumptuous repast and rubbed his hands together. In the contemplation of the numerous viands, the rich meats, preserved limes and highly spiced cakes he quite forgot the existence of his bride. One might find a woman any time but only once in a decade could one chance upon such a feast as this.

Dien Daung ate loudly and gluttonously. His eyes fairly popped from their sockets in their enthusiasm. Occasionally a bit of fruit juice or grease dripped from the corners of his mouth. He paid no attention to any conversation which took place at the table, nor did he listen to the weird music which several musicians in a far corner played upon their lutes. Dien Daung was stunned by the excellence of the repast. His mind was ravished by the savory smells until it was quite useless.

Between his food gorging, Dien Daung drank wine until he was maudlin drunk. His usually inarticulate tongue was loosened. He sang ribald songs in a bellowing voice. He stamped his feet, beat the table with his fists until the dishes rattled, and laughed uproariously. Finally he was carried from the table to the bridal chamber in a drunken stupor.

Yu Lon gazed upon his inert form in disgust. She could not spend the night by the side of a man in such a condition, no matter how handsome he might be. However, she was a bit of a philosopher. She did not imagine that her future was entirely ruined because of this unfortunate occurrence on her wedding night.

Still she had no intention of remaining in the bridal chamber. She decided impulsively to spend the night in the garden.

She extinguished the lamps that lighted the chamber and drew aside the tapestries that obscured the window. The moonlight splashed into the room, a radiant flood. She was hot, almost feverish; the excitement of the day had rather spoiled her nerves. She decided that she would put on a cool garment for the garden interlude. Slowly she cast aside her clothes even as a flower might cast its petals to the wind. Finally she stepped from the last bit of silk, a slim amber girl, gorgeous in the moonlight. For a few moments she stood by the open window, little porcelain lady, breathing in the fragrance of the garden. Her form against the moonlight was a silhouette worthy of the most graceful cameo carving.

At last she put on a kimono, a blue, soft, clinging wisp of a cloak, that would blend in color with the night sky and in texture with the dusk of moonrise. In a few moments she was in the garden, walking slowly down toward the river. She was not lonesome, despite the fact that it was the witching hour of night, for the air was full of whispers, wind voices, flower voices and lullabies in the willows. She threw herself at full length on the smooth moss bank of the river. The sky was without a blemish. The stars gleamed forth in startling brilliance. The moon was like a great white crystal globe. She sighed softly. The night was magnificent. And as she sighed, the stillness was shattered by a wondrous song. Jui Vung, the fisherman, was keeping his promise. He was coming back. On the clear air, "The Song of the Indian Night" rolled out until the very flowers trembled. All Nature paused to listen. Yu Lon felt as though her heart had ceased to beat. She was dead. Lying before the gates of Jade City, listening to a Celestial anthem. She did not stop to consider whether Jui Vung had found his youth once more or not. What matter? She was in love with a mood, not a man; a song and not a physical being. The old Amah was right. There is no age to music. It is ageless because it is immortal. And when Yu Lon was in love with a song, she was in love with youth.

AS JUI VUNG saw Yu Lon, he turned his boat in toward the bank. The next moment she was in his arms, her head pillowed against his breast. In sheer ecstasy she clung to him. In the shadows of the garden, he seemed almost young. She did not gaze into his face. She did not need to. She saw him with an inner vision. The night is kind insofar as it hides parchment skin, withered cheeks, wrinkles. The sun may be the mother of all life but it is a rather cruel parent. It shows up every defect, every weakness. The moon is colder, it lacks the fire, but it is more kind. It woos one gently into slumber.

The arms of Jui Vung encircled the fragile body of Yu Lon. The cobweb thinness of her kimono only emphasized the smoothness and grace of her body. And it seemed as if something of her youth and warmth flowed into the body of the fisherman. Once more he sang, and now "The Song of the Indian Night" was more glorious than ever. Here was the voice of India calling, calling, the love songs of India, chanted in a mighty symphony.

Thus Yu Lon, on her bridal night, forsook her stupefied husband and passed the night in the garden with the old fisherman, the old fisherman who had succeeded in getting beyond the cloak of reality into the magic fields beyond. Truly it almost seemed as though the simple Jui Vung had found the keys to Jade City.

In the morning, at the request of Yu Lon the old Amah hired the fisherman to be a servant in the house of the tiny porcelain lady he loved. By noon Dien Daung had arisen, bathed and drunk deeply of black coffee. He felt none the worse for his night of carousing, nor was he even slightly penitent because of the sorry spectacle he had made of himself. Dien Daung believed as do all Chinamen that women are subordinate to men. He was now Yu Lon's master. It was not right for her to question him about the quantity of his drinking. Fortunately for the peace of the household she did not attempt to do so. The fact that he had not consummated the marriage in the nuptial chamber worried him not at all. There were other days. One woman or another was quite the same as long as she were beautiful. He was pleased with the picture Yu Lon presented as she walked about the garden. She seemed perfectly happy. And Yu Lon *was* happy. It was not hard to be contented under existing conditions. Her husband, Dien Daung, was as handsome as the full moon. One would have to travel far to view a man more pleasing in appearance. What matter that he was inarticulate, that his conversation was boring? As she walked with him through the white marble paths at the sunset hour, the voice of the fisherman-servant drifted plaintively to their ears, crystal-clear. Even Dien Daung liked the music. It was pleasant to loll about the grass by the lotus pond and listen to the notes of that marvelous voice. Yu Lon was perfectly contented. She could look on the handsome face of her husband and give vent to wistful musings. It was not necessary for him to speak. That one lovely voice of the fisherman was music enough for any garden. Sometimes she tried to imagine that the voice really belonged to Dien Daung whose face was so handsome to gaze upon.

DIEN DAUNG gave long hours to eating and drinking. From every quarter of the country he drew the most tasty dishes. He was in this one thing an epicurean. He was a good judge of food and women, but his first love was always food. Sometimes he crept from the garden and repaired to a place where he had a rendezvous with a lady who had meant much to him prior to his meeting with Yu Lon. The lady's name was Mei Roong. Yu Lon was unaware of these stolen interludes, but not so the Amah, who understood the stars and could divine everything. She shook her head dolefully. She sat like a crouching Buddha in the sun, questing for warmth, and usually muttering and murmuring. Occasionally it almost seemed as though she moaned.

Then one day sadness swooped down into that garden. As Yu Lon walked by the side of the lotus pond she slipped and fell and her forehead struck sharply against the marble bench that stood beneath a willow. The blow stunned her. Now it so happened that Jui Vung, the fisherman, was passing. He saw her fall and rushed to her assistance. He picked her up in his arms as though she had been a broken flower crushed by a wind gone mad. Even as he held her to his breast and carried her into the house, he crooned softly to her. Once he pressed his lips to hers in a burst of worship.

When Yu Lon regained consciousness, the fisherman still sat by her bedside. But everything appeared to be in darkness.

"Is it night?" she asked.

The fisherman was horrified at her question, for the sun was blazing into the room as brightly as ever.

"No," he said softly, "it is midday."

"I can not see a thing," she said. "I am blind."

He placed his hands upon her warm brow. They seemed wonderfully cool and tender.

"Hush!" he whispered. "In a few days you will be able to see once more. Your nerves are shocked, that is all."

Later that day a noted English physician visited the house and examined her eyes. "At any moment," he said, "you may get back your sight. Your blindness will not be permanent. Of that I am sure. But I can not predict the exact time at which your sight will be restored. The main thing now is not to worry. Just wait and hope. In a few days, get up and walk about the garden. The air will do you good."

From that day forth the fisherman was her constant companion. He was her eyes, her guide. Softly he sang to her as they walked slowly through the garden. The very flowers and trees seemed saddened by the calamity that had befallen their beloved porcelain lady. But Yu Lon stood the ordeal stoically. Infinite patience is a Chinese virtue. She remained true to tradition. Some day her sight would be restored. Yet there was one strange thing about this blindness. Even though a black veil had fallen over her sight, it seemed as though she could see Jui Vung more clearly than ever. After all, the body is but the wrapper in which the bundle of man is tied up. For the real man one must look deeper. Jui Vung, the simple fisherman, was really of towering stature. He had a voice so mighty that it reached the stars. What matter age? Does one worry over the age of the sun? Could it glow more warmly if it were young?

But for Dien Daung the blindness of Yu Lon spelled tragedy. All he had to recommend him was a hollow beauty of form and face. He had an unpleasant voice. He never gave vent to a distinctive utterance. Her blindness simply blotted him out of that garden. When she could no longer gaze upon him he no longer continued to exist. However, he too was a philosopher. He had no way of telling the duration of her blindness. It was not his desire to be tied down permanently to a blind wife. Fortunately he still had Mei Roong, lady of desultory pleasures, to turn to. Now he conceived the idea of bringing her to the garden, of hiding her in the little abandoned boat house down near the river's edge. When the lady was acquainted with his plans she approved them at once. It was not hard for her to move to the garden, for she had very few possessions which she cared about taking other than the usual stock in trade of a lady of her enterprise.

Yu Lon, walking on a dream path with the fisherman, did not know that Dien Daung had brought his mistress in to soil that fragrant garden. But the old Amah, drowsing in the sun in quest of heat, was aware of all that went on about her even though she bobbed her head drowsily and murmured as though she were sleeping. This was sacrilege. Her little Yu Lon, alone, should rule over that garden. Were the spirits of the air stunned that they did not rise to smite this base husband who traded gold for tinsel? Why did the serpent that sleeps beneath Canton not tremble and rage at such a disgusting intrigue? She waited daily for the sky to fall in. Still nothing happened. It was then that she decided to take matters into her own hands. One day while Dien Daung and Mei Roong were visiting the colorful shops in Lantern Street she crept into the boat house and slipped a subtle poison into a flask of wine that stood upon a table.

In the evening when the clandestine lovers had repaired to the rendezvous for a night of love, they first drank deeply of that deadly wine. The effect of the poison was slow. It caused sleep to creep over them before death. The Amah watched at the window. When she beheld them sleeping in each other's arms, she applied a torch to the fragile structure of the house. In a moment, the flames leaped up joyfully to meet the moon. The Amah stood gazing at the conflagration. Her lips drew back, showing toothless pink gums. She extended her arms toward the burning building. For the first time in her life, her body was absorbing warmth. It was all the more piquant in view of the fact that it was caused by the burning of her enemies. She drew the warmth into her body as though it were the most soothing of tonics. Now the servants of the house were jumping about jabbering and colliding with one another in a frenzy of incompetency. People from the street outside flocked into the garden that they might behold the spectacle. Next came a troupe of firemen. They immediately proceeded to stage a play that the Fire Demon's mind might be diverted from the flames. And then for lack of interest, the fire would flicker out. But their efforts were in vain. The flames continued to mount upward. The crackling of the dried rafters was almost like the laughter of evil spirits. No one thought for a moment of trying to extinguish the fire with water. Had they done so, they would have laughed the idea aside as a futile gesture. And still the Amah stood close by the weird scene and grew warm at last.

THUS Dien Daung and his purple lady passed from that garden, never to return. Their going caused as little ripple as parched autumn leaves swept away by the wind. Yu Lon felt no great grief at Dien Daung's departure. From her life he had already been blotted out. Now for her there was temporarily only the fragrance of the garden, the cool breeze of evening, and the exquisite voice of the fisherman softly chanting "The Song of the Indian Night."

Through her blindness she had gained vision. Now she could see on a spiritual plane. She was only blind to slag and dross. The greatest things in the universe were unaltered. She was not blind to poetry and music. Neither was she blind to love. Jui Vung was not old. He could not be old, for he was ageless. He was music, beauty and love. He brought youth to everything he touched. Wherever he passed, he left an indefinable spiritual beauty in his path. Man to be supremely happy must learn to throw off the yoke of years. There is no such thing as growing old. Compared to the age of the world, man is everlastingly young.

In the calm of the azure nights, the fisherman held her in his arms down by the water's edge. The Milky Way like a milky river swept out through the cold night sky. The moon, a silver stallion, leaped across the blue meadows in quest of romance. Everything in the universe was restlessly moving onward, searching for something.

The fisherman held Yu Lon closely in his arms. It was as though a gnarled matted oak were wooing a flower. But Yu Lon thrilled at his touch. She asked nothing more than to give herself utterly to Jui Vung. Softly, softly he was singing "The Song of the Indian Night," the eternal love song of the ages.

Thus in that Chinese garden, love bridged the years, and made them of an age at last, even as the burning of her enemies had brought warmth to the cold body of the Amah.

Shaykh Ahmad and the Pious Companions

By E. HOFFMANN PRICE

A weird tale of the Sultan Shams ud Din and how he was taken from the Hall of Illusions by the Darwish Ismeddin

AS SIR JOHN LINDSAY approached the Isfayan Gate, he saw sitting there in the dust a hunchback whose tattered *djellab* and decrepit turban were grimier than his hands and matted beard. His left eye glared fiercely at Sir John. The other, or rather, the lack of the other, was masked by a patch.

Sir John shuddered at the thought of the heavy purses of golden *mohurs* he had in the past three days vainly tossed to the beggars of Bir el Asad; but on the principle of throwing in the tail with the hide, there would be no virtue in ignoring this especially villainous fellow at the city gate. And besides, this one might as well be Ismeddin as any of the others he might in his search encounter, so he tossed him a *mohur*, which tinkled against the side of the bowl the beggar clutched in his grimy talon, and came to rest among the disreputable scraps of food and copper coins the day's begging had netted.

Sir John knew that a beggar thanks Allah, and not the giver of alms. But instead of thanks to any one——

"*La anahu 'llahu!*" enunciated the beggar very clearly. "May God not bless him!" And then he sonorously intoned, "*I betake me to the Lord of the Daybreak for refuge against the mischiefs of Creation!*"

As he spoke, the beggar picked the coin from its nest of fragments of *khubz* and grains of rice, and flipped it spinning into the dust across the street.

And by those signs Sir John knew that his quest was ended.

"Old man," he said, "call on me this evening at the Residency."

The beggar's left eyebrow rose in a saracenic arch. He almost replied, then thought better of it.

Sir John wheeled his horse about, and returned to his headquarters to contemplate anew the diverse problems of the Resident in Bir el Asad, capital of the tiny, turbulent sultanate of that same name.

There was the ticklish task of preserving the neutrality of the sultanate: a status that would be upset overnight by a hot-headed sultan riding out with a detachment of the Guard to exact a blood indemnity from the hill tribes just across the border, who were subjects of a Power that coveted the rich mineral deposits now being worked in Bir el Asad by a British syndicate.

And then, of course, he had in public to address the sultan as "Majesty," and in private explain very clearly that while a reasonable number of hangings, and beheadings, and executions by firing squad would be acceptable in the course of justice, the gory, picturesque sentences so dear to the former sultan were decidedly *de trop*. Bir el Asad, in a word, was to become enlightened as rapidly as possible, and weaned away from its sanguinary spectacular barbarities and antique customs.

694

"The Sultan charged down the avenue."

Therefore when Maqsoud succeeded to the throne, Sir John anticipated the end of these trying encounters which had marked his dealings with Maqsoud's predecessor and uncle, Shams ud Din, the tempestuous son of the Old Tiger, who considered a throne as a symbol, and as an actual seat preferred the back of a horse. And thus it was that one night, after a stormy encounter with the Resident, Shams ud Din literally vanished without a trace, and when Maqsoud on the following day was proclaimed Sword of the Faith and Lion of the Desert, the Resident saw no reason for inquiring into the disappearance of the trouble-maker.

"Since there is no evidence of assassination . . . no *corpus delicti*, so to speak,"
reflected Sir John, "comment certainly isn't called for."

And like the wise Resident that he was, Sir John reported that Shams ud Din had abdicated; for well enough, reflected Sir John, had best be let alone.

Thus for a whole year: and then Sir John sensed, with the sixth sense inherent in all good Residents, that all was not well in Bir el Asad. He couldn't report that he smelled trouble. Residents are not supposed to have olfactory nerves, except strictly in private. Yet he knew that if something was not done about it, soon, it would be too late to do anything.

The concessions would be sacked and burned, a holy war proclaimed . . . and after the machine-guns and mountain batteries had had their say, a new Resident would be appointed, with instructions to avoid Sir John's errors.

One couldn't, for instance, report that lean old men with scar-seamed faces sat in the *souk*, interminably smoking their fuming, bubbling *narghilehs* and muttering of the great days of Shams ud Din, and his father before him. Reminiscence is no crime. . . .

Neither could one demand reprisals because when the Resident went abroad in the city, those same ancient, leather-faced ruffians . . . the pious Companions of the Old Tiger . . . ceased for a moment their interminable smoking, and spat with ceremonious ostentation at the Resident's shadow as it passed them.

And then, the Companions would at times be inclined to theological discussion . . . like all pious Muslimeen . . . "Ya 'Umar!" they would ejaculate betimes, invoking the sainted Omar, the conqueror and standard-bearer of the Faith. Only . . . when the Resident passed by . . . they mispronounced 'Umar in a curious way . . . the Arabic language has odd turns . . . so that it sounded strangely like "Ya humar!" And shaded off to a delicate suggestion of "Ya himar!"

Which was yet again something else. Though Sir John couldn't prove that it was he whom the pious companions were calling a jackass.

"A DISREPUTABLE beggar seeks audience of the Presence," announced Sir John's *khadim* that evening. "Shall I flog him, or give him a *dirhem?*"

"Neither. Admit him," directed Sir John.

"I am Ismeddin!" proclaimed the beggar as he strode to the center of the carpet. "You were pleased to summon me."

"His late majesty," began Sir John,

"often spoke of Ismeddin the Darwish; but——"

"But he said nothing," interrupted the beggar, "of a hunchback or a missing eye?"

"Exactly," assented Sir John.

"*Wallahi!* And that also can be explained!"

With a swift gesture he reached into his *djellab*, right hand over left shoulder; twisted his deformed back; shrugged his shoulders, and bent forward — and suddenly straightened, erect as a spear, clutching in his fist the lacing loops of an embroidered Shirazi saddle-bag, which he tossed at the feet of the Resident. Then he snatched from his right eye the patch that had concealed it, and looked Sir John full in the face: no beggar, but a lean, hard-bitten fighting man whose dingy rags were but the expression of an eccentric whim.

"My word!" exclaimed Sir John, as he regarded the bird of prey before him. "That was fast work. In another move you'd be captain of the sultan's guard."

"Excellency," confessed Ismeddin, "I have numerous talents."

"Then test them on this," challenged Sir John. "There were four black slaves in the Sultan Maqsoud's garden—four mute slaves who once served Shams ud Din. One of them was drawing on the sand, which was called to my attention by a pebble that another tossed, striking the leg of my boot. The third touched his lips with his forefinger. And the fourth pointed at what the first had traced on the sand. Then His Majesty strolled down the path toward the fountain to meet me: and he saw also.

"Since that day, one has not seen any of those four black mutes," concluded Sir John.

Ismeddin made a significant, swift motion with his hands: such as one might make in drawing snugly about some one's throat a hard-spun cord with a running noose.

"Quite," agreed Sir John.

"And what," queried Ismeddin, "might that slave have marked on the sand? Good Arabic or Persian, which Your Excellency could have read?"

"Neither," replied Sir John. "He had drawn a picture."

"*Subhan 'ullah!*" ejaculated Ismeddin. "God alone is Wise, All-Knowing!"

"It was a building," replied Sir John to the implied question, "whose domes and towers resembled none in Bir el Asad or in any other place I have ever seen."

"And was that all?" queried Ismeddin.

"No. There were three figures: a man standing, with a sword in his hand; a man who sat; and beside him who stood, there was a woman. All drawn like a schoolboy might scribble on a wall. A circle for a head, and straight strokes for trunk and limbs."

"Which proves to Your Excellency that Shams ud Din is living in some noteworthy house which has curious domes and towers?"

"Rather," amended Sir John, "that His Majesty disposed of four black mutes lest they draw more pictures."

"Therefore," resumed Ismeddin, "your Excellency was pleased to make a lavish alms-giving. For the sake of marks on the sand . . ."

"I learned," explained the Resident, "that Ismeddin the Darwish would do such and such when one tossed him a coin. And further, that Ismeddin was in Bir el Asad, and could be identified by the curious thing he would do with a gold piece."

"*Aywah!*" assented Ismeddin. "I knew that my head was not worth seven hundred odd *mohurs* to you; so that at the end of three days of Your Excellency's

lavishness, I was fairly certain—though God alone is Wise, All-Knowing—that you wanted me to serve you, rather than vengeance. How therefore may I serve Your Excellency?"

"You must prevail upon Shams ud Din to return to his throne."

"It is curious," mused the Darwish, "how the noble British government wishes the Son of the Old Tiger to return . . ." And then, to Sir John: "Since Shams ud Din left of his own desire, might he not also elect to remain where he is? Why should he wish to return, seeing that the lordly estate of kings is departed? The noble British government —may it endure forever!—thwarted his vengeances, and frustrated his lavishness. He proposed to build a Peacock Throne like that of his ancestor. Your Excellency reminded him that Shah Jahan had done that too perfectly for repetition. And there was talk of roads, and schools, and hospitals to be built instead.

"Shams ud Din therefore could not keep his word to the Companions of the Old Tiger, they who had for years given him their share of plunder to be hoarded until their Sultan had amassed enough to build a throne like that of Shah Jahan. . . .

"*Aywallahi!* And made of him an old woman, by thwarting his stern reprisal against his kinsmen, the robbers from the hills. . . .

"And then his nephew Maqsoud—may God not bless him!—fired at him from a minaret of the mosque, and missed. Whereat Shams ud Din took one vengeance which your Excellency did not thwart: he sentenced Maqsoud to occupy the throne he coveted, knowing that in these evil days a throne is a damnation devised by Satan the Stoned.

"*Aywah! Aywah! Aywah! I betake me to the Lord of the Daybreak for refuge against the envier when he envieth!*" intoned Ismeddin. And then he resumed: "Shams ud Din in his weariness found solace in a vengeance, and in a jest; for where he is, he spends his time pleasantly, and contemplates Maqsoud's dancing to the tunes piped by him who stands behind the throne."

"But I say," protested Sir John, "really, now, this is most unusual. Of course, I may have made a tactless request of His Majesty——"

"And now, Excellency, you command me to entice Shams ud Din back to this madhouse. What inducement am I to offer? To offer him a throne would be like offering me a gold piece. . . ."

The Darwish picked up the saddle-bags at Sir John's feet, and therefrom a pouch which he thrust into Sir John's hands.

"Excellency, speaking of gold pieces . . . here are your *mohurs*. Be pleased to count them."

And shouldering his saddle-bags, Ismeddin stalked from the Presence.

Sir John opened the pouch, and examined half a dozen of the coins picked at random: and saw that each was of the same minting as those he had drawn to toss to the beggars.

"Strike me blind! Salvaging seven hundred *mohurs* from the beggars of this town—the very selfsame coins. . . ."

Sir John smelled trouble no less than before.

"That beggar Shams ud Din is causing more trouble in his hole in the ground than he ever did on his throne," pondered the Resident sourly. "And"—he glanced again at the bag of *mohurs*— "that old highwayman of an Ismeddin could start a holy war over night—if there isn't a *jihad* well under way already . . ."

Sir John then and there dispatched a courier to Dar es Suyoof, and began drawing up a detailed report. And as he wrote, there came from afar the persistent, barely audible thump-thump-thump of kettledrums.

"Hell to pay in the hills," muttered Sir John. "Abd ur Rahman's at it again. . . ."

A second courier, bearing a copy of the message carried by the first, set out for Dar es Suyoof by a route different from the first. With luck, at least one of the couriers could get through.

"*LAILU wa khailu wa baida'u tarifuni*," chanted Shams ud Din as with slow, deft strokes he whetted the blade of his simitar. "*Night, and the horses, and the desert know me. . . .*"

But Shams ud Din had become sultan of the shadows: and neither horses nor the desert knew him any more. He looked up from the depths of the pit at the tiny patch of moonlit sky, no larger than a silver dirhem, then glanced at the great staircase that, spiralling around the walls of the pit, led to the courtyard far above.

Shams ud Din tried the edge of his simitar, and remembered that he had as little need of sharpening a blade as he had opportunity of dulling one. Whereupon Shams ud Din who had been sultan of Bir el Asad sheathed his simitar and strode down a passageway that led deviously winding from the pit to the great hall where the Presence sat endlessly dreaming.

The passage opened into a chamber whose vaulted ceiling swelled broad and high. Planets, and a new moon slim as a simitar blade marched across the curved, abysmal blueness. Stars arranged in unheard-of constellations glittered frostily. And as he had always done on entering the vault, Shams ud Din paused a moment to wonder if the prodigious dome above him was the firmament of another world, or whether it also was illusion.

Then Shams ud Din strode across the expanse of tiled floor and approached the foot of the dais at the further extremity of the vault, where sat, cross-legged, the white-bearded Lord of Illusion, the Presence that dominated the shadow world in which Shams ud Din had betaken himself for refuge against the vanity of thrones, and the envy of the envious.

The Presence had always sat thus: head bowed so that should he ever open his eyes and awaken from his dream, he would be looking into the great rock crystal globe which hung suspended from a slim golden chain whose other end was fastened to the curved ceiling of the vault.

In the beginning it had all seemed preposterous, this talk of the Lord of Illusion; but Bint el Kafir was lovelier even than the women of Tcherkess and Gurjestan, so that, no reasonable person could have taken exception to some of her pagan fancies.

"It is all very simple, *sidi!*" she would explain. "You have but to kneel on this small rug at the foot of the dais, and eat but three of these dried plums. And then fix your eyes on that globe of crystal, while I make gestures . . . thus. . . . And then you will see in the crystal some of his dream.

"Whatever he dreams is truth made manifest; for the world is but his illusion, and when he awakes from his sleep, there will be neither heaven nor earth, but only an emptiness whereof he will create whatever new worlds he fancies.

"Even as your own dreams when you awaken from them become nothing and less than nothing, and lose the brief span of life which your fancy gave them, so likewise will we, the creatures of his dream, vanish at his awakening . . . this

is the Law of Illusion, and he is the Lord of Illusion and creator of gods and angels, djinn and men. . . ."

In the beginning it had been a pre-posterous, pleasing game, this mummery of eating three dried plums . . . and watching the great globe whirl and throb and glow and enlarge until it blotted out even the ancient Dreamer, and the abysmal, blue vault with its strange constellations . . . and hearing Bint el Kafir chanting as from a great distance, in rippling, purring voice . . . and then seeing emerge from the shifting opalescence the Audience Hall at Bir el Asad . . . where Maqsoud published from the throne what the Resident whispered in his ear. . . . And once the ritual of illusion had revealed the garden of the palace at Bir el Asad . . . Maqsoud was walking by moonlight . . . some one whose nude, oiled body gleamed as he passed stealthily and swiftly across the lighted spaces between clusters of shrubbery was stalking Maqsoud . . . stalking him until he should pass close enough for the gurgle and tinkle of the spraying fountain to mask the sound of the last three paces to be covered before the slayer would be upon the slain. . . .

Maqsoud whirled, drew his revolver, and fired thrice. . . .

And Shams ud Din was glad that Maqsoud had escaped; for the vengeance was in seeing Maqsoud glancing from time to time over his shoulder, and the jest was knowing that Maqsoud had envied Shams ud Din.

At first Shams ud Din had been critical.

"It is curious," he observed, "that some one should stalk Maqsoud exactly as I myself was once stalked. And that he should fire thrice, and miss . . . just as I fired thrice——"

"Nonsense!" laughed the girl, as she poured another glass of Shirazi wine, and with silver tongs trimmed the fire of the *narghileh.* "Why shouldn't the dream of the Lord of Illusion betimes repeat itself? *Ya amir,* has there then been such limitless variety in your own fancies? And now put aside the stem of that everlasting pipe and see if kissing me once would poison you. . . ."

And thus and thus . . . so that in the end, Shams ud Din could think of nothing in the world more reasonable than that *"all this world and its thrones and powers and people are the creatures of some high god's dream; so that when He awakes from his sleep, we the creatures of his dream will vanish into a nothingness from which in his next dream he will create worlds anew."*

"She is as young as this morning's dawn, and as old as the first sunset," Shams ud Din would muse. "And there are none like her, not even in Gurjestan. . . ."

Whereat he would settle back among his cushions, strike his hands thrice together, and call, *"Ya Bint el Kafir! 'Atîni qahawat!*

"Sam 'an wa tâ 'atan, ya sidi!"

And as the girl with ringing strokes of a brazen pestle crushed the roasted beans of Harari coffee in a brazen mortar, Shams ud Din would sink further back among his cushions and meditate on the follies of sultans on their thrones; so that in the end, when Shams ud Din at times thought of night, and the horses, and the desert, they were illusion, while that which surrounded him now was reality.

NEVERTHELESS, it was good to see Ismeddin once more, and hear his salutation as he entered the Hall of Illusion.

Shams ud Din returned the peace, uncoiled from his wrist the tube of his *narghileh,* and offered Ismeddin the jade mouthpiece.

"Welcome, Ismeddin! And what are you doing in this devil-haunted ruin of a devil-built city?"

"I come from one even more devil-haunted, *ya sidi!"* grinned the ancient darwish as he seated himself on a corner of the Sultan's rug and accepted the stem of the *narghileh.*

"And what news of my pious nephew, Maqsoud? The last time I saw him, some one had just dropped a sizable block of stone from the roof of the palace just as he was stepping out into the courtyard. It barely missed him. Now he glances overhead from time to time, as well as over his shoulder——"

"You *saw?"* interrupted Ismeddin.

"Aywallahi!" asserted Shams ud Din. "In the globe of illusion."

"Even so," agreed Ismeddin. "I had forgotten for the moment."

"Strange," resumed Shams ud Din. "That very same thing happened to me. A block of limestone some one had pried loose from the coping. Still, there is after all not such a variety of things to make one's existence a nightmare. . . . And Maqsoud envied me!"

Ismeddin was stroking his long white beard and muttering something to himself.

"What was that, old friend?" queried Shams ud Din.

"Nothing at all, *sidi.* Merely an old man's fancy. . . ." And then, to himself, "Curious I didn't hear of it. . . ."

The *narghileh* purred gently for a matter of several minutes. And then Ismeddin: *"sidi,* Abd ur Rahman and a troop of his cutthroats came down from the mountains and raided Djebel Dukhan. Turned it inside out and then set fire to whatever was too heavy to carry off."

"There is neither might nor majesty save in Allah, the Merciful, the Compassionate," observed Shams ud Din after a moment's reflection.

"And Maqsoud turned out all but a handful of the Guard, with old Zaid in command. He arrived just as Djebel Dukhan was well aflame and crackling merrily. There was some pretty fighting. And just as Zaid was forming his troops to take up the pursuit, along came a courier from the Resident, ordering him in the name of the Sultan to refrain from crossing the border after the raiders——"

"And what did Zaid do?" interrupted Shams ud Din.

"*Sidi;*" replied Ismeddin, "you know Zaid as well as I do. There will be the devil to pay when the Resident's courier returns with Zaid's answer. And Maqsoud will fancy that his throne is an ant-heap."

"*Wallahi!*" exclaimed Shams ud Din. "But that infidel Sir John serves some purpose after all."

"And now, my lord," resumed Ismeddin, "it is high time for you to return to Bir el Asad——"

"What? I return to—Allah and by Allah and again by Allah!" swore the Sultan. "I, return to that madhouse?"

"Yes. Return at once to Bir el Asad," reiterated Ismeddin. "For the Guard had scarcely been an hour on the march to Djebel Dukhan when an old man— Shaykh Ahmad, they called him—arose from his pipe and coffee and addressed the crowd in the *souk. Mashallah!* What a speech!"

"And what was he talking about?" queried Shams ud Din.

"About the Old Tiger, your father, on whom be peace and prayer! And about your own self, *sidi.* But he didn't finish his speech. About the time he started discussing Maqsoud and the Resident, the pious Companions took things in hand, and rioting broke out.

"When I left Bir el Asad, they had burned and looted the *souk,* and one wing of the palace, and—God is Wise, All-Knowing—having from somewhere gotten hold of a few machine-guns, were riddling everything in sight."

"Stout fellows," observed Shams ud Din. "But what have I to do with all this playfulness?"

"Just this, my lord: when Zaid and the Guard return, Maqsoud will have to restore order, or the Resident will have him deposed. There will be a good deal of street fighting, and in the end, a general slaughter. And the ringleaders will of course face a firing squad to satisfy British justice."

"And again," demanded Shams ud Din, "what has that to do with me? What is it to me what happens in that den of madmen? In the end, they and Maqsoud will exterminate each other, and the Resident will perish in the stench, and—*el hamdu lilahi!*—I will be bothered with no more tales about Bir el Asad."

The sultan paused, and grinned sourly.

"Now by Allah and by Abaddon!" shouted Ismeddin as he thrust aside the *narghileh* and leaped to his feet. "You, the son of the Old Tiger, stand by and see the Companions of the Old Tiger cut to pieces——"

"Foolishness!" scoffed Shams ud Din. "Zaid and the Guard will join the rioters, and then there will be great days in town."

"It is you who are foolish, oh, mockery of a prince!" raged Ismeddin. "The Resident will call in *Feringhi* troops to outnumber them ten to one. And in the end, the ringleaders—stout fellows who followed your father out of the hills—will face a squad of British rifles.

"This jest and vengeance of yours goes too far! Shams ud Din—Sun of the Faith, in total eclipse—all for vengeance and weariness . . . wherefore this weariness? . . . *The* Lord, the Amir Timur—did he perahps spend fifty years in the saddle, all fresh and unwearied? The Old Tiger your father—did he forsake his Companions for the sake of treason which lurked in every corner? For Maqsoud to be the butt of your jest and the theme of your vengeance—very good. But for the white-haired companions—oh, father of many little pigs, what manner of prince are you?"

Shams ud Din turned the color of an old saddle, and half unsheathed his simitar.

"What have you to do with swords, *ya aj002?*" mocked the darwish. "Old woman—fling your turban into the dust, and stay here to play with your Gurjestani dancing girl——"

Shams ud Din's blade clanged back into its scabbard.

"You are right, Ismeddin. I will go, and face the Feringhi rifles with those white-haired old ruffians."

"My lord," replied Ismeddin, "rather than die like a man, go out and live like a man. If you appear, and restore order, the Resident will not demand reprisals. And you will sit more securely on your throne than before."

"Done, by Allah, and by my Beard! And you shall be my chief *wazir*——"

"Not I," protested Ismeddin. "Not until the wind which has whitened my beard ends by blowing away my brains, *ya amir!*"

Ismeddin turned toward the passage that led to the pit, and thence to the court-yard, far above.

Then came a whirring, and a clang, and a sinister click: and the exit was closed by a grille-work of bronze.

There was a tinkling of anklets, and the poison sweetness of an overwhelming perfume, and the poison sweetness of a woman's mocking laugh.

THEY turned from the barred passage, and faced Bint el Kafir, resplendent in smoldering rubies and cool, unblinking sapphires, and wearing the tall, curiously wrought head-dress she wore whenever one of the kings, her lovers, was sentenced to leave the Presence and join the circle of those who sat on small pedestals in the courtyard far above: for such was the tradition from ancient times.

"Such unceremonious leave-taking, Shams ud Din," she purred. "You have tired of your jest and your vengeance, and now you seek to evade the bargain, and your pedestal, and your everlasting watch in the courtyard. And without even bothering to bid me farewell."

And then, to Ismeddin: "Oh, darwish, spare yourself the trouble of wrenching at those bars! Fifty years ago, you might —but no, not even then. They were drawn and hammered by cunning smiths——"

Ismeddin ignored her mockery and frantically wrenched at the bars. If but one would yield, a man as lean as he or Shams ud Din could squeeze through.

"It's no use, Ismeddin," said the Sultan. "Ten men couldn't break those bars." And then to the girl: "It is not for myself that I am leaving. My people need me. A foolish, rattle-brained people. A horde of cutthroats they are . . . pork-eaters, wine-bibbers, and heretics. But they are the Companions of the Old Tiger. Therefore open that door. Not for my sake, but for the obligation of an *amir* to his people."

"Flames and damnation!" stormed Ismeddin, still vainly wrenching at the bars. "Hear Shams ud Din asking favors of a woman! *Wallahi! Billahi! Yallahi!*"

"Very noble, Shams ud Din," agreed the girl.

She paused to adjust the tall, quaintly wrought head-dress that towered above the twining midnight of her hair. And her smile became even sweeter, and her voice purred more softly.

"Very noble, Shams ud Din. But the Lord of Illusion has dreamed otherwise for you. Nor will I whisper anything to change his dream. Think well, you prince of a state that could be encircled by a beggar's loincloth tied to a scholar's turban . . . what is it to the Lord of Illusion if a handful of your father's followers face a firing squad each one of them merited forty years ago . . . is that to interrupt his dream and make him change its course?"

She turned to the solemn, sleeping Lord of Illusion.

"More than high god, you once dreamed that a top-heavy empire collapsed, and Dhoul Karnayn with his long spears marched resistlessly to fulfil your fancy. Once your fancy turned to slaughter, and Genghis Khan swept over the earth with his Golden Horde, and what slaughter the Mighty Manslayer made! Oh, Lord Dreamer, will you change this fellow's fate that he may delay for a few years the just doom of the pious companions of his pious father?"

"And so," said Shams ud Din, "I can not serve my people?"

"Thou hast said," affirmed the girl. "The Amir Timur . . . *the* Lord . . . he who succeeded in everything he attempted . . . failed when he sought to leave me. And marched to his place in the courtyard, for he was bound by a strong doom that neither gods nor men can evade, for whatever the Dreamer dreams, that moment becomes fate made manifest."

So saying, she began to make curious passes and gestures, and chanted in ca-denced syllables of a doom that none had ever evaded.

Ismeddin stepped back from the unshaken bars. Then he drew his simitar, and tried its edge, and eyed for a moment the slim, curved blade and the veined markings that banded it, ladder-like.

"They call you Ladder to Heaven . . . now if it please Allah——"

The darwish assaulted the grille-work.

"You have split stout skulls and their vain helmets, *ya sayf!*" he shouted as the blade rang clear against the bars. "Now shear again! *Ya sayf!* Cut deep!"

And through the clang of steel, Ismeddin heard the voice of Bint el Kafir purring like throbbing music from a great distance:

"Shams ud Din, you are worthy of your predecessors . . . and I will be very lonely as I wait for another king, your equal . . . I will often think of you up there on your pedestal, Shams ud Din . . . it is wise and excellent to yield to your fate, Shams ud Din . . ."

Then Ismeddin heard the girl chanting in a strange, rippling language such as he had never heard before; and a great fear seized Ismeddin.

"Once more, *ya sayf!*" he shouted to drown that deadly chant.

The last stroke. He flung his sword ringing to the tiles, gripped the bar, wrenched it until its sheared end touched the floor, and turned to face the Sultan.

Shams ud Din stood staring fixedly into the great crystal globe of illusion. His head nodded to the cadence of the girl's silky voice as she chanted in that ancient tongue, and stroked his cheeks with weaving gestures. His features were immobile——

"In the great name of Allah I take refuge from Satan the Damned!" intoned Ismeddin in a voice that would carry across a battlefield. "Shams ud Din! Wake up!"

He could as well have whispered. And then the globe of illusion, suspended from its golden chain, began rotating; pulsing, glowing like a ball of cold, sinister fire.

In another moment the Sultan would have crossed the Border.

Ismeddin drew the Sultan's simitar from its scabbard.

"To the Lord of the Daybreak I betake me for refuge——"

The blade flamed out and clipped the golden chain. The globe of illusion crashed and splintered against the tiles.

The girl's scream followed them up the winding stairs as Ismeddin half carried, half dragged Shams ud Din after him.

"Wallahi!" gasped Ismeddin as he reached the courtyard. "The world, it seems, has not yet vanished, in spite of my cracking the crystal and the Dreamer's dream which he was dreaming."

Then he shook Shams ud Din vigorously.

"To horse, *ya amir!* In another second you would have been petrified."

He rolled the Sultan into the saddle, mounted his own beast, and led the way, clattering down the stone-paved avenue leading out of the ruined citadel and into the jungle.

"It seems," began Shams ud Din at last, regaining some command of himself, "that for the figment of some one's dream, I am still passably substantial. I heard you, but I couldn't answer. I tried to tell you—Allah! What *did* I try to tell you? . . . In another instant it would have been too late. I'm chilled through, and my flesh is still about half stone. Ismeddin, what's the secret? It's more than the doings of a juggler in the *souk* or a faquir from Hindustan. . . ."

The sultan shivered.

"Who knows?" countered Ismeddin.

"Unless it might be that Bint el Kafir fed you too many of those strange-tasting dried plums, and whispered too often in your ear as you slept."

Then, as they emerged from the jungle, Ismeddin set spurs to his horse, and followed by Shams ud Din, galloped eastward toward Bir el Asad.

SHAMS UD DIN and the darwish reined in their foaming horses at the Isfayan Gate, where, looking down the broad avenue toward the palace and the Residency, they commanded a full view of the scene whose red glow on the sky had served them as a beacon during the last hour of their ride to Bir el Asad.

Great slabs of paving had been torn up and piled to form barricades to block the streets leading to the square in front of the palace. The sultry glow of the *souk*, now in smoldering ruins, was seconded by the bright flames that were lapping up Harat ul 'Ajemi. The roar of muzzle-loaders and the shouts of the besiegers all along the line was accented by the intermittent rattle of a pair of machine-guns nested at the further flank. Spurts of flame from windows and the parapet of the palace showed that some of Maqsoud's handful of troops were loyal. Bullets ricocheted from the façade of the palace, and whined away into the darkness.

A rocket serpentined from the courtyard of the palace, and burst high overhead. A green and two red stars hung in the darkness for a few moments, and vanished. Then from a great distance came the silvery whisper of a bugle.

"Feringhi horse!" exclaimed Ismeddin. "That call is the signal to take up the gallop. A large outfit, or they wouldn't use bugle signals. The Resident's couriers must have wormed their way through Abd ur Rahman's outposts. Now get busy before the Resident knows relief is on the way."

O. S.—**8**

From within the palace came the brazen, reverberant note of a great gong whose sonorous clang drowned the shouting and musketry and the kettledrums of the besiegers.

"Maqsoud calling for a parley," declared the darwish. "He didn't hear that bugle."

"Maqsoud had better keep his head behind the parapet," observed Shams ud Din. "Look! By Allah! It *is* Maqsoud!"

"Then stand fast, *sidi*," counselled Ismeddin. "His foolhardiness may serve us well enough."

Shouts and howls from the barricades. The besiegers accelerated their heavy, ragged volleys: a storm of one-ounce slugs kept the defenders under cover, knocked loose splinters of masonry that spoiled their aim.

"No, they didn't get Maqsoud," said Ismeddin. "He didn't drop; he ducked. Look! The Resident! Strolling down the parapet with his orderly and a flag of truce. The idiot! What do they know about flags of truce? . . . *Wallahi!* If they hit him, the whole British army will clean us out to the last man——"

The Sultan leaned forward in the saddle, spurred his weary horse, and charged down the avenue, straight toward the square and into the field of fire.

"Back, fool!" roared Ismeddin.

And then the darwish charged after Shams ud Din.

Sir John still rode up and down the parapet; but now he directed the fire of the defenders, seeing the futility of flags of truce.

Into the cross fire rode Shams ud Din, and after him clattered Ismeddin, blowing hoarse blasts on a ram's horn.

"Cease firing, oh sons of pigs!" shouted Shams ud Din as he reined his horse back to his haunches and wheeled to the right to face the besiegers.

"Come out from behind that barricade,

O. S.—**9**

oh eaters of pork! Allah and by Allah, and again by Allah!" raged Shams ud Din. "I'll have every last man of you flayed alive and crucified——"

The firing in front of him ceased; and then, all along the line it died out.

"*Mashallah!* Shams ud Din——"

"Yes, by God! He *will* crucify us all——"

"*There* is an amir for you!"

"He will flay us alive!"

"Just like his father——"

"May Allah be pleased with him!"

And tossing their weapons ahead of them, the rioters clambered over the barricade, noisily acclaiming the son of their old chief.

Shams ud Din very sternly regarded his father's white-bearded companions as they knelt in the square about his horse's hoofs.

"Oh, crack-brains! Oh dogs, and sons of dogs! You who burn my city the moment my back is turned! Back to your houses while I deal with that infidel up there on the wall. And as for you——"

Shams ud Din wheeled his horse about, and followed by Ismeddin, rode toward the entrance of the palace.

"Oh, excellent prince!"

"He is our father and our grandfather!"

"He will forgive us——"

And the Companions adjourned, content with a rich, riotous day resurrected from the limbo of the past, and confident that the wrath of their suddenly materialized sultan would not demand an unreasonable number of beheadings and impalements.

"*SIDI*," announced Ismeddin as he stalked into the Sultan's private audience hall, where he was receiving the jewellers detailed to erect the long-planned Peacock Throne, "with your permission I am setting out for Herat in the morning."

The jewellers withdrew at the Sultan's gesture of dismissal.

"And so I can't persuade you to quit robbing caravans, and to stay here as my chief *wazir?*"

"*Sidi,* a *wazir* must appear at court in rich dress, and an elegant turban, and wear a curled beard, as befits the dignity of his office."

"Well," said the Sultan, "doubtless you would miss that ragged *djellab* which was last washed in the reign of my saintly grandfather. Still——"

"No, my lord," protested Ismeddin.

"In court dress I would bear a startling semblance to the venerable Shaykh Ahmad, and the noble British government would know more than it should."

"Shaykh Ahmad?" queried the Sultan.

"Yes, by your head and by your beard, *ya sidi!* Shaykh Ahmad, who started the rioting on the *souk.* And now that Maqsoud's head adorns the Isfayan Gate, and you will soon adorn the Peacock Throne, I must keep my engagement in Herat."

With a ceremonious bow, Ismeddin left the Presence.

"May Allah preserve Herat!" muttered the Sultan, as he clapped his hands to summon the jewellers.

YUNG CHI

By HUNG LONG TOM

Yung Chi had heard a legend
Of a chest, heaped high
With beauty and with wealth,
Buried within the walls of old Peking.
The legend ruled his life.
He toiled for years,
Sweated and toiled
Nor ever ceased to dig,
Searching for beauty,
While above him
Pink dawns and sunsets,
Purple splendor rolled
And stars that glowed
Like flowers in a field.
Above him was the glory
Of the sky. More beauty
Than a thousand casks
Might hold.

At the Fortunate Frog

By COUTTS BRISBANE

How Doctor Fung Lee matched wits against the other physicians
of Sen Yang, who were in a conspiracy to bring about his death

THE last of the long line of patients had departed, writhing but relieved. Doctor Fung Lee sat himself down on the low couch that had served all morning as operating-table, lit the pipe which his servant Sung presented to him with the cautery iron which had done yeoman service, and puffing a cloud of smoke, permitted himself to smile.

That morning at daybreak he had opened his clinic for the first time in his own house, after years spent as an itinerant practitioner proclaiming his merits in every market-place of the great province of Honan.

He had done well. Already he had thought of settling down in some large city, when a stroke of fortune had trebled his capital and he no longer hesitated.

He had purchased a small but well situated house in the Street of the Evening Star, in Sen Yang, hired a hairy, two-humped camel and sent it forth through the crowded city ways, led by his faithful ex-barrowman, Sung, to announce his arrival.

There was no false modesty about the advertisement. Large placards hung on either side of the beast proclaimed in red letters:

"Doctor Fung Lee, Mighty Healer of bodies, is come to live among you, in the house of the Fortunate Frog, in Evening Star Street. Doctor Fung Lee, Healer of Mandarins, the Best Doctor in the World. All Diseases cured. Pain abolished. Doctor Fung Lee, who formerly sat in the market-place, receives the sick at the sign of the Fortunate Frog, or heals the incurable in their own homes.

"Doctor Fung Lee, the Greatest Doctor in the World, is in Evening Star Street at the sign of the Fortunate Frog. He cures Everything!"

And since Doctor Fung Lee was already widely known as a successful if somewhat drastic dealer with human infirmities, business had started with sunrise. He had reason to smile.

"We begin well, Sung!" he observed. "And we will do better. The Fortunate Frog is well named."

"Frogs become the prey of serpents," murmured Sung. "There are three in Sen Yang who will willingly attempt to seat you in the saddle of the Heaven-Aspiring Steed without unnecessary delay. I have already seen them observing the crowd at your door and their faces were as those of men who wear the wooden collar of torment."

"Doubtless you speak of my honorable brethren in the art of body-restoring? I have seen them before when we sat at the corner of the market-place. Twice they have endeavored to drive me away by the blows of hired men with clubs. But the people protected me. It will be the same again."

"The tiger may miss his spring at one who runs. The sleeping man is a sure prey," grunted Sung. "Also they now have time to consult together. Yet the chief of these men, the honorable Yat Foo, is elderly and rich. May this humble one suggest that soft words and a not inconsiderable present may incline his heart you-wards, or at the least move him to abstain from such actions as may end in my inconsiderable self having with great grief to arrange with an undertaker on your behalf?"

"Since he is the elder of the honorable brethren, etiquette plainly demands that I should call upon him," said Fung Lee softly. "And a bag of taels of superior silver and good weight would be a suitable indication of the reverence due to one far gone in years, even though he may have advanced into second childhood. I will go. You will go also, remaining at the door in an attitude of respect."

"And wearing beneath my coat a short sword of superior sharpness," agreed Sung. "I will fetch your horse that you may go with fitting dignity."

FOR near half a century, Doctor Yat Foo had practised in Sen Yang, so it was not surprizing that he had a fine house surrounded by a high wall and excellently designed garden, with several servants whose manners were polished as jade.

Doctor Fung Lee was conducted to an inner apartment, the windows of which looked upon the garden, and there left while the servant sought his master. Doctor Fung looked forth and beheld a sight entrancing even to one who had in his professional capacity seen many of the pearls adorning the yamens of wealthy merchants and great mandarins, for the maiden reclining by the fish pond far outshone them all in pulchritude and the modesty of the regard with which she returned Doctor Fung Lee's respectful yet adoring gaze.

Rising with a grace that recalled the rhythmic movements of a slim bamboo swayed by the breeze of morning, the maiden approached the window.

"Honorable sir, be not impatient if my revered father delays giving himself the ineffable pleasure of beholding your moon-like countenance," she said in a voice in which blended the sweetest notes of singing birds. "At this hour he permits himself to repose after the labors of the morning."

"I trust his sleep may be sound and prolonged so that I may the longer enjoy the delight of looking upon you and hearing words that are as the sounds of a lute of jade and gold," replied Doctor Fung. "This despicable person's only claim to consideration is that he belongs to the same profession as your revered and honorable progenitor, having practised it with not inconsiderable success about the province. Now he has ventured to establish himself in this city and so has come to pay his respects to the great Doctor Yat Foo. The name is Fung Lee, favorably known as a healer of mandarins."

At these last words, the maiden's countenance, of a peach-like smoothness and rotundity, which had so far exhibited only the degree of interest demanded by politeness to a not ill-looking stranger, became animated by curiosity and concern, for indeed the name of Fung Lee had been spoken in that house in terms of no kindliness.

"My revered father is well stricken in years. It may be that age has soured a once-benevolent disposition, yet he has permitted himself to speak of the honorable Doctor Fung Lee in terms such as might be employed by the High Ones in reprimanding an inferior insect," she said hesitatingly. "Would it not be well therefore to prepare yourself for a rebuff?"

"Do you, most marvelous blossom of the gardens of Paradise, share this inhospitable sentiment?" asked Fung Lee eagerly.

"I rejoice to talk to one so renowned as to cause the venerable one to break a jade vase of considerable value but unequalled ugliness and even to bestow hard words upon the humble person who addresses you," she replied, lowering her eyes as modesty required, but allowing a smile to uplift the corners of a mouth comparable only to the petals of a vermilion flower. "And this humble one ventures to assure Doctor Fung Lee that in the household of

Yat Foo she will remain his admiring friend."

"The house of the Fortunate Frog is lonely. It lacks a mistress. Is it possible that this lowly one might hope one day to adorn his hearth with a graceful shoot from the gnarled trunk of the venerable Yat Foo?" asked Fung. Practise with the more exacting tools of his profession had taught him to reach his objective with speed and precision.

"It is written that many things, though possible, are too often difficult of accomplishment," she murmured. "Yet to a person of such attainments as the honorable Doctor Fung Lee, such a transplantation might not be impossible. But now I must go. If it was known to the venerable and irascible one that I had talked with you, many blows from a heavy cane would be my portion."

"But I must see you again. I do not know your name!" said Fung Lee urgently.

"About the falling of night I will be in that summer house. And the name is Willow Leaf," whispered the girl and slipped softly out of sight.

A MOMENT later a servant, whose countenance having once encountered a sword, was destitute of a nose, appeared and in tones of dislike bade Doctor Fung Lee follow him to the presence of the master.

Doctor Yat Foo's person, despite a plenitude of good food, was of a meager habit, while his thin face, creased with many wrinkles, was distorted by malevolence as he glared at his visitor. Yet habit was strong and he could not refrain from making the usual gestures of courtesy. He bowed.

"This humble and despicable roof is honored by the presence of the learned and benevolent Doctor Fung Lee," he said. "To what happy cause may I at-tribute the delight of beholding his luminous and sagacious countenance?"

"To the desire of basking for a moment in the rays of wisdom emanating from the person of the world-famed Doctor Yat Foo and of hearing his mellifluous voice," replied Fung Lee. "Also, as a mark of the esteem in which I hold him, to lay at his feet this small token of regard."

Doctor Foo took the bag eagerly enough, weighed it speculatively, laid it beside him.

"It shall be expended in works of benevolence," he murmured. "Doubtless, my son, you are proceeding further northward in a day or so?"

"I had proposed to bask in the effulgence of the light cast upon Sen Yang by your learned self for a number of years only to be limited by the decree of the Rulers of the Upper Sphere," murmured Fung Lee. "I have thrown my good money away!" he thought.

"You reside in the house named the Fortunate Frog, I am told. That is a misfortune. The house is an unlucky one. Short is the span of those who dwell there," went on Yat Foo.

"I will consult an astrologer. Perhaps the luck may be made to change," suggested Fung Lee with a smile.

"I am something of an astrologer and I have read in the stars that the town of Sen Yang is unlucky for any one of the honorable house of Fung," replied Yat Foo in a voice of doom.

"Is it permitted to ask what form this ill luck will take?" asked Fung Lee, still smiling, though he had received notice to quit.

"The voice of the stars has spoken with no incertitude. Head and body batterings, slicing with swords and knives, and a funeral marred by the absence of a head from the honored remains are but too plainly indicated. Be warned, my son. In the fine province of Sze Chuan fortune awaits you. Seek it without delay."

"One hundred and five persons sought my aid this morning. Numerous others will undoubtedly arrive tomorrow, while I have received requests to visit several wealthy men in their own yamens. Shall I leave them to perish because the stars have spoken? Perhaps, oh venerated Yat Foo, your ears have mistaken the words. Have I your leave to withdraw my humble and despicable person from your honored roof?"

"Your going will be as the withdrawal of the sun. May your health continue to be excellent—yet I fear it will not," quoth Yat Foo and so bowed him out.

Escorted by the no-nosed servant, Doctor Fung Lee reached the street and the waiting Sung, mounted his horse and rode home through a rosy dream inspired not by the prospect of dissolution offered by Yat Foo's words but by the thought of presently seeing Yat Foo's daughter. He ordered a light repast, and having eaten, lay down to repose for a little before setting out to visit Yat Foo's garden.

Meanwhile, Yat Foo had summoned the other two old established doctors of Sen Yang, men of substance both, Doctor See Hop and Doctor Lu. Younger than Foo, they might be assumed to have a greater interest in suppressing competition before it could affect them adversely. Yat Foo came to the point with admirable—and unusual—brevity.

"This mangy dog, Fung Lee, who calls himself a healer, has been here. I told him that the climate of Sen Yang was unhealthful for him. He will not take the warning. If he remains, there are lean days for all of us; for the people, unmindful of what we have done for them in the past, flock to him. My man Chai can break a head very skilfully. The river will carry a body far."

"That is not the way!" said Doctor See Hop. "The fellow has great friends. He procured for one great lord the felicity of a son and another he has certainly cured of jaundice. Also, the mandarin of the province, Sun Lo Chi, is said to be about to visit us and he might be moved to make loud noises if a healer disappears, accompanied by questioning and slicings. Already Doctor Lu and I have considered the matter."

"Thus!" intoned Doctor Lu pompously, for he was a person of girth. "Let us stir up the people against him. Let a body be procured, one of a traveller who is a stranger. Let the body be bestowed in the outhouse of the house of Fung Lee. Then let an old woman—my sister will play the part, for she seldom stirs from my house and few know her—let her make an outcry, swearing that Fung Lee has slain the man to calcine his bones for medicine and that he is her sister's son. She shall make much outcry. The people will follow her to the garden of Fung Lee. There they will find the body. And because they are stupid and ignorant and there is good loot in Fung Lee's house, they will fall upon him. And perhaps in the riot, some one will deal Fung Lee a blow that will send him to the Upper Air without more ado. At least, no more people will crowd about his door for healing."

"Your words are wise," murmured Yat Foo. "I see but one difficulty. We have no body prepared, yet we should move swiftly before Sun Lo Chi comes to us."

"We have your headbreaker, Chai. Let him go forth in the dusk and make a body ready. Travellers are often late upon the road. Then let him take the body to Fung's garden and leave the rest to me—and the people."

"It is good!" agreed Yat Foo. "So it shall be. Now let us instruct Chai. He is stupid, but when once he understands he remembers."

SEN YANG had a wall. Once this wall had been strong and high, a protection against brigands and spoilers. But time and neglect, and the attentions of builders who found in it a quarry, had made many gaps in it, and though the gates were solemnly shut at sundown, belated travellers usually entered by the nearest hole.

Doctor Fung Lee had noted that Doctor Foo's garden backed against the town wall. He had also observed that though there was no gap just there, the upper tiers of stones had been removed, while cracks offered a ready foothold. As darkness fell he climbed into the garden and sought the summer house. Willow Leaf, clad in shimmering gray silk, gleamed in the obscurity.

"Flower of Paradise!" began Doctor Fung Lee. "Redolent garden of sweet herbs! Moon of———"

"Hush! At another time, honorable Doctor Fung Lee, I will listen to sweet words. But now listen to mine. Mischief is intended toward you. I do not know what, but Chai, who is a person of evil countenance and a heart of stone, goes presently forth to accomplish it. Be silent! Let us watch the going out. He comes!"

The execrable Chai appeared walking upon feet of silence and bearing a short but heavy club which might be concealed in the sleeve. He climbed the wall.

"Moon of Endless Delight!" murmured Doctor Fung Lee. "I will follow. It may be that the Watchers will offer to this person an opportunity of connecting the edge of this sword with the head of the abominable Chai. Tomorrow at this hour I will return."

And without further ado, for the need was pressing, he too surmounted the wall and followed the shadowy figure moving silently in the direction of the town's eastern gate. At a little distance from it, Chai took to the road and there loitered. Doctor Fung Lee, perceiving that the time was not yet come for any attempt upon the fellow, crouched by the wayside.

Two travellers, well mounted and carrying drawn swords against the chances of the road, passed at a trot. The execrable Chai, perceiving the gleam of steel, with admirable discretion withdrew himself from their observation behind a clump of weeds. They passed into the town through a convenient hole in the wall.

For a little was silence. Then came a solitary figure walking with the gait of one whose honorable feet are incommoded by the roughness of the way. Even in the gloom it was plain that he was a beggar, for his clothing was ragged and he bore a bowl.

CHAI rose from his lurking-place as he passed, and suddenly, without warning or even a polite word to indicate to the stranger that he was about to pass into a state of no-existence, smote him heavily upon the head with his loaded club.

Doctor Fung Lee, greatly interested in this manifestation of the essential baseness of the execrable Chai, remained quiet until, having hoisted the victim upon his broad shoulders, the slayer set off once more around the walls. Doctor Fung Lee followed at a discreet distance. Thus he perceived the execrable Chai enter the town once more by a gap in the wall well shrouded by creepers and scale the wall of a garden beyond.

And now Doctor Fung Lee's interest quickened, for though time had been lacking to explore the vicinity of the Street of the Evening Star, the dilapidated summer house to which Chai bore the defunct man was all too familiar, for it was his own. Doctor Fung hesitated. Should he draw his sword and, hamstringing Chai, call for help? Or, slaying him outright, dispose of the bodies with the help of Sung, thus leaving the atrocious Doctor Yat Foo in doubt of the fate of his emissary?

But while he hesitated, Chai, with movements of much celerity, had sped across the garden and surmounting the wall at another place, proceeded along the street into the Everywhere.

Doctor Fung Lee meditated no longer. He ran to his house and summoning Sung, told him of what had occurred. Sung sighed.

"Honorable sir, there is but one thing which a wise man may do. Let us bear this not-breathing one to the garden of the honorable Doctor Foo and there bury him, but not deeply. A word to the magistrate that the honorable Foo employs such remains for the practise of magic, is then clearly indicated. Let us hasten."

This advice being at once sound and practical, they hastened to the summer house, bearing a light and the wherewithal for the digging of a grave. By the light, Doctor Fung Lee inspected the defunct man. And at once something which the stupidity of Chai had failed to note, became apparent. Though outwardly clad in the rags of a beggar, the body was inwardly covered with garments of superior silk; while a long knife which, but for a fallacious reliance upon the protection afforded by his poor appearance, might have saved his life, was of excellent quality and adorned with jewels of price.

"Such garments are too good for the tomb," murmured Sung.

"Are we robbers? Be silent!" quoth Doctor Fung sternly. "Yet it may be that he wears some amulet by which doubtless sorrowing relatives—ah!" He paused, then bent a listening ear. "Amazing is the no-perception of the villain Chai. This man lives! Let us bear him within and struggle with the Demon for his life."

Shortly after, faint groans, presently rising to prolonged howls, arose from the house of the Fortunate Frog as, relieved by timely blood-letting and stimulated by skilful touches of a cautery iron, the victim of ill-directed endeavor struggled back to consciousness.

Toward dawn, revived by wine, sustained by a bowl of chicken soup and four black eggs warranted a century old, which Doctor Fung Lee kept in stock for his better-class patients, the apparently dead man recovered sufficiently to give an account of himself and pour out his thanks to his preserver.

THE rosy flush of dawn suffused the Upper Air as, leaving the sleeping man in the charge of the wife of Sung, a person of discreet years and well versed in cookery, Doctor Fung Lee and the faithful Sung, well armed though their garments concealed their weapons, proceeded to the residence of the honorable Doctor Yat Foo.

Early though the hour, there were yet signs of activity by the gate of the dean of Sen Yang. Two chairs stood there, each with its chairman. Doctor Fung Lee recognized them. They belonged to the honorable Doctors See Hop and Lu. Glowering in the gateway was the execrable Chai.

"Lead me to the presence of the learned and venerable doctor, your honorable master!" said Doctor Fung Lee, smiling with the affability of a tiger of the hills confronting a well-fed but unarmed traveller. "Celerity is indicated. If it is not forthcoming, the stars prophesy disaster to his palatial dwelling and all within."

With a growl of confusion, Chai led the way into the yamen, and so to the presence of Doctor Yat Foo, who, in act of concluding the last arrangements for the stirring-up of the dregs of Sen Yang against Doctor Fung Lee, regarded him with consternation, while his eminent and honorable colleagues permitted their mouths to display their yellow teeth.

"Revered and honorable brethren!" began Doctor Fung Lee, bowing ceremoniously to each in turn. "Your very humble and ignorant brother comes to render thanks to you for the kindness displayed in the dark hours. Well does this person know that each of you could have revived the honorable and eminent person sent to him by the hands of the strong and dexterous no-nose, Chai. Yet perceiving that he was young and in need of help, your magnanimity selected Fung Lee. The great Sun Lo Chi has been pleased to thank him in terms that modesty does not allow him to repeat, while promising him other rewards of a more substantial if less gratifying sort."

The three forgot politeness. They glared, they stared.

"Sun Lo Chi?" cried Yat Foo. "The mandarin who comes to dwell in our midst?"

"The same," quoth Doctor Fung Lee blandly. "A person of surpassing merit who, that he might the better observe the extortions of minor officials, has been traversing his province in the garb of a beggar—with his soldiers and yamen men a little behind him. They are already in the city. Sun Lo Chi will presently send them forth to seek a person with no nose, who, he has told me, assaulted him with head batterings. Absence is indicated for that person, lest there be slicings. Assault upon the body of a high official is bitterly punished."

There was a stir by the door. Chai became suddenly notable by his absence. With one accord the three smiled and nodded to each other. With no word spoken, they were agreed.

"My son," said Yat Foo, "in the name of us three, the healers of Sen Yang, this person bids you welcome. Presents of a quality befitting one of your transcendent merits shall soon be within your honorable house. Commend us to the noble Sun Lo Chi, in case there should be some of his household too mean in degree to deserve your skill."

"Truly it shall be so," murmured Doctor Fung Lee. "There is but one thing more. This person lacks a wife to adorn his hearth and furnish him with sons who shall make the offerings when he has by the decree of the High Ones become an ancestor. The Willow is a tree of grateful shade and peculiar fertility. A Willow Leaf is a graceful and fitting decoration for an abode, mean yet not unfurnished with all that may be required by the household of a humble yet flourishing healer of bodies."

"To be allied with the ancient and honorable house of Fung is the one wish which this person desires to gratify," said Doctor Yat Foo. "A go-between of renowned skill and delicacy shall wait upon the honorable Doctor Fung Lee within the hour. All shall be concluded swiftly. And now, what say the Sages? 'Of all precious things, nought is better than a cup of wine drunk by brethren in amity'."

And solemnly, fraternally, the medical faculty of Sen Yang drank together.

THE SOUK

A LETTER from J. Allen Hanna, of Detroit, asks: "Is the Arabian method of preparing coffee different from other methods? I notice in Otis Adelbert Kline's stories about Hamed the Dragoman constant references to the strength and bitterness of coffee. For instance, in *The Dragoman's Secret,* Hamed asks for coffee 'bitter as aloes, black as a Nubian at midnight, and hot as the hinges of Johannim's innermost gate.' In *The Dragoman's Revenge,* Hamed orders: 'Let there be coffee, bitter as death, black as Eblis, and hot as Johannim.' The coffee-shop of Silat must be an interesting place indeed, where coffee is made of such flavor as to call forth such encomiums."

Now the editor of ORIENTAL STORIES, having drunk Arabian coffee brewed by Otis Adelbert Kline himself, already knew something of the bitterness and blackness of the brew, and shared Mr. Hanna's curiosity about the coffee-shop of Silat in Jerusalem. In the first place, the Arabs and Turks pound their coffee to a fine powder in a mortar, after the beans are roasted. Then this powdered coffee is mixed with an equal amount of sugar, a teaspoonful of each to a demi-tasse of water, and allowed to come very slowly to a boil. The creamy foam, *Kafmak,* which rises is skimmed off and placed in small cups, after which the coffee is allowed to come to a boil, for an instant, twice or thrice more. In Istanbul it is usually served very sweet, whereas in Syria less sugar is used. Cairene, or Egyptian, coffee, besides being roasted very black, contains no sugar at all. The best Arabian coffee comes from al Yemen. The desert Arabs drink their coffee in cups but little larger than a thimble; and they mix it with a seed which gives it an aromatic flavor. Among the Bedouins coffee is served to guests as a sign of hospitality. Major E. Alexander Powell, in his book describing his trip across the Syrian desert, tells how his party was captured by Bedouins. After much discussion, the sheykh ordered coffee to be prepared, much to the relief of Major Powell and his friends, for this meant they were to be released. The Arabs will not drink coffee with those whom they intend to murder or pillage.

A letter from Joseph E. Loftus, of Lakeland, Florida, says: "Will you kindly allow me to take exception to Henry S. Whitehead's remarks apropos Frank Owen's *The China Kid?* I found this tale exceptionally true to the life of the men about whom he wrote; and please believe me, I have had adequate experience in that mode of life. Perhaps Mr. Whitehead has never been 'on the beach,' though he knows

(Please turn to page 716)

IN OUR NEXT ISSUE

THEY all saw Gyi, instantly. There was no mistaking that burly figure running like a galloping gorilla! He was speeding through an abandoned patch of scraggly banana trees, men running behind him with spears, men kneeling to aim crossbows, darts whizzing around him like stabs of light.

Newt hastened to raise his rifle and sight on the nearest of Gyi's pursuers. The bellow of his piece was seconded by the sharp whip of the lighter repeater fired by Nwé beside him. He heard her lever snap viciously as he picked another mark with the heavy double rifle. Men stumbled and fell.

Gyi dashed on, twisting and turning through the banana-stalks, coming like the wind for the bank. The raft was turning in, its oarsmen breaking their backs at the long sweeps. And then Gyi had burst through the fringe of low bushes and was swimming out, in great splashing strokes, across the narrow lane of water between raft and shore. He crawled out on the logs as Newt discouraged the last of his pursuers and the oarsmen reversed bow oars with grunting effort.

What happened to Gyi, the cutthroat and desperado who risked his life by invading a country single-handed that teemed with enemies where there was a price on his head for his many murders, all for the sake of rescuing a little baby boy who was heir to the throne of Möng Nam—all this will be fascinatingly told in this complete novel of thrilling surprises, vivid action and hair-breadth escapes in the next issue. Don't miss

The White Sawbwa of Möng Nam

A story of the Shan states of Burma
By WARREN HASTINGS MILLER

—ALSO—

THE TEST OF A GHOST
By S. B. H. Hurst

A dramatic story of Dost Mohamet, one of the Ghosts of Intelligence—the murder of the English mission to Afghanistan, and Lord Roberts' advance on Kabul.

BREAKFAST FOR ONE
By Kennis Gorman

The soft witchery of India claims its own—a tale of love and passion in the East.

THE SONG OF THE CAKES
By Nat Schachner and Arthur L. Zagat

A vivid tale of the Manchu conquest of China, and the fulfilment of the old Ming prophecy, when blood ran red in Peking.

THE BLOOD OF BELSHAZZAR
By Robert E. Howard

A red-blooded story of the time of the Crusades, and of a fierce bandit hold among the frowning foothills of the Taurus Mountains.

RATS AT THE SILVER CHEESE
By Bassett Morgan

An unusual story, about a half-caste Chinese clerk who claimed the estates of a Manchu noble.

THE DEATH-HEADS' MARCH
By Geoffrey Vace

A thrill-tale of the Khyber Pass and Juggut Hai, the bandit who lay in wait for the life of Chowkander King.

Autumn Issue ORIENTAL STORIES Out October 15

(Continued from page 714)

his West Indies and writes very entertainingly about the strange beliefs of their people. Mr. Owen has the courage to write the truth of his characters instead of the vastly simpler and more popular formula story. Drunken men on the beach will tell you that yarn is likely true. Things happen just like that, and with as little reason; these men react very similarly, according to their individual habits of thought, although it all may seem without reason to us. Almost any man on the beach could recite a tale parallel to *The China Kid,* but few of them talk about themselves, and the ones that ever write are rare; when they do take up pen they write court intrigues or country club romances."

Writes Joan D. Prosper, of Seattle: "I have just discovered ORIENTAL STORIES, and find that the type of fiction contained in it is helpful to me as an escape—a complete mental change—from the grind of professional cares. I particularly enjoyed *This Example* and *Tsang, Sea Captain,* in the last issue. This sort of fiction is a new experience to me, and I was surprized to find the stories so skilfully written."

"I like ORIENTAL STORIES immensely," writes Gordon Philip England, of Waterville, Quebec. "Of all your authors, Hurst appeals to me most. His latest story, *This Example,* is the best yet; I do not know when I have enjoyed reading a story so much."

"Here is what I think about serials in ORIENTAL STORIES," writes Jack Darrow, of Chicago. "It would be a long wait between installments, and many readers would not like this, but there is another way to publish book-length novels. That is, publish them complete in one installment. This would crowd out many of the short stories, but if only one was published in about every third issue, you could make up for it in the other issues."

Mrs. H. Lambert, of Terre Haute, Indiana, asks: "Why not write some stories about the Human Leopards of the Congo? I have only read one story about them and did not know it was based on fact until last week. I found out then that there is a mysterious cult called that. *The Finger of Kali,* by Bernice Banning, was interesting. Write some more about Kali." [The Congo region of Africa is not strictly Oriental; therefore a story about the Leopard Society would be out of place in this magazine. The littoral of North Africa, however, is Oriental in character and language, though not in geography; and we will publish several interesting stories of this region; notably those by Paul Ernst and G. G. Pendarves.—THE EDITORS.]

S. B. H. Hurst, in a letter to the editor, gives the following explanation of his story in this issue, *The Ball of Fire:* "This yarn had its inception in the looting after the capture of Mandalay. Certain Irish soldiers claimed to have seen the ruby. It is doubtful if they did, but there seems to be no doubt at all that King Thibaw entrusted it to one of his ten attendant priests, as in this story. Thibaw was sent to Ratnagiri, and died soon after. There was a rumor once that the Pet had passed into the hands of the priests of Buddha in Cambodia. This I doubt, as the priests in Burma have about as much use for their Cambodian co-religionists as a Roman Catholic has for a Baptist, or vice versa. The Burma priests are a very decent lot, quite different from the Lamaist sects, and they have taught free school to the Burmese

(Please turn to page 718)

Win $3,700⁰⁰

OR BUICK 8 SEDAN AND $2,500 IN CASH

Can you find 5 faces in the picture?

Sensational money-making opportunity for everybody! You may win $3,700 if you prefer all cash or handsome latest model Buick 8 Sedan and $2,500 in cash. This offer is made by a prominent business house for advertising purposes. Someone is going to win $3,700—why not you?

I want to send you this prize. Act quick! Send your answer today and qualify to win.

All you do to qualify for an opportunity in this great cash prize advertising plan is to find five faces in picture.

People riding in the auto above got out of the car. Their faces are shown in odd places about the picture. Some faces are upside down, others look sideways, some look straight at you. If you can pick out 5 or more faces, mark them, clip the picture and send to me together with your name and address. Sharp eyes will find them. Can you?

Easy to Win - $12,960 in 103 Cash Prizes

We will give away $12,960 in cash. You are sure to profit if you take an active part. In case of ties duplicate prizes will be given. You get $3,700 if you win grand first prize. In addition there are 102 other wonderful cash prizes. Grand second prize $1,000 in cash. Grand third prize $500 in cash. Also four other prizes of $500.00 each and many others. All told $12,960 in cash. Money to pay you is already on deposit in the Mercantile Trust and Savings Bank, a big Chicago bank.

SEND NO MONEY
The main thing is—send in your answer today. You can share in this advertising cash distribution. Hurry! and take no chance of losing the extra reward of $1,000 for promptness if you win grand first prize. Act now! You don't need to send a penny of your money to win! Just find five faces in the picture above and mail with coupon at once for particulars.

$1,000⁰⁰ for Promptness
Send your answer at once. Make sure to qualify for $1,000 extra given for promptness if you win the Buick Sedan —a total of $3,700 if you prefer all cash.

Indiana Farmer Wins $3,500!

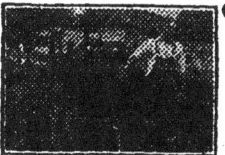

● This is a picture of Mr. C. H. Essig, Argos, Ind., taken on his farm. He writes: "Wish to acknowledge receipt of your $3,500 prize check. Oh, boy! This is the biggest sum of money I ever had in my hands. It is indeed a fortune to me."

Hundreds have been rewarded in our past advertising campaigns. Mrs. Edna D. Ziler, of Kentucky, won $1,950. Miss Tillie Bohle, of Iowa, $1,500. Be Prompt! Answer today!

Send Coupon Today

THOMAS LEE, Mgr.
427 W. Randolph St., Dept. 2380, Chicago, Ill.
I have found five faces in the $3,700.00 prize picture and am anxious to win a prize. Please advise me how I stand.

Name..

Address.......................................

Town...........................State............

717

(Continued from page 716)

kids for two thousand years. Due to this the Burmese women had achieved a freedom forty years ago—I should say hundreds of years ago, forty years referring to the dacoit period when I was there—which American women have only recently managed to get. As I have mentioned before, the wizards rule the souls of the people, however."

"I have just finished my copy of ORIENTAL STORIES and there was not a dull moment in it," writes Mrs. A. Mannicini, of Philadelphia. "I have been waiting for its appearance for over a month. I have read all the issues to date, and it is a worthy sister to WEIRD TALES."

Robert W. Nelson, of St. Charles, Illinois, writes to the Souk: "By all means keep von Gelb, your cover-portrait artist. He is superb. *Hawks of Outremer*, I think, carries off first honors in the Spring Issue of ORIENTAL STORIES, though it does not measure up to the peerless *Red Blades of Black Cathay*, which appeared in the preceding issue. Stewart's *Bibi Love* was very fine."

A letter from Hugh T. Sappings, of Olympia, Washington, says: "As a rule I have no use for love stories; but, being neither a prude nor a fanatic, I am willing to admit that I occasionally find one I can enjoy, such as *This Example* and *Bibi Love*, in your Spring Issue. Incidentally, I thought Hurst's *William* the best story in your last number. *Della Wu, Chinese Courtezan*, ranks next to *William*."

Readers, what is your favorite story in this issue? In the Spring Issue, two stories are in an exact tie for first place, as shown by your votes and letters. These are *Hawks of Outremer*, Robert E. Howard's red-blooded story of the Crusades; and *This Example*, S. B. H. Hurst's tender story of a Burmese woman's love for her man.

MY FAVORITE TALES IN THE SUMMER ISSUE OF ORIENTAL STORIES ARE:

Story	Remarks
(1) _____	_____
(2) _____	_____
(3) _____	_____

I do not like the following stories:

(1) _____	Why? _____
(2) _____	_____

It will help us to know what kind of stories you want in Oriental Stories if you will fill out this coupon and mail it to The Souk, Oriental Stories, 840 N. Michigan Ave., Chicago, Ill.

Reader's name and address:

_____

_____

_____

The Dragoman's Slave Girl

(Continued from page 603)

there in his wet, mud-stained garments with the water sifting down on him through the leaky roof.

Moving on, I was soon at the door of Selma Hanoum's house, where a slave took my shoes and cloak, and ushered me through the *salamlik* into the *majlis*.

In a moment, a slender, veiled figure came down the stairs and walked toward me. It was Selma.

"Your slave girl welcomes you to her house, Master," she said, taking my hand and conducting me to a *diwan*.

Then she clapped her hands, whereupon slaves brought a pipe, coffee things, and a brazier of glowing charcoal. She waved the slaves away, and with her own fair hands lighted the pipe for me. Then she prepared coffee over the glowing brazier while I told her of my meeting with the deposed Pasha.

"It is the justice of *Allah*," she said. "Through his own misdeeds the Cretan's son has been reduced to beggary. Most folk believe that he deserves worse, but *Allah* is all-knowing."

She moved a taboret up close to the *diwan*, and sitting on a cushion before me, poured coffee. Then she handed me a steaming cup. I sipped in silence, waiting for her to speak, for I was positive that she had sent for me that she might purchase her freedom. She was tantalizingly close, and Shaitan tempted me to crush her in my arms. But I forbore.

Presently she asked: "Is there aught else that your slave girl can do for you, Master?"

Allah! How I loved her—desired her above everything in this world or the next. But I knew such thoughts were

madness. Returning my cup to the taboret, I stood up.

"Let us have done with this pretense of master and slave, *hanoum*," I said.

"Why, if you wish, my lord," she replied, also rising. "You bought me at quite a reasonable figure, and I am willing to pay you a good profit on the investment. What do you say to a thousand pounds, Turkish?"

"I say: 'Keep your gold,'" I replied. "For I give you back to yourself, free of all debt or obligation."

"But you are without funds. Surely you will accept a reward for your brave services."

"I have my reward, *hanoum*. It is better than gold, for it can never be taken from me—better than friendship, for it can never prove false. It is my memory of one beautiful and exquisite rose, which I have seen, loved, and lost."

With that, I turned and strode toward the door.

There was a patter of footsteps behind me. A little hand was laid on my arm.

I whirled to see her standing there, unveiled in all her loveliness. And in her eyes there shone a light which a man may see but once, yet never misunderstand.

"Oh my Master!" she cried. "Leave me not desolate!"

Tender, yielding, lovely as a rose pearled with dew, she came to me—gave me her sweet lips.

"Take me, Hamed," she murmured. "Never let me go. All that I am, all that I have, is yours."

And so, *effendi*, Selma, the one beautiful and exquisite rose, became mine, bringing me happiness indescribable and wealth untold. And we lived together a life of joy and contentment until Allah Almighty saw fit to receive her into His mercy.

Ho, Silat! Bring the sweet and take the full.

www.ingramcontent.com/pod-product-compliance
Lightning Source LLC
Chambersburg PA
CBHW080910020726
47502CB00008B/2417